Footnotes to Sex

Mia Farlane was born in New Zealand. When she was twelve, her play *The Only Thing in Common*, about a husband and wife who kill each other, was shown on New Zealand national television. She has a degree in French Language and Literature from Victoria University, Wellington, and lived for several years in France. She now lives in London, where she completed an MA in Creative Writing at Middlesex University. *Footnotes to Sex* is her first novel.

otes to Sex

FARLANE

VIKING

an imprint of

PENGUIN BOOKS

VIKING

Published by the Penguin Group
Penguin Books Ltd, 80 Strand, London WC2R ORL, England
Penguin Group (USA) Inc., 375 Hudson Street, New York, New York 10014, USA
Penguin Group (Canada), 90 Eglinton Avenue East, Suite 700, Toronto, Ontario, Canada M4P 2Y3
(a division of Pearson Penguin Canada Inc.)
Penguin Ireland, 25 St Stephen's Green, Dublin 2, Ireland (a division of Penguin Books Ltd)
Penguin Group (Australia), 250 Camberwell Road, Camberwell, Victoria 3124, Australia
(a division of Pearson Australia Group Pty Ltd)
Penguin Books India Pvt Ltd, 11 Community Centre, Panchsheel Park, New Delhi – 110 017, India
Penguin Group (NZ), 67 Apollo Drive, Rosedale, North Shore 0632, New Zealand
(a division of Pearson New Zealand Ltd)
Penguin Books (South Africa) (Pty) Ltd, 24 Sturdee Avenue, Rosebank, Johannesburg 2196, South Africa

Penguin Books Ltd, Registered Offices: 80 Strand, London WC2R ORL, England

www.penguin.com

First published in 2009
1

Printed in Great Britain by Clays Ltd, St Ives plc

A CIP catalogue record for this book is available from the British Library

ISBN: 978-0-670-91793-8

www.greenpenguin.co.uk

Mixed Sources
Product group from well-managed
forests and other controlled sources
www.fsc.org Cert no. SA-COC-1592
© 1996 Forest Stewardship Council.
FSC

Penguin Books is committed to a sustainable future
for our business, our readers and our planet.
The book in your hands is made from paper
certified by the Forest Stewardship Council.

To K.A.P.

Acknowledgements

The extracts by Lucie Delarue-Mardrus are quoted with the kind authorization of Éditions de la lieutenance, 57 rue de l'homme de bois, 14600 Honfleur, www.editionsdelalieutenance.com

Thanks to Christina Dunhill, Jo Broadwood, Reuben Lane and Alan McCormick. Thanks to Christelle Didier, Emma Soundy, Tara Kaufmann, Linda Leatherbarrow, Magda Devas and Mark Handsley. Special thanks to Judith Murray, my agent, and to Kate Barker, my editor at Viking. Thanks, with love, to Marilyn Duckworth.

Contents

I

The Letter

May lay awake waiting for Jansen to get back. *Chère Francine*, she went through the letter in her head, *J'ai bien reçu ta lettre qui m'a fait très plaisir*. She was running out of days. If she had wanted to send the letter, she should have sent it that morning, on her way to work, or yesterday; last week, if she'd wanted Francine to get it on time. *How are you? And how was the conference in Canada? I am well, and still of course planning on doing the PhD* ... Having wasted another day of her life, going over 'exam techniques' with nine-year-olds, May listened to the guitar-player upstairs practising his endless scales. She could always have put in her earplugs, but Jansen would be home in less than an hour, and that meant May couldn't get to sleep anyway. She was aware that at any moment there might be the clickety-clack of the door key, and then Jansen would appear, as she finally did, in her navy-blue uniform, a large leather bag in one hand, a quiet ...

'Booboo?'

May pretended to be asleep. Jansen went towards the bathroom with a newspaper. She'd be ages.

'I'm awake.'

'Can I turn on the light?'

'No, I'm sleeping.'

'May, I'm sorry, but I need to iron my shirt for tomorrow.'

'Can't you wear that one again?'

Jansen clicked on the bedside lamp.

'Why can't you do it tomorrow?' May pulled herself up in bed.

'I could, but why don't we have a hot drink together. I really need to unwind.' Jansen set up the ironing board next to the kitchenette, and got the iron out from under the sink. 'People are in such a rush out there! I was at the lights on my way to a pickup this morning, and there was this woman and I could see her. She was looking at me, and she was waving her arms around, she was going, "Come on! Come on!" I just glided slowly past her, and I thought, poor woman, if she's getting so upset about five seconds! The other day I was pulling out from a park, and I'd looked both ways. I pulled out, and then suddenly BEEEEEEEP! I had a passenger in the car at the time. I said to him, "Boy! I didn't even see that coming," and he said, "He must've been booting it round the corner!"' She held the iron under the tap, and filled the steam-chamber with water.

'I didn't send it, by the way,' May told her.

'Mm-hmm.' Jansen plugged in the iron.

'Does that mean you don't want to talk about it?' May said.

Jansen started ironing the collar. The iron wouldn't be hot yet. There was no point. She rearranged the shirt, and started on the sleeves.

'That iron's not hot enough yet, is it?'

'May, would you just leave me to iron my shirt? I can do it without your help.'

'It's not doing anything, is it though? You may as well be doing something else . . . while it heats up.'

Jansen began ironing the other sleeve.

'You could be getting me a hot drink,' May suggested.

'Would you like a hot drink, May?'

'Yes, please.' May didn't really want a hot drink, but Jansen liked to have one in the evening.

'I'll make you half a cup. You never finish it anyway. Shall we share one?' Jansen got a cup out of the cupboard.

'I'm just wondering whether I should send it to her at all.'

'May, I'm really exhausted. I don't feel like talking about Francine.'

'My PhD,' May corrected her.

'Or the PhD.'

'I've just got to decide whether I'm going to send it or not.'

'You don't have to decide tonight.'

May's throat hurt. 'Could I just tell you what I've put again?'

'I know what you've put.'

'I've changed it slightly.'

'I don't want to hear it, May.' (That was a definite 'no'. May waited in silence for her coffee.) 'They sent four of us out to the airport,' Jansen laughed as she crouched down to get the milk out of the fridge, 'but it turned out they only needed one car. So three of us had to go back to the bin to wait for another job.' She put the coffee on the bedside table, and went back to ironing again, a smile lingering.

'That's not funny. That's irritating, isn't it?' It was irritating the way Jansen laughed off annoying situations.

'It's what happens, May.' (Jansen would be wearing a jersey over that shirt. There was no point in ironing it. Or she could just iron the collar.) 'Then I got three lawyers,' Jansen went on, 'in a row: no tips, no tips, no tips. And that was my day.' She unplugged the iron, and stood it on the bench.

'How come four of you were sent out? Shouldn't it be more organized?'

'Yes.'

Jansen got into her pyjamas and came to bed. Then, as always, they had a long talk: one of Jansen's passengers had left her a pamphlet on Trees for London, she said, and she was wondering about giving people birch trees for Easter; you didn't actually get a tree, but you got a little card saying a tree had been planted for you. What did May think? May said she liked the idea and could she please just tell Jansen what she had added to the letter – only the addition – and Jansen said no, because that would get May thinking about it, and then she wouldn't sleep; and then May said she was thinking about it anyway, and Jansen said go on then, and

May did. She was so lucky really; who else had a wonderful Jansen in her life? Even if Jansen just crept into bed, she and May would often end up talking and talking late into the night, until perhaps Jansen would start drifting off, and May would say, as she did this evening: 'Are you going to sleep now? I hate going to sleep. It means it'll be morning when I wake up.' She was a realist; she liked to be prepared for all disasters, even if it meant she was grinding her teeth down to little stumps in the process. No wonder she needed so much sleep.

'You're so unromantic! How could I have got together with someone so unromantic?'

May wasn't a performer, that was for sure, but she did love Jansen.

'You're so wonderful, darling! I love you! I love you! I love you!' She kissed Jansen on the cheek, and put her earplugs in.

That night, May had another one of her rat dreams. In this one she had recently adopted a kitten. Unfortunately, she hadn't realized at the time that it was really a rat, and now she didn't know how to get rid of it (that might also be dangerous); she felt slightly sick about the whole thing, so she fed it, but decided it would be an outdoor cat, and would, with luck, get run over.

2
Successful People

It was last August that May had first met Francine. May went to Paris, she went there on her own, and stayed for two weeks at a cheap hotel in the nineteenth *arrondissement*; and during this time – it was, after all, the sole purpose of her trip – she met Francine.

'Je t'admire et je t'admirerai toujours,' May had told her. She could easily be frank in this role.

Francine made it clear she didn't want anyone bringing flowers to her shrine, which only warmed May further to her. May was starry-eyed (the expression is exact).

She was twenty years older than May; it was just a crush, so Jansen wasn't too concerned. 'You admire her. Which is understandable.'

It was Jansen who had encouraged May to contact Francine in the first place:

'But don't waste her time. Make sure you're prepared. Successful people haven't got time to waste. Ring her with a short list of questions.'

Was that good advice? May made up her list of questions, a résumé of who she was, how she had Francine Brion's telephone number, an introductory blurb to read off for the phone call; and then she went and spoke to Jansen again.

'No, May! She won't mind you ringing her. She's probably a very approachable person. Say you've read her books, you loved them et cetera, you're planning on coming to Paris, and you'd really like to meet her, because you're going to do a PhD – you're thinking maybe on her: she'll be flattered.'

'She doesn't need flattering. She's an intellectual.'

'She'll still be flattered! It's always good to have someone do a thesis on you.'

'If I *do* – I haven't even got a supervisor yet – I'm not even sure why I'm thinking of doing it.'

'You know why you're doing it.'

'Because although I'm not really capable of doing a PhD –'

'You're doing it because you've always wanted to do a PhD, May – and because you are capable of doing one.'

'I don't know that I *am* capable of doing one.'

'In that case, why have we been living in a bedsit for the last seven months?'

'Are you now saying you're annoyed about living in a bedsit? You suggested we move into a bedsit, so I could save money. And now I've got to do a PhD; I've got no choice.'

'I am not saying that. I would just like you to meet Francine Brio first, before you decide – in advance – that you're incapable of doing a PhD.'

'Brio*n*.'

'(Brio*n*.) You were all excited before, when you found her address and telephone number on the Internet.'

'I don't really have a topic I know anything much about, and I don't have a supervisor. All I've got is the money.'

'That's pretty impressive; hardly anyone saves up for going to university.'

'It doesn't require intelligence.'

'And you've done lots and lots of reading.'

'What have I read?'

'I'm not even going to answer that – May, we've had this conversation before.'

- my name is May Woodlea.
- I'm writing a proposal for a PhD.
- on your views of gender in French lesbian literature.

- I know you have written a great deal on this subject.
- could I – at some time – ask you about your work?

Her introductory speech. May looked over her list; she was ready. Her thumping heart told her she was being brave. She picked up the receiver.

Francine Brion sounded pleased to get May's call:

'Have you read my latest book?' she asked.

'I've read it several times,' May said, breathless with excitement.

Francine Brion asked when exactly May was arriving.

May said, 'It could be this Saturday, in the afternoon.'

Francine suggested they meet on Saturday evening then, at La Fourmi Ailée.

And May booked her ticket.

That Saturday afternoon in Paris, May prepared herself in her hotel room: a beige T-shirt bought on the way to the hotel, from Camaïeu; brown trousers, from the same shop; emerald stud earrings to bring out her eyes; a discreet bit of wax on the tips of her hair, to tidy up what was supposed to have been a 'Louise Brooks' haircut; a just perceptible hint of *fond de teint*; the tiniest, most subtle bit of rouge; and a dab of Chanel 19. May drank some tap water from the basin in her room, and ate a few dates, before leaving.

Métro Belleville. She went down the steps, and sat on the stretch of low tiled benches, where she waited for the train with four or five silent others. Undemanding moments, she savoured them. Large advertisements opposite showed happy young women swooping out of Le Printemps wearing their latest purchases; hand-held children stood bedazzled outside the entrance to Le Parc Astérix.

A train arrived; 'ch-clunk', various doors were opened by people going in or out. May stepped into a carriage, and flipped down a *strapontin* seat away from the doors. The doors closed. She took out her book, *Les Démons de la solitude*, but couldn't concentrate; she looked at people in the carriage, and at more advertisements.

She put her book back. Rambuteau: one more stop. The thought of meeting Francine Brion was giving her stomach ache.

May walked across the river, past Notre-Dame with its tourists, her stomach ache for company, and arrived at La Fourmi Ailée. She was very early, but she looked around, just in case. Some-where, quite possibly, hidden in the café, sat the author of *Le/Les – Féminin-s*. May found a waiter. Determinedly unselfconscious, she requested:

'Une table pour deux.'

Did she want to order anything just yet? Or would she rather wait?

She'd wait. Thank you.

Now all she had to do was sit there. She had a corner seat by the entrance.

A tall woman with a brown leather hat came through the door – too young – and went to join a table of three. La Fourmi Ailée, May noted the name again on the paper menu in front of her. Fear tidal-waved from her stomach to the top of her throat. Francine was 'probably really approachable', and she had a warm voice on the phone, May reminded herself.

To her right, a family all had their eyes humbly lowered to their table. They must have been saying grace. A particularly religious family, May supposed, they were stopping, amidst all the noise, as a 'solid family unit', to thank God for their meal. It was a surpris-ingly long grace though. May looked again, and saw they had no food before them. They were studying the menu.

Finally, *she* entered the café. There was no question about it: Francine Brion; a neat package of a woman – tailored shirt, belted trousers and thick-soled shoes – walked comfortably into the café; she knew the place well, or perhaps she was just comfortable everywhere, and located May at once:

'Bonjour.'

'Bonjour.' May gave her hand. This was possibly very English of her, but 'quaint', she hoped.

A large smile sprang out onto the writer's face. Ash-grey eyes.

It was rather dark in this corner. Did May agree? Should they find a table somewhere else? So they did. In silence, they made their way to a table further along, next to the windows.

'Un café.' And May had the same.

They sat opposite each other. Francine observed her in silence; perhaps she was reading her face. May tried not to think anything. Francine looked like an intellectual, May was thinking; and she was thinking that Francine had an 'intelligent haircut': short and neat and easy to look after. She stopped thinking and held her breath. A few seconds passed. Then Francine spoke:

'How old are you?' she asked.

'Thirty-one.'

'Just!'

Meaning?

'What sign are you?' she then asked, and, 'Show me your palm ... Ah!' Francine held May's palm open like an oyster shell in one hand, while she traced above the lines with the other. 'I see an intuitive side, and an artistic side,' she read. And then, 'Ah! Ah!' Strangely enough, May could not now recall the rest. She was perhaps not paying attention. *Ah-Ah*, something.

Francine brought out a folder. 'I have a few of my articles here for your university task: "Cavete, feminae" (Beware, Women), "Le Féminin au rabais", "Le Féminin et ses enjeux", "Le Féminin invalide: comment lui redonner sa valeur" ...' Francine started arranging the essays from most recent to the earliest. 'I have been very busy, as you can see,' she stated with no false humility. 'And now you will be busy until our next meeting. You will give me your opinion.'

May took the papers, and started flicking through the titles. Francine, who had done her work, sat back and drank her coffee.

'What do you want to do with your life?' she now asked May, who was carefully sliding the hefty folder into her bag.

May tried to think up something she should desire.

'What do you want to make of your life?' Francine reworded her question.

'I'm reading quite a bit, for the PhD.'

'What is your deepest desire?' Francine made the question clearer.

May sat there.

'I'm going to give you some homework. Do you agree with this plan? You are going to look up the word "desire" and you are going to write about what it means to you. And you are going to keep a note of your *dreams* – but of course!' she added at that point; not that May had disagreed with her. 'Because if you want to understand others, you first have to understand yourself.'

Thus, unexpectedly, May had found herself a spiritual guide.

3
Absorbing Information

May woke up one delicious morning, the second week of her visit, to find someone had slid a note under the door of her hotel room:

Francine asks you to buy Le Point *and to come to lunch at her apartment (call her for the code to the entrance gates).*

The interview – Francine had mentioned it would be out soon. May went to a nearby *bar-tabac* and bought the magazine. She bought a postcard for Jansen at the same time, and a croissant for breakfast. She went back to the hotel, opened up the magazine and found the photo: 'Francine Brion: speaking of the andro-gyne . . .' Francine had her head on a very slight tilt; her eyes fixed intently on some question. Eventually, May skimmed through the interview. She read the message from Francine again. She reread it as she ate her croissant. She placed the note inside her journal, and took out her *Plan de Paris.* It was already eleven o'clock; beautiful outside: calm. She had the windows of her room wide open. Later, the day would begin. For now, she merely glided. She was still dreaming. She was a character in a novel, who wanders in Paris, who crosses a bridge, who drinks in a café with a newspaper before her that she doesn't read, who flicks through the newspaper, who wanders through the pages, and hums.

Before leaving, May opened the guide at page forty-five: the sixth *arrondissement*; K8, Métro Saint-Michel, go south to place de la Sorbonne, turn right is rue de Vaugirard. She put the book back into her bag, not that she'd need it: Métro Saint-Michel, south to

Sorbonne, turn right; south to Sorbonne, turn right, south to Sorbonne, turn right – it was easy enough to remember.

Behind the large wooden gates, there was a courtyard, which, crossed diagonally to the left, would lead, Francine had explained, to her apartment. It was like a secret. May pressed the code – 38, 64, A – and the lock clicked open. She went through the gates, and across the glare of the cobbled courtyard. If Francine had looked down then, she would have seen her. May pressed the intercom.

'Allô.'

'C'est moi.'

'It's on the third floor!' Francine's voice sang.

The buzzer went, and May pushed open the door. She made her way up the narrow wooden stairs. It was refreshingly cool, silent and dark, like the inside of a turret. One. Two. Three. Francine had left the door ajar. May took off her sandals, and stepped barefoot into a carpeted sitting room. 'Come through,' Francine called out.

May went into a small kitchen, where Francine was sitting at a table, closing down her laptop computer.

'I have just finished a section. C'est parfait,' she said.

May said nothing. She half smiled. She looked out of the open windows at the apartments opposite, with their window boxes of geraniums, and at the yard she had just crossed.

'I could sense you were arriving.' Francine shut the lid of the laptop, and disconnected the plugs. 'I knew you were about to press the bell. I could feel that you were thinking about me.'

'Yes, I was.' Well, that was true. Then May added, 'Of course, because I was coming to see you.'

'Mm.' Francine cleared the papers off the table.

May went to take off her jacket, and put down her bag. She sat neatly on the low sofa in the sitting room.

'How are you?' Francine asked her from the kitchen.

'Very well, thank you,' May replied. She sat looking at the

floor-to-ceiling bookshelves to the left and right of her: Marguerite Yourcenar, Monique Wittig, George Sand ... Nina Bouraoui, Michèle Causse, Jocelyne François, Violette Leduc ...

'Come and talk to me. You can come and help.'

May got up. Francine was pulling a bowl of buckwheat out of the fridge. 'Do you like artichoke?'

'Yes.'

'Good.' Francine poured the boiled wheat into a frying pan. 'I'll give you this.' She handed her a wooden spoon.

May stirred, while Francine stood on the bench to reach down some bowls. 'You have to be a gymnast in this kitchen,' she said.

May smiled, but again only slightly. Stir, stir: weakly; Francine had not really given her anything to do; she'd simply given her something to seem to be doing, which was kind of her; she'd given her something to hold on to: May was grateful.

Francine stepped down carefully from the bench to the stool to the floor, and placed the two bowls on the table. 'I received a call this morning,' she told May. 'From an ex-lover. She congratulates me on the magazine interview. Ah, Sophie! She is living in Canada now, but somehow she manages to find out about the interview! She calls to pick me up on one of my comments. Note, she's very, very sharp, very intelligent, this woman. It's her intelligence that I was so attracted to, moreover. We met at a protest.'

Arms linked, in their thick coats, their hats and boots, banners held high, *Les Féministes Révolutionnaires*! May pictured Francine, a dot among thousands, progressing towards the Assemblée Nationale.

'I've done ten lifetimes of protests. I leave marches to the young now. But the young women of today are asleep. Vivement le retour de la droite! That might wake them up. No, I am quite serious,' Francine raged prophetically.

'I've been on marches,' May defended herself. 'I used to go on lots of marches. I marched last year in the LGP.'

Francine made no comment.

May had not, it was true, noticed much passion on that particular march. The Lesbian and Gay Pride being, after all, a mere celebratory event, a publicity job at best. She and Jansen had sauntered nonchalantly in the procession, towards Hyde Park. They had slipped out of the crowd, at one point, for coffee, at Starbucks. London Cleaners were right behind the festivities, sweeping up handouts and dropped flags. The afternoon had hardly had a militant feel about it. No, that day could not be held up to Francine as an update on May's political action CV.

'I've read the interview,' May stated.

Francine waited for more.

'And I found it very clear . . . You say what you mean, you include yourself in what you say.'

Francine waited.

'I loved what you said about "Beware, Women". The examples.'

'Which ones?' Francine set two cloth mats on the table.

'It's hard to say. There were so many. I could go and get it. I've made notes.'

'You'll show me later.' Francine took the spoon from May, and switched off the stove. 'Are you hungry?' May hovered. 'Sit down. I'll serve you.' She started piling May's bowl with vegetables and buckwheat.

'Thanks, that's enough.' May was not hungry. What she wanted was a cigarette, although she'd never smoked.

'Oh the wine!' Francine went over to the fridge. 'I'm going to have a little wine. Do you want some wine?'

'No, thank you. I prefer water,' May replied.

'No? Not even a little? You must learn how to relax. You are so tense. Look at the way you are holding your feet.' It sounded like an accusation.

May looked under the table at her feet: her toes were curled tightly inwards like claws. She uncurled them and placed her feet back on the floor.

Francine was now focusing on May's face. 'You block your vital energy,' she explained, 'when you do that. You don't realize! Your energy cannot move freely through you. You are far too reserved,' she continued. 'You should allow yourself to let go of the reins. A little wine would do you good.' Francine started eating. 'Bon appétit.'

'Bon appétit.' May took a tiny mouthful. She wondered how she was going to finish all this food. Then she decided she'd say something. 'Water is better for your health,' she said.

'Don't be ridiculous! A little wine is very good for your health. To deny yourself absolutely: *that* is an excessive reaction.'

After lunch – buckwheat with vegetables, yoghurt, then coffee – Francine washed the dishes while May dried; like two nuns in a chapel, May thought, silently preparing for some ritual, one washed, the other dried, in intimate silence.

'That's very good.' Francine took the tea towel from May, and wiped her hands. 'And now, *ma belle*, I am going to have to throw you out. It's late.' Francine got some *chocolat noir* from a shelf, and snapped off a couple of large flat squares: 'For your journey back to your hotel.'

May didn't want the chocolate.

Francine handed her the little package wrapped in silver tinfoil: 'Voila!' She kissed her on the left cheek, and then on the right.

'I'm returning to London on Sunday,' May announced. 'I'm leaving in less than a week. And then non-life will start up again; I have to go back to teaching.'

'You lack imagination,' Francine said. Very kindly, but it was also a challenge: May had failed to imagine something. 'In any case,' Francine went on, 'you will come back to Paris to visit me many times – I'm not about to die, after all – and we shall discuss your thesis on my ideas.' She smiled then, as if only kindness, and not intelligence, were important. 'I'll be in Le Finistère for the next few days,' she said, 'for the eclipse on the eleventh. Finish reading the articles while I'm away, and call me on Saturday. We shall see each other again before you leave.'

May went to a telephone box after breakfast the following morning, and rang Jansen, who took down the number and called her straight back.

'How's it going?' Jansen asked.

'She thinks I'm stupid.'

'Oh, "she thinks you're stupid"? What makes you think that?'

'Because I am stupid.'

'May, you're not stupid; you know you're not stupid! You've got a Master's degree that you got in your early twenties, and now you're going to go on and do a PhD; you can't be that stupid.'

'Yeah, and I'm working in a primary school.'

'Yes. So what?'

'What am I doing working in a primary school? I get an MA in French Literature and then I go and teach English in a narrow-minded private school. Is that intelligent?'

'It's a job, May. What am I doing working as a chauffeur? Do you think I'm stupid because I work as a chauffeur?'

'No, I don't. Obviously.'

'Well then,' Jansen said, as if she had proved something.

'Because you're not stupid, and anyway it's only temporary.'

'You could do something else if you wanted to; you might decide, after you've got your PhD, that you want to do something completely different for a while. Like I am.'

'Hm.'

'You'd lose your long holidays though. When I started in HR at People First I only had three weeks a year – and they'd have kept it like that, but it was only because of the "working time directive" that they increased it to four.'

'She made some suggestions about my PhD topic,' May said, 'that she thinks I ought to change: because it's already been done and my topic's too broad, she said. She's far more interested in cross-dressing than in gender anyway, so she's given me some ideas for me to work on.'

'Yeah.'

'She's going away this afternoon, for a few days. She wants me to write a page about her interview in *Le Point*, what I thought about it, and she's given me some more stuff to read, and a list of authors.'

'Oh, yeah; show it to me when you get back.'

'You don't want to hear about it right now?'

'Not really, no.'

'I could just tell you the titles perhaps?'

'All right, if you want to.'

'Are you interested though, or "not really"?'

Jansen sighed.

'Okay, I won't tell you the titles.'

'It's not that I'm not interested, May. I just don't think there's much point over the telephone. I'm more interested in hearing about how you are.'

'I'm missing you.'

'I miss you, too,' Jansen said. 'Only five more days.'

Francine went to Le Finistère, where she would have a better view of the eclipse on the Thursday, and May spent this time café-crawling, and reading the last of the articles, 'On Re-evaluation'. It would definitely be useful for a PhD on Francine's work: there was a concise summary of all her writing and, at the end, a bibliography of every single thing Francine had ever had published – her feminist tracts, the essays in *Le Torchon brûle* – everything was included.

On Wednesday, May went to the Bibliothèque Publique d'Information in the Pompidou Centre. She sat at a long table in the reference section on the first floor, and with a couple of enormous dictionaries open in front of her attempted to gain some clarity on her PhD topic.

Gender portrayal in French lesbian literature was what she had had to begin with.

Brion's translation of cross-dressing – Francine had suggested something more precise – *in twentieth-century French lesbian literature.* 'You would want to look for both literal and figurative instances in the novels I mention,' Francine had told her. 'Rather than focusing on where "the material represents the abstract", my essays approach the subject from a new angle: "the abstract representing the material". That is far more interesting; that is where you impress your readers.' May's palms were sweating. Perhaps if she narrowed down her area:

Looking in particular at novels written between . . . 1930–1980: Jeanne Galzy, Célia Bertin, Eveline Mayhère, Anne Huré, Violette Leduc, Simone de Beauvoir, Christiane Rochefort, Gisèle Bienne, Monique Wittig . . . She could also include (another recommendation from Francine) *some reference to feminist articles/publications – Le Torchon brûle, Tout* – that might be a good idea. *Plus all of Francine Brion's writing, as it relates to the above.*

May had established her – crater-like – subject area; she had read some books. Now, what was the premise of her PhD? What was its central question? For some reason, that was where she couldn't think. Her mind refused; it blurred out of focus. Her throat hurt. She looked around at the real students in the library: a slender man in his mid- or early twenties sat at the other end of the table, copying out real notes from a book he would no doubt refer to in his essay or his thesis; a chic nouveau-punk stood next to a photocopying machine, pulled a card out of her wallet; some people were wandering among the shelves in search of information needed for real university papers due in this week or next month, for real courses on which they were enrolled. May had been in the library for nearly an hour.

Cross-dressing (to be defined, because everything always needed defining – or didn't it?); and the central question was . . .

She'd go and get a coffee. Perhaps if she relaxed her mind, the perfect idea would surface.

However, standing alone, the following day, in front of the statue of Charles Baudelaire in the Jardin du Luxembourg (the eclipse barely noticeable through the clouds), May admitted to herself – and the sky seemed to agree – that she would probably never write the PhD, it was all beyond her; even to write the proposal was beyond her; she might never even write the proposal . . . although she would still want to see Francine of course, because Francine was a piece of walking history, she was a font of knowledge; and it was natural that May would want to get to know her, if only a bit. All the same – and was this a problem? – it was less natural for May to want to think about doing the PhD, if she was honest; just as one would be fairly unlikely to want to become an astronaut if one was afraid of flying (for example). And yet, May tried to remain positive, although it was more probable that she would not do the PhD, there was always the possibility that she would. She was unsure. She was unsure, and while she was unsure – she put the 'CE-approved' safety glasses back into her bag – she should at least allow herself to continue visiting Francine; since, in the worst-case scenario – May began walking back towards the exit – she'd learn something.

'Allô, Francine. It's May.' It was Saturday morning, and she was standing in a telephone booth near to the hotel. 'I knew you would have left your answering machine on,' she explained. 'And it is for that reason that I allowed myself to call you, since, although I didn't want to disturb you (I know that you work in the mornings), I told myself that you would have put your answering machine on if you were working, so . . . the weather is incredibly beautiful today, it's not weather for staying inside, I told myself, so I wondered,' May got to her point, 'whether you would like to go out for a walk somewhere. It's what I am going to do, in any case –' She was cut off.

If she had thought about it – and she wished, after she got off the phone, that she had thought about it – she would have prepared a succinct message before picking up the phone. Instead, she had gabbled out her thoughts. She went back to the hotel, where she spent the rest of the morning in her sunless room, waiting for Francine to call, listening to the hum of the traffic outside, and nibbling her way through a bag of figs.

At two o'clock, someone knocked on her door; it was the man from reception: 'There is *une dame* on the phone for you,' he said.

'Une dame': it would be Jansen or Francine. May followed the man downstairs to reception, 'Merci,' and took the receiver.

It was Francine: 'I have just listened to your message.' She stopped to laugh.

'What?'

'No, I'm laughing. And it does me such good to laugh,' she said. 'I could yawn, if you like, but it's surely better that I laugh. Still, what would you prefer?' Francine sounded angry.

May didn't know whether she was meant to reply to the question, or not.

'You have spent all morning in your hotel room, waiting for my telephone call. Is that right?'

'No, I've been working,' May defended herself.

'That's very good. So much the better.'

'I've just finished "Re-evaluation",' May told her.

'Good. Very good.'

'Perhaps we could meet in the Jardin du Luxembourg?'

'Yes, we could,' Francine replied.

'Or I could come to your place and we could go there together?'

'I'll wait for you at the gardens, near the orchard, in front of the Baudelaire statue. Do you know where that is?'

'Yes.'

Francine was sprawled on a green wrought-iron chair, her head tilted towards the sun. She opened her eyes as May approached. 'I'm sorry. I didn't find a chair for you,' she said. 'There's one over there, look.' She pointed with her chin to one further down the path, and May went over to get it. Francine watched her return with the chair, place it on the gravel path, and sit down. 'I'm going to sleep a little while,' she told May. Then she closed her eyes again. She looked faintly amused. As if she had completed an experiment, and she had learned what she had wanted to learn. May sat there, thinking out an improbable conversation. Eventually, she closed her eyes, and began listening to the birds.

May had returned to Paris only a few more times after that – over the Bank Holidays and in her mid-term break – and stayed each time at the same hotel in the nineteenth *arrondissement*. She got to know the hotel's uniform rooms: the wardrobes, with the thin doors that creaked when you opened them; the linoleum floors, with their dips and slants; the basins with the plastic tubs below; the varyingly sagging beds; the spindly tables with their flowery-bright yellow or green tablecloths; and the glass ashtrays, advertising 'Pernod'. She sat at a table every morning, drinking tap water and peeling endless mandarins into ashtrays as she scrawled hopeless notes into an exercise book. At 1 p.m., she visited Francine, who would then explain – over rice and courgettes, or radishes followed by an omelette with bread – the various paragraphs that May had not understood.

Then, fortunately – even though May did like to visit her; it just wasn't easy, it was never a relaxing experience – at the end of November Francine went to Canada; but two months would pass quickly, she assured May, and if May wrote to her, she would reply. 'Work on your PhD,' she said, 'and we shall see each other again in February.'

4
The Letter

The day after her rat dream May returned from work, with the letter to Francine still in her bag. She opened the door to the bedsit, and flicked the light switch. Nothing happened. A second later the hall light, on timer, clicked itself off. This was so symbolically 'right', she thought as she stood there in the dark; it was the material representing the abstract (her life), but maybe she was just cold, and tired and hungry. She pressed the hall light back on again, looked in her wallet for a one-pound coin, and quickly topped up the electricity meter. During this time May received a text message from her younger sister Elizabeth in Cambridge:

Will call at 8. Be there, or be square! Ex

May considered 'being out'; perhaps she could go to the Portuguese café round the corner? While she was considering this, her mobile rang.

'Are you at home?' It was Elizabeth.

'I've only just got in. Can you call back in ten minutes?' At least then she could get herself a coffee.

'Well, call me when you're ready.' Elizabeth didn't want to pay for the call.

'No, I'll be ready in ten minutes, next to the hall phone with my coffee. You can call that phone.'

'All right. Okay.' Elizabeth hung up, without saying goodbye.

Her mobile rang again. It was Jansen. 'May, I'll probably have to get off the phone soon,' she said, 'so I can't talk –'

'You're ringing to say you can't talk?' May really needed a hot drink.

'I'm ringing to let you know I've got a pickup in Hertfordshire, which means I won't get back until ten, ten thirty.'

'Okay.' Information received.

'I'm sorry I'm going to be late.'

'Hmm.'

'May, I've got to go.' Her next passenger had arrived. 'Could you put my pyjamas in the bathroom?'

That was a totally unsatisfying call. May got her coffee, and went to wait on the landing for the phone to ring. While she sat there, the hall light went on and off as various tenants from the other rooms came and went. The guitar-player passed her on his way upstairs where he started 'Knockin' on Heaven's Door' for the twenty-seventh time that week; the young Australian woman from the next-door studio hiked by, carrying a large rucksack. She'd have been to the laundrette. 'Hi,' she said. May said, 'Hi.' That was as far as communication went in this house, and it suited May. 'Well, call me then!' she said aloud, after the woman had gone into her studio. 'If you're going to.' The guitar-player moved on to 'No Woman, No Cry'. May looked at her watch: that was twenty minutes. She got up and went back to the studio, switched on the bedside lamp, found the envelope she had once more forgotten to post, and opened it.

Chère Francine, she read.

Well that was already a problem: Francine wrote '*ma* chère May'. But is that what an older woman does? Is allowed to do?

'*My* dear Francine' – did May (she didn't think she did), did she have the right to 'embrace' Francine, to own her with such an expression?

'Write to me your thoughts as they unfold,' Francine had told her in a postcard from Canada; basically, she wanted stream-of-consciousness authenticity:

I wanted to let you know . . . How are you? Welcome back! (May had started again) *I expect you are very busy, as always . . . Dear Francine, How are you? How was Canada? I'm fine. In two weeks I am on holiday.*

*I won't be going anywhere . . . Dear Francine, How are you? I'm very
well. The holidays are coming up, which I'm very . . . How are you? I'll
be interested to hear about your time in Canada. I'm well. The holidays
are coming up, which I'm pleased about . . . Dear Francine, Thank you
for the letter (and the postcard). I'm writing to let you know . . . I'm
writing because . . . I wanted to let you know that I have decided to defer
the PhD. I now realize that I feel unprepared, and perhaps I'll always be
unprepared . . . I have decided to defer the PhD, because I have come to
realize . . . Because I feel unready, I have decided, having embarked on
background reading, that I . . . I have come to realize* (May had tried
again) *that, although I have read quite a lot around my PhD topic (not
yet quite defined) . . .*

May now looked at her letter. It was draft number five; she had
freely written six or seven pages, and then cut the unacceptable, which
brought it down to a page. After that, she had shifted paragraphs
about, inserted some niceties, and the result was what she had in her
hand. She just wanted to check now, once more, that she was happy
with the final product, which (literally translated) went:

> *Dear Francine,*
> *I received your letter, which very much pleased me.*

She skimmed past the greetings, read the watered-down confession about deferring her PhD, and then added a PS:

> *The other night I had a strange dream –* blah, blah, blah, the rat dream
> *– What do you think? I don't know what to make of it.*

A lie, of course. Francine was back from Canada, and May had
made no progress with the PhD; the rat was Francine, and May was
frightened of her. It didn't take a genius. Also, if May admired Francine (which she did) that was understandable, but if it was anything
more than admiration (which perhaps it was), that was worrying – if
May could dare to think about it – because Francine was, in fact, a

powerful woman. And the only thing that kept May safe was that Francine couldn't possibly like her. May wished she hadn't added the dream – and perhaps she shouldn't have mentioned the deferral; she slid the letter back into the envelope and resealed it. If she went out briefly now, to post it, Elizabeth would call while she was out. She put on her coat, and went out anyway.

May got back ten minutes later, still holding the envelope. She had decided against posting it. But she could always use some of what she'd written in the new version. A note was pinned to the door: *Call Elizabeth*. May sent her sister a text:

Back now. Call if like.

She made herself another coffee, and waited once more on the landing, to the sound of 'Lady in Red'. Valentine's Day was coming up, but she and Jansen didn't buy each other cards or flowers – only sometimes, if it occurred to them. Shortly before they'd got together – May was twenty-three, living in a bedsit near London Bridge and doing her PGCE, and Jansen was still in the army – Jansen had sent her a tiny pewter bear; he was the size of a thumbnail. May kept him in her wallet. And when they moved into their first home, a pokey flat in Islington (central, and on the line to Jansen's work), May sat him above the fake fireplace, on the mantelpiece next to Jansen's teddy bear. After that they'd moved to a ground-floor flat in Pimlico (it was closer to work for both of them, plus it had a sunny front room with bay windows); and that was where – May felt sick whenever she thought about it – she had thrown (it was almost a year ago now) the tiny bear out of the window into the back garden. What she'd meant to do was just express her anger, and then she was going to go and find him; but he was the size of a thumbnail, and the garden was overgrown with rose bushes. 'I'm going to go and look for him,' May announced, and their argument was put on hold. After a while Jansen came out and helped; it got dark, and they never found him.

Which was why they were now living in a cheap (-ish) bedsit in

Stockwell, with most of their books and some of their furniture in storage: Jansen was sorry for having laughed when May had told her about how her lecturer had once said she had a 'fine mind'; they'd talked about possibilities; and Jansen had suggested they move somewhere cheap so that May could save for the university fees to do a PhD. It had also meant Jansen could finally give up her stressful Human Resources job and –

The phone rang.

'Hello.'

'Oh, hi-ee!' It was a high-pitched girly voice. 'Is Mandy there? Room ten?'

'Just a moment.' May knocked at room ten. 'Phone for you', she said, and went back to the studio to get herself some supper: sardines on toast. She sat on the bed, switched off her mobile – eliminating the possibilities for disturbance while she ate – and stared at the envelope; she didn't have the energy to start another letter that evening. Nor did she at all have the energy for Elizabeth, who probably wanted to sort out some free accommodation in London, because there was going to be a gig, or a wacky exhibition or something. Well, if she wanted to talk, she'd persevere, and eventually get through to the hall phone.

May ripped open the envelope for the last time. It would go into her Francine file.

'Thank God for that! I've got you at last!' (May looked at her watch. It was nearly ten.) 'I've left you *three* messages. Then I tried the hall phone again. (It's engaged *all* the time, by the way. Did you know that?) Finally someone answers the phone, and I have to wait twenty minutes while they go and get you! Oh well, no problem – you can't call me back though, can you?'

'No,' May said.

Silence. Then, 'Are you in a bad mood? Is this a bad time to call?'

'No. I am just not paying for the call. Sorry.'

'Yeah,' inhaling of cigarette smoke, 'sure. Just a moment.' (. . .)

'Right. I've just got my ashtray. So how's Jansen? How are you?' she went.

'How are you?' May asked. 'What are you calling about?'

'Nothing much. Just a catch-up.' (That was unlikely.) 'And to see if you felt like a visit this weekend.'

'I'll be in Paris.'

'Again! What's in Paris? Or should I say "who"?'

May didn't reply.

'I'm just kidding: joke,' Elizabeth said. 'Okay, what about the following weekend?'

'Jansen's not working and we're spending it together.'

'Right.'

They were silent again. May realized that if she were Jansen, she would be attempting light chat, she'd be asking interested questions about Elizabeth's night class, her sculpting, she'd be finding out more about the flat. May felt under no such obligation; if Elizabeth was not going to talk, May would respond with a polite muteness.

'Right. Well, I guess I'll find somewhere else . . . Listen, I won't keep you then.'

May was going to see Francine. That was the first thing she thought after Elizabeth had more or less hung up on her. Paris: Francine. May hadn't seen her since November, and now she would be there in less than five days, having lunch with her in her apartment. Her arms tingled at the thought. It was four days, in fact, less than four. So, perhaps there was no point in sending the letter; perhaps she could decide on the spot whether to mention the deferral or not, once she was in Paris; and perhaps, also, there was no real need to mention the deferral just yet – when maybe she'd really get started on the PhD . . . Anyway – she did a happy little jump – *la joie*! She folded Jansen's pyjamas, placed them lovingly on the edge of the bath, and went to wait in the dark for her return.

5

Her Head

Francine looked across the kitchen table at her: 'The English don't know how to cut hair.' She dipped a radish into a small bowl of salt. 'It looks as if they've put a bowl on your head and cut around it!' Francine bit into the radish.

May smiled at this wonderful directness.

'That is a lot better already, put to one side,' Francine said, rearranging the fringe. 'Turn around. Oh yes!' Throwing her head back, dismayed, to the side, eyebrows lifted. 'They've given you a boy's cut!'

May let her hair be flicked about this way and that.

'Next time, you must come to my hairdresser's. You look like a boy. I do know it's the fashion among young lesbians, but there are people who don't suit short hair. Do you wish to look like a boy? Is that what you want?' Francine of course had short hair – dark brown, just beginning to go grey – she had very short hair; and yes, it suited her. Perfectly.

It was a mistake, May now realized, to have got her hair cut in England. It was not an elegant cut. She could have been beautiful with an exquisite, refined, sharp-soft, flick-to-the-side look (achieved at a French coiffeur's) that would have suited her long oval face, and accentuated her cheekbones. Her actual cut – ten pounds at the local hairdresser's – was, on this occasion, an auburn 'Joan of Arc' (a Jean Seberg). She did feel more comfortable with this rough short cut. She would be too seductive otherwise; she flattered herself, not really believing it.

'How is Jansen?' Francine took another radish. She had not yet met Jansen, but she always asked after her.

'Fine,' May said. 'She's still driving for now, says she's happier doing that. She wonders what she's doing with her life though, I think – we're a bit the same in that way.'

'What do you mean "the same"? You're doing a PhD, aren't you? Although, apart from that, you have not the slightest idea of what you want to do, none at all, as far as you tell me.'

May smiled, trying to look pleased. She would tell her about the deferral later. 'No, but I have to get on and do something with my life. I'm doing the PhD, which is good, even though I'm only doing it part-time, which does slow things down of course. But still . . .'

May gave her a cheerfully philosophic look. She knew she must irritate someone like Francine, who was preparing two books for publication at the same time; an article she had written was 'exploding into a book'. Her collection of essays was coming out in less than a month. Her visit to Canada had gone 'extrêmement bien'. They were inviting her back, all expenses paid.

'Ah! I have something for you.' Francine left the kitchen, then returned a few seconds later with an old French paperback, and a copy of yet another article she had written: 'on Lucie Delarue-Mardrus'. Did May know the writer? She did at least know the name?

'Peut-être.' And perhaps not.

Francine handed her the book. '*L'Ange et les pervers*.' She announced the title. 'Nineteen thirty-four. Out of print, quite obviously. You will return it to me on your next visit.'

'Thank you very much.' May carefully opened the precious edition.

'Show it to your supervisor. She will know her.'

'Yes.' May shrugged. 'I imagine. Yes, she's sure to. I don't know.'

'If she's supervising a thesis on cross-dressing in French lesbian literature, one would hope so.'

May put the book into her bag. 'Well, yes,' she said, 'in that case, she will know her. That's good.' As she didn't have a supervisor, she wanted to get off the subject.

'One would expect,' Francine continued. 'What is your super-visor's name? I know her perhaps.'

'I can't quite remember now – Pattrick or Fitzpattrick?' May invented. 'I haven't actually met her yet. She's been very busy. I've been more or less working on my own ...'

'But she must expect you to send her your work? She ought to be commenting on what you've written. It's her job to do that! You should complain. (In your position, I certainly would.) You must send her a short letter or an e-mail – to this Pattrick-Fitzpattrick character – telling her you expect to meet her at least once a month. You haven't met her yet? It's farcical!'

May decided now to mention her fears about doing the PhD.

After some discussion on the subject of courage, ability, perspi-ration and perseverance, Francine came to her conclusion: 'It's true you aren't an intellectual, but after all you don't have to be one in order to write a thesis.' Francine, direct as always, weeded out May's unnecessary obsessions.

Later that afternoon, May, clearly not an intellectual, walked back to the hotel Henri IV, taking in the knowledge. She crossed the Pont-Neuf. Paris at dusk. She felt relieved. Much like how she had felt when 'Purgatory' (as she now referred to her ex) had left her for another student at university. Aching in the same way as one might ache after having nerves removed from under a tooth. In dulled pain, she had gone out and chosen a sea-green jacket with buttons not one alike, to celebrate the event. Purgatory would not have liked the jacket; May had bought it. And this release from being an intellectual, the latest 'surgical removal', would free up a consid-erable amount of headspace. If she had told Jansen she was not intellectual material, Jansen would not have laughed – she was too kind; she would have replied, 'But you could be if you really wanted to be.' May might have wanted to be an intellectual if she had been capable of it, but she wasn't. Anyway, intellectuals don't go around wondering if they are intellectuals or not. They have more pressing matters to ponder over. Thirty-one, and she was just realizing that ever since primary school, she had been hoping that, somewhere inside herself, she was a latent intellectual, that one day it would all come out. But she was not an intellectual. It hurt.

'If I'm not an intellectual, can I still be intelligent?' she had asked Francine as she left her apartment.

'Of course! What did they teach you in school?'

May didn't understand. She cried.

6

Head to Head

Jansen wasn't working on Sunday evening, so she met May at the Eurostar terminal, Waterloo, and drove her, in their orange Skoda, D reg, to a 'very special restaurant', which specialized in seafood, and where there was live music; one of her passengers had told her about it, she said, and she wanted to take May there, as an early Valentine's present.

The tiny restaurant was in the basement of a four- or five-storeyed house in Chelsea. There was just one remaining free table, next to a wooden platform with an upright piano on it. The waiter lit their table's candle, and left them to peruse the menus.

May considered hers. 'I don't mind at all if we don't eat here,' she reassured Jansen.

'You're not paying for this, May. You can just enjoy it.' That sounded like an order. Jansen was pre-menstrual perhaps.

'I'll only have a main then – and a cappuccino perhaps.' Even that was expensive.

'Have anything you like – this is on me. I'm going to have a main and a pudding,' Jansen said.

May looked at the desserts. 'Perhaps we could share a pudding? That would be romantic.'

'I might want one of my own.'

Jansen would want the crème caramel.

Someone dimmed the lights slightly.

'That's better.' May smiled. 'Now we can all look beautiful.'

Jansen laughed. 'I like the way you've done your hair, on the side like that,' she said. 'It's a bit different.'

'And you really don't think it's too short?'

'No. No, I don't. It works.'

'Francine thinks it's too short.'

'Do *you*?'

'It could be a bit longer. It could be that I'm conforming to a certain dress code, was what she thought; although I don't think so. I hope not.'

Jansen went back to studying the menu.

'But *you* think it's okay?' May asked.

'I've just said that, yes.'

'You suit your hair,' May said. 'It's a bit longer at the moment, but it looks good. I like your hair long, and I like it short, too.'

'Thank you.' Jansen acknowledged the compliment.

Presently, the waiter returned. May said she'd 'go for the "pan-tossed freshwater trout with rocket and potato salad drizzled with balsamic vinegar and olive oil", please', and Jansen chose a 'fillet of wild turbot and an aubergine, chilli and chive flatbread'. After that, a man in an evening suit stepped up onto the wooden platform, and started playing 'Moonlight Serenade'. Jansen smiled at May. Then she clearly decided the timing was right and she mentioned Tamsin. 'She's coming down to London for an interview at the end of the month. I thought we could invite her to dinner. Perhaps she could even stay at our place – I haven't said anything to her yet . . .'

May thought silence might express better than words how she felt about that idea.

Jansen expressed other thoughts, also using silence.

'I can't mind-read,' May said.

'Neither can I. Could you please tell me how you would feel about her staying? And I'd appreciate it if you'd give it some thought, before you say no. You did invite Francine to stay.'

'Ha, ha, ha.' That was obviously different; Francine was so obviously not going to accept the invitation.

'No, "ha-ha-ha" nothing. You invited her without asking me.'

Jansen picked up the jug of iced water that was placed on the table between them, and filled their glasses. 'At the very least, I'd like to invite her round to dinner. You didn't see her last time she came to London.'

'You haven't even met Francine yet.'

'If you'd like me to come to Paris with you next time, that would be fine.'

May let the suggestion waft past.

The pianist came to the end of his first piece, a few people clapped, he played the opening notes of 'My Funny Valentine', paused for the amused laughter, smiled, and went on.

'Maybe you and Tamsin could go to Saint James's Piccadilly together, and hear a truly provoking sermon.' May shared her thought.

Jansen ignored the thought.

'No, maybe you could: it's not a bad church, as far as I know; it's not all eternal smiling; they deal with the real world.'

'Is that an attack on Tamsin? Because if so, it isn't amusing – or accurate.'

'I wasn't attacking her; I was coming up with an idea – not that I'd be interested in accompanying you though.' May took a sip of the water. It was so cold it made her teeth hurt.

'So, if you could think seriously about her staying. I need to know before Friday. You've got a whole week.'

After a while, the waiter came back to their table with two very large – 'careful; very hot' – dishes, a minimalist arrangement. May set her face into an expression of impressed appreciation. Jansen thanked him, and he went away.

'I've got another article from Francine to read, something she wrote in Canada.'

Jansen made no comment.

'And a book.'

'I may as well not have spoken,' Jansen said.

May sighed.

'I don't know whether you do it deliberately . . .'

The pianist moved on to some light jazz.

'Do you have any idea that you're doing it?' Jansen persisted.

'You said I've got a week to think about it.'

'Mm-hmm. I'd like some sign that you've heard what I've said. I think that's a reasonable expectation.'

'"How was your weekend in Paris, May? How was it with Francine?"' May decided to go on the counter-offensive.

Jansen began to eat her flatbread.

'Bon appétit.'

'When is it you're going to Paris again?' Jansen pursued the subject.

'I thought I'd go there in a couple of weeks. That'd give me time to read the article and the book she gave me. I'm supposed to give her a ring, once I've decided on the date. But I think two weeks, rather than three.'

Jansen nodded. 'Right. So you're thinking of going to Paris the very weekend Tamsin would be here?'

'What evening would she be coming to dinner?' May asked. 'I'd be back by Sunday evening – not that I'll be feeling like socializing . . .'

'I guess we could make it Sunday. I think she's got her interview on Friday though. I'll need to talk to her about it.'

'She wouldn't stay the weekend though, would she? In the bedsit?'

'You don't want her to. Quite clearly.'

'Where would she sleep?'

'On the sofa bed. Like Elizabeth.'

'Yes, but Elizabeth's my sister.'

'If you don't want Tamsin to stay in the bedsit while you're away, I won't ask her.'

'Thank you. Can I talk about my time with Francine now? Can we talk about something else?'

Jansen said nothing.

'I can't? What?'

'You're unbelievable,' Jansen said.

'We've arranged the dinner with Tamsin, haven't we?'

'Yes, we have.'

'"I look forward to seeing her",' May said. 'Is that what I'm supposed to say? And, "I'm so happy for you that she's moving to London."'

Jansen scratched the back of her neck. 'Maybe,' she said. 'Yes.'

'Anyway, thank you for this lovely meal.' May had another sip of her water. 'I'm sorry that we're having an argument and ruining the evening.'

'We're not having an argument; we're having a discussion. And we are not ruining the evening.'

'I'm worried about the PhD.'

'Yeah.'

'And I didn't tell Francine I've deferred.'

'Uh-huh.' Jansen topped up their water.

7

The Angel and the Perverts

Jansen started her four-day shift the next morning. She set the alarm early because she had to go out to the 'bin' and swap the Skoda for a company car. May decided to call in sick with a migraine.

'I've got my book to read!' she defended herself as she climbed back into bed.

Jansen nodded. 'Would you please make dinner then, since you've decided to take the day off?' She tucked her teddy bear into bed.

'If I'm going to Paris in two weeks,' May continued, 'I have to spend a bit of extra time preparing for it. I'm going to sleep, and then I'm going to spend the rest of the day reading. *L'Ange et les pervers*, Francine's said it's of interest – on the subject of cross-dressing.'

'I thought you decided you definitely weren't interested in doing the PhD.'

'Until I've told Francine I've deferred I have to keep working on it, don't I?'

'Mm-hmm.' Jansen gave that some thought.

'What?'

'No, I was just wondering . . . I'm just curious. The thing is: you've got the ideal situation, where you can actually meet up with the person you want to do your PhD on, and she's even willing to help you: she keeps lending you books and articles; she asks you when you're next going to visit. That's rare.'

'What are you saying?'

Jansen said nothing.

'What are you saying?' This was annoying. 'If you're going to start an idea, can you finish it?'

'It has to be your decision, May. I don't want to tell you what to do.'

'You've started telling me, so just tell me!'

'You'll say no straight away.'

'You think I ought to do the PhD.' May guessed the obvious.

'Have you ever thought of asking her if she'd mind looking at your proposal?'

'I haven't got a proposal!' And Jansen knew that.

'You've made lots of notes for one though, haven't you?'

'Notes, yes.' Which meant nothing.

'She could have some advice. That's all. Now that's she's back in Paris she might even be able to help you get started, help you with the exact wording . . .'

May laughed. 'No, Francine is not like that. No.'

'Well, I knew you'd say that.' Jansen put on her chauffeur's blazer, and picked up her bag.

'No, because I'm the one who has to do it. "Oh, please write my proposal for me": no, that's not acceptable. Anyway she already has helped me with it: I'm doing "cross-dressing".'

'All right. I knew you'd reject my idea; but I just thought, if you're now changing your mind and you're thinking again about doing the PhD, maybe you could ask her for some specific help.'

'I'd have to write the proposal first, wouldn't I? I'd have to make some attempt. Obviously.'

'Yes, you would – darling, I've got to go.'

'And why would I be asking for feedback on my proposal, if I'd already submitted it last September? I'm *doing* the PhD, remember! I'm in the middle of it!'

'Yeah. You'd have to let her know you hadn't started it yet.' Jansen kissed May on the cheek. 'Anything simple: you could do pasta with pesto sauce, and you could do a salad. Sleep well. Do you want me to turn off the light?'

★ ★ ★

Some time later May woke up; it was twelve o'clock: she'd wasted the morning. Her brain kicked straight back into gear, nagging her to do something with her life. Someone with a more positive way of phrasing things might have called it a 'yearning desire', but she felt it like a pain in her heart and throat: a daily pressure to come a little closer to her real path. In the meantime, she had the day off work and should be using it. There was the article from Francine; and the novel to read – first, she should read it first: because it would help her understand the article, or it should do; but then, of course, reading the article would help her understand the book; it should do, or it might not. Why, when she had the time, did she have to turn everything into a long drawn-out problem? She had been the same at university, leaving essays until the night before they were due in, until the anxiety had built up into an unbearable pressure:

'Hello, it's May.' She'd rung her lecturer once, after bingeing on a packet of chocolate biscuits and arriving at the desperate crazy point.

'Hello, *how* are you?' Madame Sacquin puffed out her aitches.

'I can't write this essay.' She stated it like a diver waiting to go off a high-diving board.

'Have you read the book?'

'Yes.'

'Have you understood it?'

'Yes.'

'Do you understand the question?'

'Yes.'

'Well then, you just *have* to answer the question. You start at the beginning. You decide what you are going to cover, you say what you are going to do and you do it, and then you conclude.'

'Hm.'

'It is always the most capable who worry the most,' Madame Sacquin had told her. 'I could tell you not to worry, but I know you will worry: because you *have* a fine mind.'

A fine mind. You have a fine mind. I know you will worry, because you have a fine mind. For a while – a bit like a placebo – it had worked: May had completed her degree; a Masters; then, at twenty-two, she had scrawled out a proposal for a PhD, moved her 'fine mind' with its enormous potential to Lille; and within six months she had given up on her studies; because, despite her promising tendency to worry, she hadn't believed she could do it.

And ever since then she'd been unable to do nothing – which was what she had gone on and done – without worrying all the time about what she ought to have been doing, with her 'fine mind'.

Which was why it was so important, now, that she finally do something perhaps.

May got up, and opened the curtains. It was raining. She'd stay in bed – she'd made her decision – and read the book. She sat up with her earplugs still in, pulled the duvet over her knees, and opened at the beginning of *L'Ange et les pervers*:

Il a rêvé souvent que sa mère, (He often dreamed that his mother,)
ou plutôt la bête aveugle (or rather the blind beast)
qui agit en nous (that acts in us)
indépendamment de notre esprit, (independently of our spirit,)
a dû, (must have,)
lorsqu'elle le portait, (when she was carrying him,)
préméditer des jumeaux, (premeditated twins,)
car, (for,)
depuis l'âge (since the age)
où l'humain entre dans (when the human enters into)
l'angoisse de l'âme, (the anxiety of the soul,)
son instinct lui a fait sentir (his instinct had made him feel / made him aware of)
à ses côtés (at his side)
un mystérieux second lui-même. (a mysterious second self.)

Outside, behind the barred windows, the sycamore in the back garden waved a branch at her. Perhaps she should read the article first? May pencilled a fifth question mark into her notebook. It didn't help that there was now – despite the earplugs – a throbbing in her head; it was coming from the upstairs flat: the guitar-player. It seemed as if he was having a temper tantrum with his loudspeakers; he was demanding attention from the whole house. She would ignore him. Page two ... (if she could just concentrate). Three question marks into page three she took out her earplugs, and dropped the book onto the carpet. It sounded as if he was whacking a mallet on the floor in time to the bass-techno-thud. May found the landlord's number:

'What do you want me to do about it, darling? I can't throw him out.'

'No (. . .). Well, if you could speak to him.'

That was a waste of time. How much would it cost, May wondered as she threw handfuls of knives and forks into the sink (combining her rage with doing the dishes), if she told him not to call her 'darling'? Would they lose their bond as a result? Her soul was surely worth that much. It was prostitution to accept such familiarity.

At about this time across the Channel, in her *rive gauche* apartment, Francine would be hard at work, tapping out yet another article, to the sound of Mozart, or Bach, or Paderewski. To whatever background accompaniment she had chosen that afternoon. The only other sounds would be those, echoing up from the courtyard, of the occasional friendly exchange between residents.

Jansen, conflict-resolver extraordinaire, went upstairs that night after work, still dressed in her chauffeur uniform, May noted, which would make her a little stronger. May stood listening at the foot of the stairs.

'Hello. I'm Jansen,' (she reminded him). 'I live downstairs at number two.' (Always introduce yourself.) 'With May. We are finding your music is too loud.' (State the problem. Start with 'I/We'.)

He would be standing there glaring at Jansen – May couldn't

hear anything now, but she could just imagine how it would go: he was limiting his (repetitive) late-night guitar-practice to ten o'clock; surely he could play his sound system during the day?

Five minutes later, Jansen came back downstairs: it turned out the guitar-player was a carpenter, who had just gone self-employed. He had no idea anyone was home during the day, or he'd never have put on his sound system so loud. He'd recently broken up with his girlfriend. It was Valentine's Day, and he was just trying to keep his mind off things.

'Amazing! He doesn't say he's sorry; he tells you his life story, and hopes to get sympathy.'

'He said he'd keep his music down, but apparently he's taken on a job for fifty bedside tables –'

'Oh my God!'

'I think we should just move, May. We're not going to get him to stop, are we? Realistically?'

'So we move? We just accept it, and we move?'

'You can try and talk to him if you want.'

'Very funny.'

'Why don't we just move? It's not as if you're even doing the PhD.'

'What do you mean? I haven't enrolled yet, that's all.'

8
Preliminaries

'Allô, c'est May.' She was standing in a telephone booth outside the school. It was dark. It was raining. Her hands were cold. Her nose was cold. She couldn't put her bag on the ground because it would get wet. Perhaps she should have gone home first, got rid of her bag, eaten something, warmed up, and then gone out to call her. But it was too late; she had already dialled.

'Ah, te voilà, toi!' Francine was eating. May had called her at the wrong time.

'Hello. How are you?'

Details concerning research for her next book; she'd now been officially invited to next year's conference in Montreal, but she had decided not to go; winter was dragging. And May? How was she?

'I'm fine. I'll be in Paris again in a week and a half, on the Saturday; will you be there? I'll be there at the end of the afternoon.' The telephone card had one pound forty left on it, which was probably enough.

'Yes, I'll be here. Do you want to book me in? But of course, you are right. I have other friends in Paris, other people I may want to see.'

'Yes.' Ninety-eight pence. May was having trouble speaking, and she was feeling self-conscious about her French.

'Well, I'll be here. Telephone me once you're in Paris. In any case, I'm not going anywhere.'

May said nothing. Ninety pence. She should probably get off the phone now anyway: Francine sounded busy.

'You must receive my messages,' Francine told her. 'Because I was saying to myself that you should call this evening. Did you receive my message? Do you practise telepathy? Or perhaps it was you sending me a message, and I received it.'

May sent a wordless response via the moon, to Francine's apartment. She smiled.

'I have just broken off with a person with whom I'd had a very long relationship,' Francine went on. 'Sophie – I had just finished talking to her on the telephone, when you rang. This is perfect – now the phone will be engaged if she tries to call.'

'Should I not –'

'I told her: here is the situation; it's over – because sometimes it is necessary to clear one's life of clutter. I am making space for something else. Do you understand what I'm saying?'

Francine was making space for her. The unlikely idea shot through May's system; it was like being injected with caffeine and camomile at the same time.

'Perhaps you will understand later,' Francine said. 'So,' she moved on, 'this is what I propose: you will call me when you arrive, and I shall let you know where to come and meet me. We'll go out to dinner. How does that sound?'

'Yes, lovely.' Would Francine cut May out of her life at some point? Sixty-five pence remaining: she should have bought another phonecard.

'Bring *L'Ange et les pervers*, and we'll discuss it over dinner. The angel is a perfect example of gender conformity. Have you read my article "The Transgressive Transvestite or the Chameleon?"?'

'No, I haven't read it – not yet – because I haven't quite read the novel yet, and I'm waiting to have read that, of course, before I read your article.'

'Of course, that's logical.'

'I've had a look at it though.'

(. . .) 'Excuse me; I'm eating while I'm talking to you. I'm having an early dinner, and now I really must get off the phone.'

'Jansen and I have been looking at flats – we've found somewhere now and we're moving in less than two weeks, to the new place – so I haven't had much time,' May quickly explained. Thirty pence: they'd be cut off soon. 'I'll call you once I'm in Paris,' she said. 'Bon appétit. I'll say goodbye now.' Twenty pence.

'Yes, that's right. You will call me and we shall speak when you arrive. Au revoir, May. Je t'embrasse.'

'Goodbye. Je –'

Sunday evening: May and Jansen had finished packing up half the wardrobe and most of the chest of drawers – the summer clothes and what they wouldn't need for the week – and they were finally in bed together, reading before going to sleep. May was on page twenty-seven of the Delarue-Mardrus novel, and Jansen was reading an article in the *Guardian Weekend Supplement* about baking double-chocolate biscuits.

'Oh yeah, just to remind you,' Jansen said. 'Tamsin will be coming to dinner this Sunday.'

'. . . *La grande fille rauque siffle un taxi* . . .' ('The tall girl with the husky voice whistles for a taxi.')

'If you want to put that into your diary,' Jansen continued.

'. . . *un taxi* . . .' May continued reading. '. . . *perdu dans les solitudes du Neuilly qui touche à la Seine*.' ('A taxi . . . lost in the "solitudes" of that part of Neuilly that touches the Seine.')

'She'll be here when you get back from Paris, from seeing Francine.'

'What was that?'

'Hm, she listens when I mention Francine.'

'I'm trying to read!'

'I'll tell you about it later.' Jansen went back to her chocolate biscuits.

'No, tell me about it now.' May shut the book, leaving her index finger in the page she was up to. 'What?'

'Tamsin's coming to dinner this Sunday.'

'Okay, but could you write that down for me? I can never remember anything just before going to sleep.' May opened her book again. It was beyond her how Jansen could continue to seek out the company of such an intensely earnest woman.

'We'll be meeting up in the afternoon,' Jansen told her. 'And going to the pictures, or an art gallery. I'm finishing work a bit early.'

'So you won't be able to meet me at Waterloo?' May looked up from her book. 'Is that what you're saying?'

'We might be able to, Your Majesty. What time does your train come in?'

'Five twenty-five.' May ignored the attack. In the early days, Jansen used to say it tenderly, and with love; she'd say: 'May, you don't happen to have royal blood in you, do you?' (But perhaps May went a bit far sometimes.)

'Do you want us to meet you?' Jansen said.

'I don't want you – plural – to meet me, no. Not if you're going to be with Tamsin.'

'Okay – you don't mind not being met,' Jansen confirmed.

'There's no point, is there? Because I'm not going to be able to really talk anyway, if she's going to be there.' May wanted to be met.

'We'll see you back here for dinner then.'

'I won't be able to say anything real with Tamsin around,' May completed her gripe, although now it was inane to bother. 'It will all be dull small talk.'

'It's up to you whether you want to be real or not,' Jansen said.

'And I really don't want a late night. I've got school the next day,' May reminded her.

'If this is going to be such an ordeal for you, perhaps we just forget it; I'll take her out to dinner, and then come home. That way you won't have to see her at all.'

'I thought you wanted me to see her! Now you *don't* want me to see her.'

'Would you like to see her?'

'Yes! And I don't want a late night, is what I'm saying.' She didn't want to see Tamsin, of course she didn't, but she knew she had to see her, or Jansen would be annoyed.

They ignored each other for a while.

'You know what this feels like?' May said, after a few minutes. 'I feel like you're being quiet, in order to leave a space, like a blank page, where I'm supposed to think about my excessive negativity.'

'May, you can be very complicated sometimes.'

'I just wish you would now and then make plans that only involved us.'

'We hardly *ever* see anybody!'

'Yes, okay, but do we do anything special just the two of us?'

'And the Valentine's dinner?'

'Like stay in a bed and breakfast, I'd love that. You remember that place years and years ago, near the army camp?'

May had come up from London on the train, it was right at the beginning of their relationship; and Jansen was waiting for her in the car park: she had the driver's seat tipped right back, and a book was leaning open against her thighs, but she wasn't reading, she had her eyes shut. May tapped on the window and Jansen lifted her head, without surprise, leaned over and opened the passenger door for May, who met her halfway out of a horizontal. They had a quick pub dinner, and then went straight to the bed and breakfast, a cute little seventeenth-century cottage.

'The doors were tiny; we could touch the ceiling of our room,' May said. 'It was like being in a dolls' house, remember. You said it was like going back in time. And we pulled the mattress onto the floor,' she laughed, 'because the bed was so *awful!*'

'It would be nice if you were slightly interested in seeing her,' Jansen said.

'I've just said: I *want* to see her!' May opened up her novel again. 'Can I get on with my book then, please? I've got to get this read before next weekend.'

'I'll bring her back here for coffee.' Jansen was stiffly grateful.

'Fine. That sounds good.' It didn't sound good, it sounded boring. May went back to her book. She knew she was a horrible person.

'I'd like to turn out the light now.'

'I'm reading – five minutes.'

9

In Paris Again

'I have already ordered, for I am as hungry as a wolf,' Francine said.

May took off her coat and put it on the back of her chair. 'Me too,' she said; then, 'Bonjour. Bonsoir, I mean.' She sat down.

'You look very well,' Francine observed. 'Your hair's grown a little. It suits you far better. Now you must leave it to grow.'

'How long?'

'You will have to experiment.' Francine looked at May, and smiled at her.

May smiled. She blushed. She picked up the menu and smiled into it as she flipped through the pages. Eventually she asked, 'What are you having?'

'A tomato salad as a starter, and pasta.' Francine took some bread from the little basket on the table, ripped off a piece, and put it into her mouth.

The waiter appeared, with the starter. He placed it in front of Francine. Then he turned to May. 'Would you like to order?'

'Yes, I would like the salmon, please,' May said, pointing to the dish on the menu.

'No starter?' Francine asked her.

'No. No, thank you.' May said this to the waiter.

'No salad?' Francine was surprised.

'Yes, a salad. Yes, please.' May changed her mind.

'A tomato salad, perhaps?' the waiter suggested.

'Yes, please. No, a green salad, rather.'

'Very good.' He left.

'You will forgive me. I am not going to wait for you.' Francine began eating.

May looked around the restaurant. Every table was taken.

'Ah yes!' Francine said as she forked another segment of tomato. 'I knew I had something to tell you: I have just finished a most wonderful novel, by a new writer, Anne Béranger; it is her first novel.'

'Anne Béranger – I might have heard of her. The name sounds familiar perhaps . . .'

'That would surprise me very much, given that the novel is not yet published; it is her manuscript that I have just read. Superb. She is an excellent writer.'

'Oh.' May nodded and tried to look impressed.

'She is a star rising into the firmament,' Francine continued.

May nodded again.

The waiter arrived with the salad. 'Une salade verte!' he announced, and he left again.

'She will be coming to my book launch in April – because I have invited her of course – so you will have the opportunity to meet her. She's an old friend of mine.'

May said 'Mm', and smiled, to look interested.

'Just before Easter,' Francine went on. 'You will be on holiday.'

'Yes. But I'll come to Paris before then – in two or three weeks?'

'Is that a question?' Francine took another piece of bread and dabbed it in the oil and tomato juice left on her plate.

'No, I mean, well I'm not sure: probably in three weeks, I think. Or two.'

'It doesn't matter. I'll give you this anyway.' Francine wiped her hands on her napkin, and pulled a thick folder out of her bag.

'Is it Anne Béranger's novel?'

'These are the rest of my essays,' Francine said, handing them to May. 'The ones that have not yet been published but that will be out in April – in my collection. You are going to be able to read them and come to the launch with questions to ask me.'

'I don't think I'd see myself as capable of asking questions at a book launch.' May put the folder straight into her bag.

'You are afraid of saying something stupid.'

'It would be difficult to speak at a book launch, especially in French.' May stared at her salad. She should start eating.

'Especially when one is shy,' Francine said.

'It's the language, too.'

'Yes, yes. Give yourself excuses.'

'No, French is not my language, so it's difficult for me.' May took a piece of bread and placed it next to her bowl of salad.

'It is a lack of willingness; a lack of courage above all. Language has absolutely nothing to do with it.'

'It really is more difficult.'

'Are you not going to eat your salad?' Francine asked. 'You haven't started it yet.'

'Yes.' May picked up her fork. Then she said, 'I can talk more easily in English. It depends on the situation, as well. With Jansen, for example, I talk a lot. Because we know each other well, and we talk all the time. She talks, but I talk much more than she does. And yet, I think she's more of an extrovert than I am. We really are very different.'

'Fortunately, or there would be no interest in your being together.'

May started her salad.

'You read well,' Francine told her, and she broke off another piece of bread.

'Thank you,' May said, because that was polite – not that she was sure she'd understood the compliment. Francine seemed to be saying – if that was possible – that she was quietly impressed with the various notes and letters she'd had from her; May felt as if she'd just been told she was beautiful; she felt light; she felt perhaps even liked by Francine. 'And thank you,' she felt flattered, 'for the essays.' It was as if, in an understated way, Francine had told her she liked her. 'Actually, I haven't yet finished reading *L'Ange et les pervers,*' May thought she'd better tell her, 'but I've got it here with me, if you need it back . . .'

'Return it to me when you have read it. In three or two weeks.'

They left the restaurant at about ten thirty. May asked, 'Would you like me to walk with you back to your apartment?'

Francine said, 'Yes, you can walk with me. And will you carry my bag, too?' She smiled and held out her bag.

'Yes, I will carry your bag if you like.'

'May, no! I am teasing you. Really, you are behaving like the boyfriend I never had!'

'I wouldn't want to be behaving like a man,' May said. 'I don't see myself like that.'

Francine asked, 'How do you see yourself? This is interesting.'

'Not like a man,' May said. She felt embarrassed.

'You see yourself as a woman then?' Francine said, and she laughed.

Francine was either being mean, or she was being flirtatious. 'I am a human being,' May said.

'Yes, but you are a woman also.'

'That's true, yes.'

They walked in silence for a while. It was so cold; the wind was icy. They crossed the Pont-Neuf, past the statue of Henri IV on horseback, looking over the prow of the island, towards the Seine.

'What a wind!' Francine said. 'It's horribly cold!'

'I can give you my gloves.' May pulled them off. 'I can put my hands in my pockets.' She gave them to Francine.

'Keep your gloves. Keep them! You will need them. In any case, it is time for you to go back to your hotel. It's late and you don't need to walk me all the way to my apartment.'

'No, I'd like to accompany you.' Did Francine not want May to walk with her?

'You can walk with me as far as my street,' Francine said, and she accepted the gloves.

If Francine (May let herself think this) ever – which she wouldn't – May would probably . . . yes, she probably would, but Francine probably wouldn't in the first case, which was fortunate – but she might. May pictured it, the beginning only, opening the door in the dark, but she couldn't imagine more; that would be sacrilege, unless Francine was the one to . . . in which case . . .

They arrived at the Théâtre de l'Odéon.

'May, this is my street,' Francine said as she stopped on the corner. 'And these are your gloves.' She took them off and gave them back.

May put them on. 'I could walk with you as far as your place,' she said.

'And what is Jansen doing this evening?'

'She's been working. But she'll be sleeping right now, I suppose.'

'You suppose? And she is not accompanying a woman back to her apartment?'

May said nothing. Then she said, 'No.'

It felt safer to pretend a simple question had been asked.

'Fine. Now I am going to say *bonsoir* and *bonne nuit*. Sleep well.'

May took another sip of her *café-crème*. She was in the *bar-tabac* near the hotel. It was early and there was only the waiter and one other customer, a man perched on a stool at the bar, smoking, drinking a small black coffee, and reading *Le Parisien*. She felt tired; her face was tight and dry from lack of sleep, and the coffee was giving her a headache. She was behaving, she thought, like someone who was falling in love. (Or were moments spent with a woman like Francine bound to feel vaguely sublime?) She looked at her watch: eight forty. Six hours before the train back to London. Francine seemed to be suggesting that May was in love with her; and she judged May for it. But that wasn't fair, and May wasn't even sure she was in love (she loved Jansen). Also – it was all a bit disturbing – was Francine's behaviour completely above board? May bit the crispy tip of her *croissant au beurre*. Perhaps she'd wander along the Seine; or she could go to the Gibert-Jeunes near Saint-Michel Métro and find a few second-hand books, or to the open-air book market at the Parc Georges Brassens. Not that she needed any more books or anything else to read; she still hadn't finished *L'Ange et les pervers*, and she had semi-read but had not understood Francine's essay on Delarue-Mardrus (so she needed to reread the essay), and now Francine had given her nine more essays to read.

May opened *L'Ange et les pervers* at the beginning of chapter seven:

'*Me voilà lancée dans l'immoralité des autres . . . se dit Miss Hervin rentrée chez elle . . .*' ('Here I am launched into the immorality of others . . . Miss Hervin said to herself once she was back home . . .')

10

Tamsin

The clothes were too careful; the colours were too bold; the shirt was done up too high; she didn't eat biscuits, 'thanks'; she didn't drink coffee, 'oh, no thanks.' If they had ordinary tea though, she'd be interested. How could Jansen ever have had a thing for the woman? Her smooth, soft voice was so calm, as if she had camped in a library all her life; it was as if some disaster had occurred, and her voice had got stuck on 'soothe'. Talking to her, you started to feel like you were a crash victim. And what were her plans for the Easter holidays? A silent retreat.

Jansen set the tray of tea, coffee and rejected biscuits on the floor in front of them, and Tamsin moved forward, politely eager, from the sofa, dropping her jumper onto the tray.

Jansen leaped off her chair. 'Don't worry. I'll get it.' She picked up the jumper, and shook the crumbs out over the sink. 'You've got chocolate on it, I'm afraid,' she said, handing it back.

'Sorry,' Tamsin said. 'That's so clumsy of me.'

'No, you're fine.' Jansen poured the tea and passed a cup to Tamsin, who immediately spilt it over the biscuits.

'Blast! What's wrong with me today?' Tamsin said. 'I'm so sorry.'

'You really don't like my baking, do you?' Jansen laughed, carefully picking up the plate of soggy biscuits and taking it over to the bench.

'I'm so sorry,' Tamsin repeated. She went bright red. 'Is that all the biscuits?'

'We've got Digestives, I think. It's not a disaster.' Jansen sponged up the rest of the tea on the tray, got a packet of biscuits out of the cupboard, and sat down again. 'Oh, May!' She had thought of something they could talk about: 'Tamsin and I were remembering our army days –'

Tamsin smiled here and shook her head, closing her eyes as if it was all too ridiculously amusing, and nodded to Jansen, to get her to continue.

'We were remembering the night the SIB came to the camp, the "Special Investigation Branch" – of the Royal Military Police,' Jansen explained.

'And did a search.' Tamsin took over now, coming to life. 'A warning came through on the switchboard: "Quick! The SIB's coming!" You weren't allowed *any* alcohol *at all* in the block, but a lot of people had their secret supplies. So everything was piled into plastic bags – vodka, sherry, wine, some people had dope to get rid of, letters, cards, magazines – and Jansen drove it all out to someone's brother's for safekeeping.'

Laughter.

'Being a chauffeur's not exactly the same: long waits at Gatwick and Waterloo for late arrivals,' Jansen said. 'Missed connections –'

'Yeah but what about the rich and famous?' Tamsin reminded her. 'Who was it you had in your car the other day? Mick Jagger, wasn't it? Or Mick Fleetwood? I always get them confused,' she said, laughing at herself.

'Mick Fleetwood,' Jansen told her.

'That's right, you told me.' Tamsin blushed again. 'I'm useless with names.'

The conversation moved on to job-hunting: how to fill in an application form, the importance of following the 'person speci-fication', interview skills: it was so important what you wore; first impressions were everything, and if you could show you were enthusiastic.

At a lull in that conversation, Tamsin announced she was 'pretty whacked', that she'd head off now – if that was all right – and leave them to get on with their packing. Jansen nodded in silence, said,

'Fine, yeah' and accompanied her out of the bedsit to the front door of the house.

'Is she always like that?' May asked Jansen after she returned. 'I felt as if we were at an intensive course for job-seekers. I don't think I could've coped with much more than an hour. Thank God she was tired.'

Jansen squirted dishwashing liquid into the baking tray, and filled it with hot water.

'All she seemed to want to talk about was work.'

'She's looking for a job at the moment; of course she's going to want to talk about work. She's just had an interview.' Jansen handed May a tea towel.

'"I would really enjoy making sure each customer felt looked after." I wanted to say, I'm not thinking of employing you; you can relax now. But I think she really meant it; she was being sincere.'

'Some people enjoy going to work; just because you don't.'

May made a face. 'What irritates me is that, behind all those CV profile clichés, she really believes everyone else should live to work, like she does.'

'Is there anything you actually like about her?'

'She's got a "I'm really conservative" look about her. Sometimes I question your taste.' May yawned.

'Yeah. I question it too.'

Then Jansen left the bedsit. She left the house. Without slamming the door – she never slammed doors. It was freezing outside, and she didn't even have her jersey on.

May had been rude; she'd been rude about Tamsin – again. She hadn't meant to be quite so vocal, it was unattractive to rave on like that, but she found it hard to keep her mouth shut sometimes. May got Jansen's jersey, and her jacket; she put on her coat, and went out in the dark to the Flying Bull, the closest pub, where – yes – there was Jansen, sitting at the corner table, to the right as you come in.

May slid along the wooden bench opposite her. 'Hello,' she said. 'Sorry.'

Jansen ignored her.

'Is that an Irish Coffee?'

'Yeah.'

'I brought you your jersey – here you are – and your jacket.'

They sat there, not talking. May didn't know what to say; she couldn't start inventing compliments she didn't believe in. She knew it was because of Tamsin that Jansen had done something odd: gone into the army (as a truck driver, briefly); it was true that May's bizarre experience – staying in the barracks with Jansen, the morning bugle et cetera – might never have occurred, had it not been for Tamsin. In fact, Jansen would never have gone to Belgium over the summer, and therefore May would never have met her, in a remote lesbian nightclub somewhere in the Flemish countryside. It was the fourteenth of July 1989, the bicentenary of the French Revolution. May had had too much to drink and was crying on a falling-apart armchair, because she had never heard of Théroigne de Méricourt:

'One of *the* most well-known French Revolutionaries, one of the most important. It's astonishing you've never heard of her really – considering how very interested you are in the eighteenth century . . .' Nadine (a PhD student whom May had been hoping for months to impress) had told her, before strolling off in disgust to smoke her joint alone.

May had not heard of Théroigne de Méricourt, and through her haze of *vin rouge* she was nevertheless quickly able to work out what this would mean: she and Nadine could never be lovers now. It was a dismal certainty.

'Hello, my name is Jansen.' She had leant sympathetically across the coffee table at that moment, and firmly shaken May's hand.

This out of place gesture, the handshake, such kindness, such formality, May remembered it.

Jansen – her 'real' name was Jennifer Andersen, but no one called her that – was on leave from the army with a friend (Tamsin), and was, the following day, on her way back to Wilton, 'but we've got time for a dance now, if you like?' Such a kind smile.

'How can I get to see you again?' May suddenly developed the ability to be direct.

'I'll give you my number, but – to be fair – you'll have to give me yours.'

(Charming, the reply was charming.)

They had a few dances together – 'le rock' and one 'slow' – and sat chatting. Not having a phone in France yet, May had then given Jansen her mother's number in Canterbury, and, on the spot, determined to: give up her PhD research on Violette Leduc; forfeit her scholarship; and return to England, where she could get a teaching qualification, perhaps. May was not entirely 'compos mentis' when she made this decision to give up her PhD. But anyway, there was Jansen sitting opposite her now, nearly ten years later, calmly sipping on an Irish Coffee; and the only thing that really ever irked May was this blindness Jansen had around other people's faults – it was a real blind spot of hers – and then, of course, her inability to lose contact with Tamsin.

'You won't have noticed, but she ignored me tonight, most of the time. As usual.' May could not find anything nice to say, and she wouldn't waste her time trying.

'You haven't seen each other for a while. She probably had no idea what to say, but I think she likes you.'

'Hmm.' Jansen always thought the best of people. 'I'd probably be a university lecturer by now,' May said, 'if it wasn't for Tamsin.'

'"If it wasn't for Tamsin"? Ah, I see: it's her fault.'

'If you hadn't gone with her, to her uncle's in Mouscron –'

'If you hadn't met me: it's *my* fault,' Jansen corrected herself.

'I'm not blaming you. It's just a fact. If you hadn't gone to Belgium that year –'

'It was your decision to give up on your studies, May. No one forced you to.' Jansen picked up her cup and put it back down

59

again. 'That's why you've always been so obnoxious about her, though, isn't it? That's ridiculous.'

'I am not always obnoxious about her. And I'm not saying anything's her fault either. Or your fault. I am just saying.'

'It's not as if I got you pregnant,' Jansen said.

'Yuk! Don't be revolting.'

'Shall we go home?' Jansen gestured for the bill. 'We should really try and finish the rest of the packing this evening: because I'm not going to be able to help you much during the week. We could do the kitchen area together, if you like, and then have a hot drink and a Digestive biscuit.' She put on her jersey and her jacket.

'And I could tell you how the dinner went with Francine,' May added. 'I haven't even been able to tell you about it yet.'

'No, May. Tomorrow. I'm really tired.'

II

The Call

May wished she'd put the phone on 'no-ring'. She was in the bedroom of the new flat, sitting at the writing desk, surrounded by a mess of half-unpacked boxes of books. It was Friday evening, Jansen was putting paintings up in the sitting room, and what May should have been doing was quickly shelving all these books; so she could get on with using the rest of the weekend to finish reading the Delarue-Mardrus novel, and then Francine's essays. Because in one week she was going to Paris again, and she wasn't prepared yet, because of all the business of moving; and although it was Jansen who had done all the calling and the talking to people et cetera, May had still had to go with her to look at the places (and it was May's job to get the mail-forwarding set up, for example). In any case, May wasn't prepared.

'Kennington: that's zone two – not bad,' Elizabeth said. 'So what's it like?'

'Hmm.' There wasn't anything to say. 'It's a sixties council block. We're on the fifth floor. There's no lift. There's no balcony. It's tiny.'

'There's a sitting room though, isn't there?' Elizabeth wanted to know.

'There's a small sitting room, yes.' La Fayette, Labé; Leduc, Leduc, Leduc: she'd shelve them by century, perhaps – would be better . . .

'And how are the neighbours?'

'Quiet.' May stared out of the window at a block of flats identical to theirs.

'Great. That's why you moved, isn't it?'

'How's the sculpting class?' She had to get off the phone soon.

'Oh, I'm not going any more. I haven't been to the last three sessions.'

'What do you mean? You've dropped out?'

'Dunno – s'pose so; there are only five or six more to go anyway . . .' Elizabeth trailed off.

May made an interested, uninterested 'mm' sound.

'It's not really me,' Elizabeth said. 'And my flat's falling apart; everyone's on the verge of leaving. I think I might have to move out, too. Or I'll be caught with the lease. Anyway, I'm thinking I might move down to London and be on the dole there for a while, meet new people, see what happens . . .'

Elizabeth's first aim in life was always: to 'see what happens', and mainly just to have a good time; when she turned eight she suddenly developed an interest in the performing arts; she invited a straggle of friends to join her in a production of *Toad of Toad Hall*: some of them had significant voice parts, others were more suited to mime, or costume or prop or popcorn duty and so on (Elizabeth's specialty was scenery, plus dark-chocolate fudge) – and May's job was to supervise; it was around the time of her A-level exams, and she was supposed to welcome the diversion of being babysitter to a home-based repertory theatre. May wasn't threatened by Elizabeth, she didn't want to be like her, she just found her exhausting; it was exhausting being in the presence of all that laughter, people being constantly amused and uplifted; it was a drain. A few years later Jansen met the teenaged, multicoloured-tights version of Elizabeth; and naturally she found her 'really funny' and 'lots of fun'. At twenty-two, Elizabeth was still 'having fun', not taking life too seriously – and generally wasting it. (May was also wasting her life, quite possibly, but she wasn't *happy* about it.)

'All her flatmates are leaving,' May went and told Jansen, who was standing on a chair, banging a picture-hook nail into the wall above the sitting-room bookshelf.

Jansen stepped down off the chair.

'So – guess what? She's dropped out of her night class, and she's thinking of coming down to London.'

Jansen picked up their Rodin print and stepped back onto the chair with it.

'It's a really stupid idea. Already she's doing practically nothing, and now she wants to do nothing at all! She could at least finish the term.'

'For sure.'

'What?'

'I'm agreeing with you, May.'

'Are you saying I'm like her?'

'I'm agreeing with you.' Jansen was shifting the painting about, trying to get it straight.

'She could always move in July or June or whatever.' May went back to what she was saying. 'This is where I'm supposed to save her: I'm supposed to talk her into staying to the end of term. (Do you want me to help you with that?)'

'Yeah, could you please pass me the spirit level,' Jansen said. 'It's over there.'

'I'm not going to play that game.' May got the level from the sofa and passed it to Jansen. 'She can do whatever she wants.'

Jansen placed the level on top of the frame. She was about to make a suggestion; May could feel it coming. She waited. 'If she's really keen on moving to London' – Jansen got off the chair – 'perhaps we could ask her if she'd like to come and stay with us for few weeks – until she finds somewhere. Now that we've got a proper flat again. That might be an idea.' She looked up at the Rodin and smiled. 'What do you think?'

'We've only just moved! Everything's still in boxes.'

'Of course, if you're far too busy with that PhD . . .'

'I am busy with the PhD. What do you mean? I'm busy with it.'

'Good. Courbet over the sofa?' Jansen asked. 'Or in the bedroom?'

'Not in the bedroom!'

'Over the sofa then.' Jansen picked up *Le Sommeil*. 'Can you help me with this? You could take the other side.'

They held the large print – of two naked women entwined together in sleep – against the wall.

'Here?' Jansen said. 'Or a bit higher?'

'No, there, there. Bring it down a bit.'

'Okay I'll hold on to it, if you could do the mark. The pencil's on the bookshelf –'

May got the pencil and made a mark on the wall, and they put the print back on the floor.

'I don't want to invite Elizabeth,' May said, 'but now that you've put the idea into my head I feel as if I'm going to have to invite her.'

'May, you don't have to invite her. It was just a thought. You don't *have* to; and if you don't want to, please don't.'

'Yes, I do,' May disagreed resignedly. 'I'm going to have to. We are sisters and that is what sisters do for each other.'

'What does Elizabeth do for you? Already she gets somewhere to stay whenever she needs to be –'

'She doesn't have to do anything for me. We're not in a business negotiation. And I am her older sister.'

Jansen put a nail through a double hook and started banging it into the wall.

'The thing about Elizabeth,' May continued over the banging, 'is that she always does what she wants. She wants to learn the guitar, she does guitar; she doesn't want to do French, she stops doing French; she drops out of school one year, she comes back the next year. Oh, I've got no money, I'm on the dole, but I've always wanted to go to Thailand . . .'

'So why don't you do something different? If you're unhappy.'

'I am doing something different. I'm doing a PhD.'

'Yes, but why? Are you enjoying it? Do you want to work in a university? What do you hope to gain?'

'A PhD.'

'And then you'll be happy.'

'Yes.'

'I don't think so.' Jansen got another nail out of her pocket.

By the following Friday May had only read three more of Francine's essays, and she still hadn't finished the Delarue-Mardrus book. She called Francine.

'Allô, bonjour!'

'Bonjour, c'est May.'

'Ah, bonjour, May! Can you guess who I've just spent the morning with?' Francine asked her.

'No.'

'Anne Béranger,' Francine announced.

'Ah bon,' May said.

'I spent *four* hours with her! We had tea together. It was very interesting. You must speak of her in your dissertation.'

'She's not published yet though, is she?'

'Not yet, but she will be – and I am going to write about her – so you will have to include her.'

'Yes, I could.'

'She's coming to my book launch.'

'I know,' May said. 'I remember you told me.'

'We used to know each other very well – I didn't tell you that. She was a student of mine when I was still at the Sorbonne.'

'How many years ago was that?' May feigned bland interest. Was Francine trying to make her jealous?

'Oh I don't remember – ten years – I don't know. She wasn't made for academia. It stifled her. She was too free; she loved spontaneity.'

May said, 'She sounds really interesting.' (And like a bit of a cliché, she thought.)

Silence.

'And how are you?' Francine now asked. 'You're calling me from London?'

'Yes. I'll be in Paris tomorrow morning.'

'That's perfect. I'll put you down for three o'clock. Does that suit you?'

'Yes – thank you.'

'Do you have anything to say to me? How is Jansen?'

'Fine. My sister called me last weekend,' May said, in order to say something else. 'She's younger than me –'

'Ah, you have a sister, a little sister.' Francine wanted to know more.

'Yes, but we didn't really grow up together. She was only nine when I left home – which is why I haven't mentioned her,' May defended herself. 'Actually, she's not that little any more; she's really tall; she's taller than I am anyway, not quite as tall as Jansen, but she's not at all "little" any more, is what I mean.'

'And what is she doing now that she's "no longer little"?' Francine asked.

'She's living in Cambridge; she's doing a night-class in sculpting – except that she hasn't been to the last three classes, and now she's decided to move to London, so . . .'

'I know what you must do,' Francine said. 'You must invite Elizabeth to your place. She clearly needs an older sister; and you have a need to mother someone, I can see that.'

'By the way,' May changed the subject, 'I haven't been able to finish *L'Ange et les pervers*,' she said, 'so I won't be able to talk to you about it. I'm sorry.'

'We'll surely find other things to say to each other. It's not a very serious problem.'

'No, perhaps not.'

'Call your sister; she's waiting for you to invite her,' Francine explained.

'I don't think so.'

'I think so. This is an opportunity for you, in any case; you can show her the value of pursuing one's goals,' Francine said.

'Perhaps.'

Long silence.

'I think that's everything,' May said.

Francine laughed.

'Is it still worth my coming to visit you?' May asked. 'Even though I haven't read the book and I can't give it back to you yet?'

'It's you I have invited to dinner, not the book! You can send me a commentary with the book later.'

Hi, E. What about come short visit? Just a thought. May x.

Jansen looked at the text message: 'Mmm-hm,' she nodded, 'yeah.'

'You'd be okay with that?' May asked.

'Yeah. That'd be fine.'

'Okay. And so should I specify how long for?'

'I think, first invite her and see what she says.'

'So I shouldn't put –'

'May, you can work it out.'

May altered her text message slightly, and showed it to Jansen again.

'Fine.' Jansen gave her approval, and May pressed 'send'.

12

The Reply

The following morning there was a message on the answerphone.

You have one message; message one:

'I'm moving out of my flat, so yeah I'll come and stay. Call later.'

Message sent today, at 1.25 a.m. End of messages. To delete all messages, press 'delete'.

May pressed 'delete'. 'Thank you,' she spoke to the answerphone. 'Wonderful, wonderful.'

'What's the problem?' Jansen came into the bedroom, wearing her towel like a sarong; she'd just had a bath.

May said nothing. She had to be at Eurostar in just over half an hour and she hadn't ironed her jacket yet; she was going to Paris, having failed to read the book, and of course she hadn't finished Francine's essays. She didn't have time for this.

'Excuse me,' Jansen said. May moved away from the chest of drawers, and Jansen got some knickers and socks out of the top drawer.

'I can't believe it.' May stared at the answerphone.

Jansen put on her bra, went to the wardrobe and got a shirt off one of the hangers. 'What's happened?' She put on her shirt, and started buttoning it up.

'Elizabeth's arriving this coming Friday,' May told her.

'Oh.' Jansen pulled on her trousers, and tucked in her shirt in front of the mirror.

'It's not that I don't want to see her; I'm just terrified of being invaded.'

'I'm going to go and make breakfast. Follow me if you want to keep talking to me.' Jansen went to the kitchen.

'She has no sense of privacy; she'll take over the sitting room and leave her junk all over the place,' May said.

'We did invite her.' Jansen put some bread into the toaster, and clicked on the kettle.

'Yes, but does she say how long she's planning on staying? Because I can just see it: I'm going to end up having to tell her to move out! I said "visit", not "stay". This is why I didn't want to invite her.'

'So why did you invite her?'

'Because you suggested it. Because I am an idiot: someone suggests something to me and I just do it, I go along with it.'

'That doesn't sound like you at all.'

'It is me! I've done it!'

'. . . May, she's going to call you back. You can discuss it then.' Jansen got some plates out of the cupboard. 'Are you going to be ready in ten minutes?'

'Ten minutes!' May held her hand to her stomach. 'I haven't even had a shower yet. You know I'm not ready!' She was in her pyjamas.

'Okay, well you'd better have a quick shower then.' Jansen got the butter out of the fridge. 'I need to be at a pickup by eight o'clock this morning, so I will be leaving no later than seven thirty. If you want me to drop you off at the station you will have to be ready. I am not waiting for you.'

'It's only twelve minutes past.' May pointed to the clock on the wall.

'By the kitchen clock, yes.'

'So I haven't even got time to call Elizabeth? I can't solve this problem?'

'What problem?' The toast popped up and Jansen put it on the plates. 'Text her once you're on the train, and ask her how long she was thinking of staying. I'm leaving in nine minutes.'

'Could you put the iron on for me?' May ran off to have her shower.

13

Lost in Paris

May was in Paris again, on the Métro, going from the Gare du Nord to her hotel. The Métro, overground; it was like a large fun-ride, she thought, with life-sized Paris going by; the street market at Barbès-Rochechouart, busy stalls at a fairground. She hadn't read Francine's book, and perhaps this was in fact a good thing; it was more relaxing: because now she wouldn't have to talk about the book, and she wouldn't have to talk about the article either. She was free. Visiting Francine with no reason, except that the train ticket and the hotel were already booked. May smiled to herself. 'Je suis libre! Libre!' she thought. Jansen had bought her some dried mixed fruit for the trip. May had it in her pocket now; she took out some pieces of banana and papaya, and popped them into her mouth. It would be nice, she decided, to get Jansen a postcard – and then send it from London, she'd have to, because *La Poste Française* was shut on Saturday, wasn't it? But even from London, it would still be a little surprise: *une carte-postale de Paris, mon amour!* She could find one at the *bar-tabac* near the hotel, or she could go and find a special, beautiful one at the *carterie* near the Pompidou Centre on her way to Francine's; and then she could buy a dessert and sit around at a little café for an hour or so until two thirty.

Walking down the rue de Vaugirard a few hours later, on her way to Francine's, May now felt ill; she'd had too much coffee: she'd had *un grand crème* at the *bar-tabac* near the hotel, and then she'd gone to the Pompidou Centre and bought a postcard with an inky-blue silhouette sketch of the Sacré-Cœur for Jansen, and then she'd gone to *un salon de thé* and had *une mousse au chocolat* and another coffee – *un express* – and written on the postcard:

Une carte-postale de Paris, mon amour!

Plus, in brackets:

(Perhaps you could come to Paris with me some time – but not the next visit, because that's Francine's book launch and that will be stressful – unless you'd prefer to go somewhere entirely different. I think I'd prefer somewhere different – wouldn't you? – and then it would be our special holiday . . .)

After which, she'd had two more coffees; that was four coffees in the space of three hours: that was stupid.

She felt drugged. Walking down the endless rue de Vaugirard, in the noise, with all the cars, and the occasional bus and *mobylette* going by, she felt spaced out. And nauseous. Finally, she came to the large wooden doors that led to Francine's, and she tapped in the code – 38, 64, A – which she knew by heart.

The door didn't click open. She tried again. Perhaps the code had been changed. Or she'd tapped it out in the wrong order, or she wasn't supposed to press that large button below. May couldn't remember, and she couldn't think. She'd have to call Francine, and she'd left her mobile in London –

'I'll open it for you,' a young woman offered. She was with a friend.

'Merci,' May said.

The woman tapped out the right code, let May through the door first, and then the two women overtook her and went into the flats straight ahead.

A huge green refuse bin – that hadn't been there before? – was sitting in the corner of the courtyard just next to the entrance of Francine's block. May looked for the right buzzer; she looked for 'Brion', but she couldn't find it. That was odd.

Perhaps Francine had removed her name from the intercom for some reason. But why would she do that? May looked again: there was no 'Brion'. And it was definitely the third floor – wasn't it? May looked up. Francine's windows were shut; had she gone out? That would be a good way of sending a clear message: it could be that Francine was inside, pretending to have gone out; it was a nuisance to her that May was visiting once again, and she had therefore shut her windows to make the place look deserted.

Unless of course they really weren't her windows . . .

'Ah, there you are! I was expecting you at three o'clock.' Francine looked at her watch and then at May, who, having at last found the correct place, was pulling off her shoes at the door. 'In future, you will think to call me.' Francine let her in. 'I was about to go out shopping. You are very lucky; you've arrived just in time.'

May came into the sitting room. She felt terrible – her head ached and she felt nauseous again. She explained she'd got the time wrong, and asked, 'Comment vas-tu? How are you?' She said it in English, too, for some reason – because she was feeling very strange.

Francine said, '*Très* bien. Et toi?'

And May said (she returned to French), 'I feel strange, I feel bizarre. I have just had four cups of coffee. It makes me ill. I feel dizzy.' She sat down on the sofa. She could have fainted just then, she thought. 'Could I have some water, please?'

'Of course.' Francine went to the kitchen. '. . . I've been working on the article . . . do you realize? Four hours! That's a very long time . . .' She was talking about Anne Béranger again, but May wasn't listening. She couldn't. She closed her eyes for a moment and wished that she could lie down.

'Merci.' May took the glass of water, and drank.

'Is that better now?' Francine asked. 'You should always carry a bottle of water in your bag. I never go anywhere without water.'

May held the glass against her forehead to cool it down.

'It's idiotic, to have drunk so much coffee!' Francine told her. 'You have to learn to listen to your body. One has to be very attentive; the body is extremely important. Everything is linked.'

May drank some more of the water. 'I'll feel better soon,' she said.

'Give me your hands,' Francine told her. 'You look pale.'

May put the glass on the floor. She held her hands out, palms down, to Francine, who took them, turned them over, and with her cool fingers pressed together the webbing of May's hands. 'Close your eyes,' she said.

May closed them.

'Marathon runners find this gives them more energy,' Francine said, speaking softly. 'It also relieves headaches. Breathe in,' she said, maintaining the pressure, 'breathe in . . .'

May breathed in. Francine was probably looking at her.

'. . . Breathe in, keep breathing in. And now – breathe out.'

May breathed out.

'You're breathing out your headache – breathe in again . . . and breathe out. That's better; you're more relaxed,' Francine told her. 'Can you feel your headache leaving?'

'I'm not sure.' May kept her eyes shut.

'You have to train yourself to slow the breathing right down. If you can learn to relax during the day, you will sleep more intensely at night; and you will dream more intensely.' Francine replaced May's arms to her sides. 'You can open your eyes.'

May opened them.

'Stay there.' Francine considered her for a moment. 'Try to be aware of your breathing. I am going to prepare myself a herbal tea, a lime-blossom.' She went back to the kitchen. 'I'll make you some, too.'

May leaned back into the sofa. She closed her eyes again, and concentrated on her breathing; she tried to imagine her mind washed free of coffee.

'Here you are.'

May opened her eyes again, and Francine gave her a plate with two slices of *pain de campagne* on it. 'You should eat. It will line the stomach. I'll go and prepare the *tisane*.' Francine returned to the kitchen.

'Thank you,' May called out after her. 'That's very kind.' She ripped off a piece of the fresh brown bread, and put it into her mouth. She felt so ill, and she felt so grateful, that she almost started to cry. She choked on the bread, and then she took another sip of water.

The room was teeming with books; it was crawling with them. May was in a cave of books; like fungi, in piles around the edges of the room, they seemed to be growing – beside the front door and under the windows – creeping up the walls, and touching the ceiling. All these books that May hadn't read; it made her head swim. She imagined them, in a freak earthquake (confined to the sitting room), shaken out of the shelves, and flying out at her. Francine would come back from the kitchen, and find her drowning under the rubble of novels and essays; she'd pull May's limp body out from under, and breathe life into her.

Francine came back with the tea. She handed May a thin porcelain cup with a saucer.

'Thank you very much,' May said, and she put it on the floor. She felt a bit flushed. 'I'm not feeling very well. I'll drink it in a minute perhaps.'

'Do as you like,' Francine said. 'Don't drink it at all, if you don't want to.'

'No, thank you, I'm going to drink it.' May bent down to get the cup. She took a small sip. 'It's very good. Thank you.' Her head was spinning. 'I'm not feeling well at all.' She wanted to lie down. She put the cup back on the floor. 'I'm going to close my eyes,' she said. 'Do you mind?' She half lay down, leaving her feet on the floor, to be polite. 'If I could lie here for a while, perhaps ten minutes . . .'

May opened her eyes. The room was dark now; the curtains had been drawn. She got up and pulled them open again, disturbing a sparrow, which immediately flew off. The windows were wide open; it was late in the afternoon.

'Ah, bonjour.' Francine said this very gently; she was taking oranges out of a paper bag and putting them into a large pottery bowl on the kitchen table. 'I didn't wake you?' She began unpacking a bag of kiwi fruit, placing them on top of the oranges.

'No.'

'Well, that's very good then.' Francine folded up the paper bags and put them in a drawer.

'Was I asleep for a long time?' May asked.

'I have reworked an article, and I have been out shopping,' Francine told her. 'You see: while you sleep, others are busy at work.'

'It's bizarre; I drink too much coffee, and it puts me to sleep,' May apologized.

'No, it's not bizarre; it's quite normal: when you mistreat the body it has to recuperate; and there is nothing better for that than sleep.' Francine finished putting away the rest of the shopping. 'Sit down. I'll make you another *tisane*. I have bought us some *pâtisseries*.'

'Shall I help you?' May offered.

'No, no. Sit.' Francine pulled out a chair.

May sat down at the table. She wasn't quite awake yet. She watched Francine prepare the tea.

Francine put the teapot and cups on the table, undid the bow on a thin cardboard box and opened it out. '*Une tartelette aux framboises* and *une tartelette aux fraises*: which one do you prefer?'

May's favourite fruit was raspberry. 'They both look delicious,' she said.

'Shall we halve them?' Francine got a knife from the drying rack next to the sink. 'How is your PhD progressing?' she asked as she handed May a plate.

'Not very well. Thank you – this looks delicious.'

'Have you seen your supervisor?' Francine sat down, and poured the tea.

'No.' May took a small bite of the strawberry tart. 'Not yet,' she said.

'You still haven't seen her? It's unbelievable! Listen, I'm going to tell you what you must do: find another supervisor.'

May shrugged.

'Quite simply.' Francine ignored her. 'And you will tell this woman that she is no longer needed, for you have found someone else. She isn't fulfilling her obligations; you owe her nothing.'

'No, it's really my problem,' May said. 'It's because I haven't felt ready. She can't comment if I haven't been able to put anything very solid together; when it's all almost only in note form.'

'But that's ridiculous! She's there to guide you. She could help you with the structure. You've been working on this for months. *I* could help you with the structure – except I am not being paid for that, of course; besides which, I may be far too busy now . . .'

'No, that's kind. I'll continue working on it.'

'For how much longer?' Francine asked.

'Yes,' May agreed – that was a point.

'It is a real question,' Francine told her. 'Your supervisor's going to expect to see something very soon, surely!'

'Perhaps before the end of summer, then?'

'No: before the end of spring.'

May nodded.

'If I have one piece of advice to give you,' Francine went on, 'it would be to put more pressure on yourself. You have to, or you'll never arrive anywhere.'

May nodded again. 'Yes. No,' she said.

'Come here with your essay plan the next time you visit, and I will have a glance at it.'

'But you'll be too busy with your book launch, won't you?'

'I shall look at it after the launch, the day after.'

'Okay.'

'That is, if you want. But perhaps you don't want my help. I am not forcing you.'

'No, that could be good.'

'Good. Well, now I must get back to work. Have you finished your tea?'

'Yes, thank you.' May got up to go; she'd done something wrong. 'I might go for a walk in the fresh air,' she said, trying to sound purposeful. 'I might walk back to the hotel.'

'That's an idea,' Francine told her. '"Solvitur ambulando".'

'Hmm,' May said.

'By Saint Augustine.'

'Oh.'

'Do you know the expression?'

'Possibly. What does it mean again?'

'It means, "have a good walk",' Francine told her. 'The weather's becoming fairly mild now; you'll find it's still quite pleasant at the end of the afternoon.'

'Perhaps you would like to walk with me?' May thought aloud; perhaps that was what she was supposed to do: she was supposed to take the initiative now and then, behave more like Francine's equal. 'We could go to the Jardin du Luxembourg – or to the Tuileries,' she suggested. 'Or if there's somewhere else that you might like –'

'No, May! I can't spend all my afternoon walking around in Paris! I thank you for the invitation, but you are going to have to venture out on your own; I've got work to do.'

'Yes, of course.' Was Francine saying that it was a waste of time walking across Paris with May? 'I think a long walk will help my head,' May explained.

'Exactly.'

'Thank you for the tea,' May said. They were standing at the door now. 'And thank you for the afternoon tea, and for helping me with my headache.' She didn't want to go; she'd definitely done something wrong, and she shouldn't have suggested the walk, that was presumptuous of her, or she was supposed to have said something else, she didn't know what.

'If you're feeling better, that's good.'

'Yes, thank you.'

'Bon, au revoir,' Francine prompted her.

'Oui, au revoir.' May went out onto the landing and knelt down to get her shoes.

'I won't wait here for you,' Francine told her. 'I must get back to work.'

'Of course.' May smiled, in order to look happy. 'See you soon.' She started doing up her shoelaces.

Francine closed the door.

14
Problem-Solving

Arriving at Waterloo, she hoped Jansen would be standing there waiting for her to come through passport control; she'd take May outside to the car. 'I thought you might appreciate being met.' Soon the car heater would be whirring away. They'd stop and pick up takeaways.

May bought a ticket, and took the Underground home.

'Oh, you're back. How was it, then?'

May placed her bag on the sitting-room floor. 'How was what?'

'What d'you mean "how was what?"? How was Francine? How was it visiting her?'

'Fine.' Jansen had her answer.

Jansen sighed heavily, as if she were carrying a piano. 'Did you decide to tell her you've deferred?'

'No.'

'May, you're being monosyllabic.'

Silence.

'Shall I make dinner?'

'Hmm.'

Jansen left the room. That was really irritating; she was supposed to draw May out; she was supposed to wait for more answers, persevere. Instead, she was now in the kitchen, chopping onions. That was deliberate.

May went into the kitchen.

'So, you don't wonder how I'm feeling, after visiting Francine.

No, I still haven't told her I've deferred! And now she's asking me again about my non-existent supervisor!' Jansen didn't seem to be listening. 'Not that you're interested.'

'*What?*'

'You asked me, but you didn't really want to know. Otherwise, you'd have tried a bit harder. Perhaps it's not simple-simple, easy to talk *about*.'

'Are you saying you'd like to tell me now?'

'Not if you're not interested.'

'I *asked* you how it was!'

'Well, do you want to know?'

'May, if we're going to argue can you help me cook? I'm hungry.'

'Oh, that's why you're so grumpy.'

Jansen passed May the broccoli. 'And put some carrots in with them, too.'

'I hate cooking.' May got the carrots out of the cupboard next to the sink.

'There's a message for you, by the way. On the answerphone. It's from Elizabeth.'

'Why didn't you tell me?' May dropped the carrots into the sink and went to the bedroom. She listened to the message, wiped it, and returned to the kitchen.

Jansen had cleaned the carrots and put them on the bench.

'Elizabeth's decided she's definitely moving to London; and she's going to take up our offer to stay here until she finds a place: that's not what we offered! "Won't be there Friday. Probably more like Saturday." She's told Mark – whoever he is – that he'd be welcome to have dinner with us. "Hope that's okay," she says. "Think it's the least I could offer him." Great, she's already inviting men around.'

Jansen practised quiet detachment as she moved onions around in the pan with a wooden spoon.

'How can you stand it in here? It's awful!' May rubbed her eyes dramatically, and turned on the extractor fan.

'May, can we have a calm evening? I know you're feeling stressed, but I really don't appreciate you coming in here and ranting at me.'

'I am stressed.' She was getting all wound up again; she was being excessive, she could see it, and completely awful to be around; but she didn't know how to calm down. 'It's exhausting.'

'Yeah.'

'And I think I'm a bit pre-menstrual, too,' May told her. Maybe that was it.

'So am I: we are both pre-menstrual.'

'Oh.'

'Yes. So perhaps you could set the table.'

'All right.' May got some plates out of the cupboard and put them on the bench. 'Elderflower juice?' She tried to be nice.

'Yes, please.'

'I just wish I'd never invited her.' May got out the glasses. 'It makes my throat hurt.'

'Why don't you call her back,' Jansen said, 'and say you're looking forward to seeing her, but you'd rather she didn't invite her friend at this point?'

'Because I am *not* looking forward to seeing her? I am far too busy! I'm busy!' There were no clean forks; May found some in the sink, and gave them a quick rinse under the tap. 'Francine is expecting me to show her what I've done so far; I'm supposed to show her my outline next time I see her. I'm never going to get it done!' She put the forks on the plates.

'Okay. Well, tell Elizabeth you don't want her to come.'

'I can't do that! It's too late now; I've invited her! She's my younger sister, my "little" sister.' May made sarcastic little quote-marks in the air.

'For sure.'

May used to find it so cute – she took the glasses to the sitting room – when Jansen went 'for sure' like that; she'd found it kind of 'American' in the James Dean sense, and she'd told her so, too;

it became a joke between them, and Jansen started using it, as a come-on line; but lately she seemed to be using it to indicate that May was being over-the-top hysterical. Which was a bit depressing. 'I'll have to just call her,' May said, 'damn it, and say, sorry but we'll be out most of Saturday, so she'll have to call me on my mobile or whatever, when she arrives in London, but not a good idea to invite Mark for that reason. I'll do that.'

'Whatever you like,' Jansen called out; she was competing for pre-menstrual priority.

May went to the bedroom to get the call over and done with.

'It'll be a bit late,' Elizabeth told her. There was a pause. No one spoke. 'Okay then!' she finished, as if it were all settled. 'So I'll see you when I see you, yeah?'

'And if we're not in, maybe you can find a café nearby until we get back.' May tapped the ball gently back into Elizabeth's court.

'Look,' Elizabeth sounded put out, 'what I'll do is I'll try to remember to have my mobile on, and you can give us a call when you get back. That'd be easier . . .'

'Easier for . . . ? Elizabeth, this is getting really complicated.' She would have to ask the obvious. 'When exactly will you be getting here?'

Elizabeth laughed in an exasperated way. 'It's not my vehicle, May. Mark's offered to take me all this way, which is pretty damn kind of him, isn't it? I'm not gonna turn around now, and lay on any heavy time rules, am I?'

'Uh huh. So, you don't know when you're leaving Cambridge?'

'Is this a problem for you? This sounds like it's a problem for you,' Elizabeth accused.

'Well, I do want to be able to go to bed at some point.'

'All right, okay,' Elizabeth's tone indicated she was going to find a solution for this, 'okay, but how early do you go to bed, anyway?' She was ready to be shocked.

May didn't answer.

'Leave a key out for me somewhere. We'll be heading straight out again anyway; we're gonna see if we can catch the end of a gig that one of Mark's friends is playing in. Put the key under a mat, or above the door somewhere.'

Jansen arrived then, and stood in the doorway, carrying two plates of steaming stir-fry, which she lifted up and down, mouthing 'Dinner!' May nodded dismissively, and returned to her call.

'No, Elizabeth. This is London. We're in Lon-don!'

Jansen left the room.

'Well, leave it with your next-door neighbour,' Elizabeth suggested.

'No, I don't feel safe doing that.'

'You're making a really big deal out of this. I'll call you when we're leaving, okay, and if it's late, sorry! What can I do? It's only one night, for God's sake!'

15

The Day before the Day

Friday: it was dark outside, but May woke up because she knew the alarm was seconds away; she switched it off. 'The alarm's gone off, by the way,' she told Jansen (it was about to). She got out of bed. In less than twenty minutes she had to be out the door. School – non-life – started at 8 a.m.

Elizabeth was coming round tomorrow evening. May noticed the basin was looking grimy. The soap tray needed cleaning; she did a few wipes with the flannel, squirting cleaner into the basin. That's three minutes less I've got for breakfast, she thought. She went back into the bedroom, and stood looking in the mirror at her face: creased with fatigue, and set in a frown. She saw her reflection – this morning, the day before, the day before that – like a pack of cards being flicked through. Tired faces. 'Every morning is just the same awful repeat,' she announced to Jansen, who was lying in their warm bed, the duvet covering her chin. 'I'm really not keen on this. Do we know how long she's staying? Is she planning on getting a job?'

Jansen said nothing, which was another way of saying something; she obviously had her not so silent opinion on this.

'I guess you're thinking it's a good thing letting her come and stay?' May continued.

'I'm not thinking anything, May. I've just woken up.'

'But what do you think about it? You do think something, obviously.'

'Well, she's not going to want to stay with us for ever. And in the meantime you might even enjoy some time together. It might be fun.'

'Fun?'

'Okay, it's going to be awful. You've decided that already.'

'You're quite happy about it anyway; you always get on so beautifully together.'

'Is that a problem? Would you rather I didn't like your sister?'

May looked at her watch. 'You can't give me a lift this morning, can you?' More an accusation than a real question.

'I can't, May, no. I've got the Skoda. I've got to take it to the bin first and pick up one of the company cars . . . You do a great pout, by the way.'

May nodded. 'Hmm.'

'I've got a bit of a headache, but my first pickup's not till ten, so I can just have a slow start to the day. I might call Tamsin and see how her job-hunting's going. Maybe, if she's got another interview, she could come round here for dinner –'

'When? We've got Elizabeth coming to stay.' May wouldn't be able to have a shower now. There was no time.

'We can still invite people to dinner. I can't remember the last time we did that.'

'It's been winter; everyone hibernates in winter.'

'Oh – Alison! We should give her a call! When did she say she was getting back? Is she still in America?'

'I can't remember. I've got no idea.' Alison was someone they'd met a few years ago, during a signal failure on the tube.

'I wonder how it went with Barbara,' Jansen said; she was talking about Alison's latest.

'Mm.'

'We could have a flat warming and invite round a few people we haven't seen for a while.'

'Could we settle in first?'

'I'm not saying this week, May.' Jansen was annoyed. 'I was thinking the end of next month.'

'Sue won't want to come, if Alison's going to be around.'

'No, I know that – but we can invite them both, and they can decide. What about Patrick?' (Her cousin.)

'I don't know. Could we talk about this later? I need to get breakfast. Do you want tea?' May went to the kitchen.

She clicked on the kettle, got out two cups, plates, some bread out of the freezer, the butter. She could hear Jansen leisurely coughing in bed. In her early teens, May would be frantically getting ready for school while Elizabeth toddled around with her thumb in her mouth, or sat curled up in an armchair listening to nursery rhymes or stories on the record player: 'Under a large tree in the country, Alice sat reading a history book that her history teacher had given her to read. "Ah," thought Alice. "What good is a book without pictures?" . . .' Elizabeth put her favourites on repeat. 'Under a large tree in the country . . .' 'Under a large tree . . .' On and on.

At exactly seven fifteen May left Jansen, who was now reading a Nick Hornby in the bath, kissed her on her wet forehead, pulled the front door shut, and tapped a final goodbye on the bathroom window as she walked towards the stairwell. Happily, she didn't bump into any neighbours; it was too early to pull her face into a polite smile.

At the station, she pulled out *L'Ange et les pervers*; she had finished reading it. Now all she needed to do was read it again.

16

Elizabeth's Arrival

Elizabeth didn't arrive on Saturday; she arrived on Sunday – at 8 a.m. Once she'd hauled in a cardboard box of art books, a rucksack and a large green rubbish bag of clothes and coat-hangers, she sat down at the sitting-room table in her hipster jeans and army surplus jacket, and told May, still in pyjamas, about her journey:

'We're stuck at a service station. Kate's been doing all the driving (she's the one with the licence), but then Mark (he's really far gone by now) wants to drive. So we just sit there, while they argue it out. My mobile was out of credit, and I wasn't gonna risk leaving the van just to call you; they might have gone off without me. We sat there for ages, Mark's drinking and drinking. Finally Kate's persuaded to hand over the keys, so they swap seats . . . *then* he says, because – well, I don't know why, just *because* – he says . . .' (Elizabeth pulled herself up into role here, putting on a wide-mouthed slur) '"I'm not going anywhere until she has a few swigs of wine!" So I did, and off we went!' Elizabeth stopped to share her hilarity over this with May. 'After a few hiccups with the gears, the van's shaking it along. So Kate has to mention speed cameras of course, which gets Mark really wild: "Who's the driver?" he asks. And to prove his point, he slows right down. "Where are the speed cameras? I don't see any. Do you?" he asks me. I said, "No." Well there weren't any. Then Kate gets all snotty with me, and Mark tells her to: "Leave her alone! I asked her a question, and she answered it. Control freak!" So he just about stops, he's going so slow, and turns to her: "Slow enough for you?" he asks. That's when – "weeroo, weeroo" – we see a police car. Aah!' Elizabeth waved her arms around melodramatically. 'This is where I thank you,' she added, 'because, apart from those two swigs, I hadn't touched a drop, polite little visitor that I am. Anyway, we pull over, and Mark says to me, "You get in the driver's seat! Quick!" So there I am: *totalemente abstinenta!* Along comes a police officer: "Everything all right?" she asks me (a dyke for sure). I give her a really sincere smile, and say, "Yes, thanks. I realize I was going slowly. I was trying to give my lousy navigators here time to work out whether we were supposed to turn off at the next junction. Is the next one the M25?" She's really helpful with directions, brings out a map – ? – and helps us plan the rest of our route to Mark's. I give her a grateful smile. God it was funny! She didn't even ask for my licence! What licence? Well, here I am now,' Elizabeth reached into the inside of her jacket and took out a tobacco pouch, 'and I didn't wake you up, did I?'

'Elizabeth.' May was starting her sentence with 'Elizabeth'; it indicated that she was stepping into some sort of advisory role, which she did not want. 'Elizabeth, I'm glad you can't drive,' she decided to say it anyway, 'because if you could, you might kill someone. Also, I don't think it's very clever to get into a vehicle with a drunk driver.'

Elizabeth had nothing to say at first. Then she said, 'There were hardly any cars on the road, May. I don't think Mark would've driven if there had been.'

'I still believe that if you get into a vehicle with a drunk driver, you're condoning it. And if someone gets killed –'

'What, so I'm supposed to say, "Thanks for getting me to this service station in the middle of nowhere. Keep the gear. I'll just stay here all night"?'

'That might've been a good idea, yes.'

Elizabeth raised her eyebrows, and pulled a lighter out of her jeans pocket.

'Oh, could you smoke outside?'

Elizabeth gave May an actively unsurprised look, and made the considerate smoker's exit.

May went to the kitchen, clicked the kettle on, and got three cups out of the cupboard. As she waited for the water to boil she got a whiff of smoke: Elizabeth had left the front door open. May went to shut it.

'I'll just close this.'

Elizabeth nodded her head as she inhaled deeply on a roll-up.

May went to the bedroom, where Jansen was sitting up in bed, the *Independent* spread out in front of her. She'd taken the day off.

'Tea?' Jansen looked up, smiling hopefully.

'She's smoking out there,' May said.

'Where?' Jansen was on the sports page.

'Outside.'

'Oh.' Jansen marked a pause. 'Tea?' she repeated.

'She's smoking outside, and she'll be at home during the day when we're not here, and then she'll probably smoke inside.'

'You're not going to get me a drink, are you?' Jansen got out of bed, put her socks on and went to the kitchen. May followed her, now talking softly:

'You think I'm being horrible. I ought to be just pleased to see her.'

Jansen chose an echinacea sachet, and stood in front of the kettle, waiting for it to come to the boil again.

'I'd have made you a hot drink, if you'd given me the chance,' May defended herself.

Jansen poured water into the pot, and returned with it to the bedroom. 'We invited her to stay.' She got back into bed.

'Yes, that was your idea – and I should have specified how long for.'

'You could say something now. You could say, three or four weeks maximum.' Jansen retrieved her handkerchief, which was wedged in between the mattress and the bed-base, and blew her nose thoroughly. 'Anyway, she did say she'd be looking for somewhere else.'

Elizabeth was knocking on the front door now.

'Can you get it?' Jansen settled back with her newspaper.

May didn't move. The knocking continued: tap! Tap-tap! Tap! Tap! TAP! TAP! TAP! Pause. Tap! Tap-tap! Tap! Tap! TAP! TAP! 'Why do I have to get it?' she said, sending a nasty look in the direction of the tapping, which kept on cheerfully.

'May! Would you answer the door!'

'Why should I get it? We both invited her.' May sat down on the bed to confirm her statement.

Jansen yanked her blankets off and went to the door.

May waited on the bed.

Jansen came back and closed the bedroom door. 'That was really rude.' She climbed back into bed. 'What? Are you going to sit there now and stare at me?'

'I was just thinking how different you and I both are.'

'Yes,' Jansen agreed; she clearly had her own set of examples in mind. 'I'd like to read now.'

'I'm so tired.' May attempted an apology. 'She doesn't bother letting us know she's staying the night somewhere else. She doesn't think perhaps we might stay awake all night worrying about her. It took me ages to get to sleep. And now my day is wasted; I'm not going to be able to get anything done: I'm too tired.' May stretched across Jansen and the newspaper to reach the clock on Jansen's side, and pulled herself back upright with it to see the time: 'Eight-fucking-thirty.' May found the spare key and went back to the sitting room with it.

Elizabeth had unpacked her clothes and accessories – trousers and wide glittery belts, various coloured bras, stretchy tops and dresses – and spread them out on the sofa. 'Hey, I'm gonna have a bath, if that's all right.'

'I'm going back to bed. Here's a key.' She put it on the table.

'Oh all right – ta. See you then. Buenas noches.'

May went back to the bedroom and shut the door. She stood the clock on the stool next to her. Then, eye-mask on, earplugs in, she lay down next to Jansen, who continued drinking her tea and reading.

A little later, May felt the bed move as Jansen got out.

'What are you doing?' May asked from behind her mask. She unplugged one ear, and lifted up the mask. 'What?'

'I didn't say anything.' Jansen turned off the light, and returned to bed.

May was pleased; she snuggled into her.

'No,' Jansen stiffened, 'I'm not in the mood to be hugged.'

'I'm sorry I've been such a grump.' May settled herself away from her.

'Apology accepted,' Jansen said.

'Now can I cuddle you?'

'No.'

17

L'Ambassadrice anglaise

By Friday evening May had Jansen's cold.

Damn.

No key. She'd locked herself out.

She knocked on the door.

No answer: Elizabeth must have gone out for the evening.

May checked her bag: tissues, lists of things to do, pens, telephone book, mobile, zinc-fortified vitamin C pills, loose change, crumbs getting under her fingernails as she hunted. No key.

'It's not true. It's not true.' She rolled her eyes. 'I can't believe it,' she chanted, hopelessly resigned to the fact.

No key.

She sighed.

She knocked again; maybe Elizabeth was having a bath or something. May listened through the letter flap. She knocked one last time, three loud knocks. She waited. Her chest clenched. Jansen was doing a late shift to make up for last Sunday; she wouldn't be back until nine thirty, or nine at the very earliest. May looked at her watch: five past eight.

The door opened. 'Oh, definitely!' Elizabeth, the phone in one hand, the receiver jammed between her shoulder and her left ear, let May pass. 'Yeah!' She laughed. 'Yep, absolutely!' She raised her eyebrows at May, tilting her head back as a hello sign, and went to the kitchen, trailing the phone extension cord, guiding it along with her foot. May followed the procession. 'Yeah.' Elizabeth dropped two slices of white bread into the toaster. 'Yeah, mm . . . she is! You are! Trust me, I know "adore" when I see it. She's into you, Mark.' Belly laughter.

May tuned out for a while. What was sickening about Elizabeth, she thought as she chose a teabag – she was making herself a lemon and ginger, since she had to give herself a purpose for being there, even though it was her kitchen – what was *sickifying* was that she was so cheerful. How could she be so cheerful when her life was such a mess?

Elizabeth was now squatting down in front of the fridge, 'mm-ing' and 'ah-ha-ing', continuing, as she chose a jar of marmalade, to give her full attention to her interlocutor, sounding just like a very supportive and available 'call me at my home, if you need to' type therapist. Back to reality: she had been registered as unemployed ever since leaving school, so that she could 'enjoy doing nothing for a while'. Just about all she owned she now dragged around in a bin liner and a cardboard box. Indefinitely 'on holiday', she seemed to have no aims, except to float. Of course, she was 'only twenty-two' – a weak excuse; she had nine more years of flapping about nowhere, before she'd hit May's age. Then she'd be sorry.

Elizabeth waved before taking her toast and conversation to the sitting room. May put her teabag in the bin, wiped down Elizabeth's toast crumbs and followed her. The difference was May didn't remember having had a fun time at Elizabeth's age. She'd never been like that. She had been insecure at that age looking at older people, and now she was insecure at this age looking at younger people. She'd never, for example, looked at someone older and considered they might be envious of her carefree existence. But then, she'd never presented an image convincingly enviable; she'd never actually been carefree. Even if, while she was at university, she had attempted to maintain herself in a state of semi-consciousness, her worries swam on, frantically flailing about, yelling and screeching as she failed to drown them in red wine. No, she'd never presented an image convincing enough. And now, Elizabeth's present lack of concern (she was chomping her toast in hearty mouthfuls, laughing and chewing as she talked) May would just have to tolerate. Wasn't there an age at which she could start looking disdainfully at people?

If she could manage it, she'd counter Elizabeth's airy attitude. May would be her own centre of gravity. She decided to practise now, with her hot drink cupped peacefully in her hands, looking cheerfully complacent.

'Nyet. Okay, babe. See ya.' Elizabeth was off the phone at last. It rang as soon as she replaced the receiver. 'That'll be for you. Nobody's been given this number.' She gave an 'all-yours' palm-up gesture towards the phone.

May answered the phone:

'Bonjour! C'est bien May?' It was Francine. Phoning May.

'Oui, bonjour,' May said. It was the first time Francine had ever called her. 'How are you?' She blushed.

Francine was well. And how was May?

'I'm fine, thank you.'

Elizabeth opened the window as wide as it could go, and leaned out with a cigarette.

'Excuse me a moment.' May turned to Elizabeth: 'Sorry, but it'll blow in, even with the window open. We're really a non-smoking flat. It's in the lease,' she lied.

Elizabeth shut the window, and dropped the cigarette into a half-full Coke bottle. 'No problemo.' She stretched her long, jean-clad legs out in front of her. May noted a book, *Corfu, My Dream* (looked like the title at a glance), as she took the phone to the bedroom.

'Sorry. I was just speaking to my sister. I'm going to another room.' May shut the door. 'Should I call you back?'

'Why? I've just called you,' Francine said.

'Yes,' May said, and then she said nothing else. She didn't know what to say.

'I am calling,' Francine told her, 'because I have a proposition to put to you.'

'Yes.'

Francine laughed. 'I would like to send you some information about all my work so far and about my forthcoming collection –'

'Yes. That would be interesting,' May said.

'You would have to make several photocopies and send all this with a little note – that you can compose yourself – to ten or so faculties across England, explaining –'

'French language faculties, you mean?'

'Or Women's Studies or Gender Studies – both; I'll leave that up to you.'

'And, in the note, what should I include?'

'I'm sure you can work it out.'

'So, I'd say perhaps –'

'First write it, and then, if you want, you can read it to me before you send them off. You're simply introducing me, and providing them with an English contact.'

'So I'd write it in English?'

'Naturally. You can translate for me what you've written. Listen, if you don't want to do this; I wouldn't have thought it that complicated however . . .'

'No, there's no problem . . . I'm just not feeling very well. I've got a bit of a cold.' May had left her tea in the other room.

'I believe it would be a good experience for you; it will extend you,' Francine went on.

'Yes.' May nodded.

'You can also put them up around your own university.'

'Yes, I could do that.' (Perhaps she could take them to Birkbeck.)

'And in return for this, I shall help you with your dissertation. Is it a deal?'

'Yes, that would be fine. Thank you.' It all sounded impossible.

'You will have to finish a section in rough draft though, before Easter – that will give you a goal to aim towards – and then we'll be able to look at the structure together.'

'Even if I just brought the outline, like I was going to, that could be useful.'

'As you like.'

The front door slammed shut. Eight forty: Jansen was home

early; she opened the bedroom door, saw May was on the phone, mouthed 'Hi', and shut the door again to give her privacy.

'Oh, I'd better go now,' May told Francine. 'Jansen's just got in.'

'I'll send you the flyers,' Francine said.

'Yes. Okay.'

'And you will bring me your dissertation next time you visit. We can spend an entire evening on it, perhaps two. How does that sound?'

'Mm-hmm.' It sounded terrible.

'Is it progressing?'

'Yes, little by little.' She could hear surprised greeting sounds coming through the walls. Jansen had discovered Elizabeth at home for the evening.

'Elizabeth's staying here now. For the moment,' May told Francine.

'Who's that? A friend of yours?'

'No, my sister.'

'Ah, yes. I remember: what was it she's doing again?'

'Sculpting, night classes – she's not going any more though. She's decided to move to London, and so we've said she could live with us until she finds somewhere.'

'That's very kind of you, very generous. You get on well, both of you?'

'I think so. Yes, quite well, I think.'

'That's all very good then. So, everything's fine. No problems?'

'No. Everything's fine. Thank you, yes.'

'You are going to be my *ambassadrice anglaise!*' Francine concluded.

After May got off the phone, she realized something: Elizabeth was running a bath. May wanted to brush her teeth and go to bed. She found the idea of a bath at this time of night irritating. She just wanted to feel that at nine o'clock – or thereabouts – night-time and peace had started. She stood in front of the closed door, and listened to the water thundering into the bath, wondering how to get her toothbrush, whether to knock, or just leave it. The sitting-room door opened. Elizabeth, now wearing a towel, passed May; she was carrying her jeans slung over one arm, a fresh T-shirt and some shampoo balanced on top of them.

'It's a door,' Elizabeth explained.

'What,' May scowled at her, 'are you talking about?'

'You look like you're analysing it: the door to the source. Shall I go in? Shall I not go in?'

May ignored her. 'Are you going out somewhere?'

Of course Elizabeth was going out, and of course Jansen was polite and called out from the sitting room to ask where, and showed interest, and then Elizabeth checked the bath temperature, turned off the cold tap and wandered back into the sitting room. She sat on the sofa with her towel outfit on, and she and Jansen settled down for a nice friendly conversation.

The bathroom was free. May brushed her teeth. She wished Elizabeth would come and watch the bath. It would overflow. It was not May's job to watch it. She wished Elizabeth would get on with having her bath, so that she and Jansen could go to bed and talk. May looked in at them. They were engaged in some laughy conver-happy-sation.

'I might just come out dancing with you,' Jansen was saying.

'I'm off to bed,' May cut in. 'I've come down with a cold.'

'Yeah, good nightee!' Elizabeth's tone was mocking.

'I'll be there in a minute,' Jansen said.

'Yeah.' May left the room.

May looked at the clock: 2.15 a.m. She was still awake. This was partly due to her blocked nose, and partly due to four or five large vitamin C tablets – she had taken them within the space of two hours. Now she was clogged up and wound up. She pulled herself to a martyred ninety-degree sitting angle. 'I know you aren't very happy about this,' Jansen had come in to say goodbye before going out, 'but I'll just sneak in, and you'll be fast asleep.' May was still not fast asleep; she was thinking about Elizabeth, who loved dancing, and who was no doubt sparkling away right now, dazzling Jansen with her funky moves and fooling around on the dance floor, making her laugh. 'No, I won't say when I'll be back, or you'll just wait for me, and then you won't sleep. I'll be late.' Yes.

'I can't breathe! Great, I'm not allowed to sleep!' May complained aloud, even though this was slightly less satisfying when there was no one there to sympathize, no one to keep awake.

She clicked on the light, and scrawled out a message to Jansen: *could you buy me some oranges?*

Her head was spinning. She switched off the light, and tried lying down. But, no, it was impossible. She hauled herself back up into the sitting position, so that she could breathe. If it wasn't so late she might almost have called Francine, just to tell her how unwell she was feeling; she was feeling so unwell, she would be capable of doing something stupid like that. Then she remembered: the draft version of her letter to Francine. She clicked on the light again. She could use this time to copy out the neat version. But could she? She could not: because, if she was going to copy it out – and the notes about *L'Ange et les pervers* – she'd have to be awake enough to do any editing, any cutting or rewriting. She would have to do it later, just as soon as she woke up. She ripped out a blank page from her diary: *copy out comments on Francine's article and on the L'Ange book TODAY!* she ordered herself (not that she'd be up to going to the post office before it closed at twelve thirty, but she could at least get it all ready to go).

18

The Morning After

Jansen's teddy bear was perched on her pillow, and underneath was a message:

Good morning, darling. I hope you had a long sleep and that you're feeling better. You were sleeping soundly when I left. I'll bring you home some oranges, xx.

It was eight o'clock; Jansen must have only just left.

Perhaps May would call Francine now. She picked up the receiver. She put it down again. She lay in bed, staring over at the phone, wishing it would ring, that Francine would call her.

And then the phone rang.

'Hello.'

'May?'

'Francine.'

'I woke you up,' Francine said.

'No, I'm awake. I just happened to be looking at the phone. I was looking at the phone. And then it rang. And then you rang. That's strange.' May smiled.

'You were waiting for a call. You were willing the phone to ring.'

'Yes. I wanted someone to call me. That's true.'

'Someone in particular?'

'I'm glad that you called,' May conceded. She couldn't help smiling. This must be what it felt like, she thought, to have an illicit phone conversation, to be pursued by someone; she let her head float off for a while.

'Perhaps I should get you to stare at my phone sometime,' Francine said. 'Would you do that for me?'

'Yes, if you like.'

It was wonderful that Francine had called. She had called last night, and now she had called again. This was the second call; Francine had called her twice.

'So,' Francine said, 'I am phoning to say that I have now sent you a few articles and interviews about me that you could use for your letters to the universities – you'll find them useful for your dissertation as well.'

'Yes, okay.' Francine had called her on business.

'And, looking through my papers this morning, I just realized that I have not included an important interview I did a couple of years ago for a Canadian publication.'

'Oh.' May felt a bit stupid now; she hoped that her smile hadn't come across earlier.

'Therefore, I would like you to wait for that to arrive before you send anything off. It won't arrive for another week, because I want to send it to you together with the invitation to my book launch; they are being printed at the end of this week, and I want you to have one of these invitations as well.'

'Okay.'

'You will have all that in about a week, no doubt.'

'Thank you.'

'And are you well?' Francine asked.

'Yes.'

'You're not very talkative this morning. You're tired perhaps?'

'Yes, I am a little tired, and I've got a cold.'

'Oh, yes I can hear it in your voice. I shan't keep you on the phone in that case.'

'No.'

'Good. I look forward to seeing you quite soon, and you're going to send me a letter with your thoughts about *L'Ange et les pervers* before then, and the book.'

'Yes.'

That was it. That was the conversation. May had drifted into fantasyland, and forgotten to ask Francine how she was. May closed her eyes. She couldn't call her back now: 'Oh, hello, Francine. It's May. I forgot to ask you how you are. So . . . how are you?' Not possible. Hopeless. She was useless.

May put on some socks that she found on the bedroom floor. She went into the kitchen, where she considered doing the dishes, or maybe she'd just rinse them. She dropped a Redoxon into half a glass of water and, while it fizzed, she stared out of the window at the housing estate lawns and the tiny square of play area; it was raining. She drank her Redoxon and frowned at the dishes: Elizabeth stacked, but she didn't get rid of leftover food, which was the obvious first thing to do. May started scraping little lumps of something into the bin. She'd fill up the sink with hot water and leave the dishes to soak. Why was she awake? She switched the kettle on and waited for the sink to fill up. Maybe she'd take toast and lemon tea back to bed, and write out the final version of her notes on *L'Ange et les pervers*. The letter to Francine *had* to be sent on Monday, and her book.

May returned to bed, and looked through her notes:

At first I thought the main character in L'Ange et les pervers *was a man – 'il' – a boy, rather, since it begins with his childhood; later, I understood that 'he' was brought up as 'he', but was in fact a girl (phys-ically) – or so I thought – and the character discovers this later, except that 'he' doesn't, because 'he' still considers himself 'he' (I'm simplifying) – or perhaps both male and female, if I understood this correctly.*

May rejected that paragraph. She kept reading:

The main character, as a 'garçonne', mixes with lesbians; and, as a 'feminine man', mixes with gay men. However, she/he has no intimate relationship of any sort with anyone from either group.

May would leave out all that, as well.

Finally, she/he (as 'she', but later returning to 'he') adopts the bastard son of the female lover (by this married woman's adulterous male lover) of the main character's friend.

Questions: (May read on)

1. *What does this adoption symbolize? The main character is parenting 'his' (sic) masculine self? Meaning?*

2. *Was the main character an unwanted girl, or was 'she' and/or 'he' an unwanted hermaphrodite?*

Or was that a confused question that demonstrated just how much May had not understood?

May would keep the first question only. And now for the letter . . .

She heard someone unlocking the front door. She got out of bed to go and have a look.

It was Elizabeth letting herself in. 'I've come back to get a bit of sleep,' she said. 'Do you want me to lock this again?'

She must have been out all night.

'Did you have a good sleep?' Elizabeth locked the door.

'No. I'm going back to bed now. I'm not feeling brilliant.'

Elizabeth walked past May. The sitting room would be out of use for the rest of the day. May went back to bed. It was a dull day, still raining, with low dark clouds: perfect weather, in any case, for not getting up. She got an envelope out of the writing desk, and addressed it to Francine. May was sitting in bed, looking in her wallet for a stamp, when there was a tap on the bedroom door.

'You'll be happy to know' – Elizabeth poked her head in the door – 'that Jansen's bringing us back some curries tonight: because of your cold. She's a lovely woman, a really lovely woman. We had a great night last night. She's quite a hot dancer.' Elizabeth seemed to be revising a previous assumption. 'What are you reading?' She came in and plonked herself on the bed.

'I've read it. I've finished it. I'm just looking through it.'

'*L'Ange et les perverse.*' Elizabeth leaned forward and picked up the book. 'Hey, I like the pictures! Great sketches.'

'"*Pervers*" – you don't pronounce the "s".'

'Per-r-r-ver-r-r,' Elizabeth overdid the 'r', as if she was being sick. '*The Angel and the Perverts*: intr-r-reeeguing.'

'Could you be careful? It doesn't belong to me.'

'Delarue-Mardrus,' Elizabeth noted. She hopped off the bed, and handed the book back to May. 'Those are uptight letters, by the way,' she pointed at the envelope lying on the bed, 'if you're interested. Your handwriting shows you're holding on to something.' She went to pull the door shut again.

May picked up the envelope and put a stamp on it.

'If you want to come across intelligent and relaxed, you need to take less care to make your handwriting so legible,' Elizabeth went on from diagnosis to helpful advice. 'You'll have noticed with very clever people – artists and doctors, lawyers for example – you can never read their handwriting, can you? Not easily,' she answered her own question.

'That's very interesting.'

'I'm not saying you're stupid. I'm saying handwriting is like body language; that's all: it will be interpreted.'

'Thank you.' And now May wanted Elizabeth to go away.

'What you say is only half of the message, probably even less than half.'

'Thanks.'

Eventually, Elizabeth picked up the other half of the message, and left the room.

'You're "quite a hot dancer", by the way,' May told Jansen that night, once the bedroom door was jammed shut with a sock, and they were sitting in bed together.

'Am I?' Jansen smiled. She picked up the clock to check the alarm was on for the next morning.

'You look pleased,' May said.

Jansen laughed. She put the clock back on the stool.

'Oh, you're *really* pleased,' May corrected herself.

'Yes. It's a compliment. And quite a good one.' Jansen got out of bed again. 'I'm going to go and brush my teeth.'

May knew Jansen was leaving the room because she was annoyed, and because that is what pacifists do when they're annoyed. It was convenient for Jansen that she had forgotten to brush her teeth.

A few minutes later, Jansen came back, turned out the light, and climbed back into bed again.

May tried to say something nice. 'You are a good dancer,' she said. 'I'm just feeling annoyed with Elizabeth,' she explained. 'It's not that she's done anything; I just need my space.' May swivelled her eyes about. 'She is my sister and I do care about her.' It was so irritating to have to say this: not because it wasn't true, but May wasn't in the mood to say it. She was only saying it because she felt pressured into being positive. 'I do love her,' she added.

'I know you do.' Jansen appreciated the effort.

'*And* I need my space. It disturbs me having her here,' May went on. 'I can't even think of doing the PhD, when I haven't got the space to get it done. Francine wants me to show her what I've been doing. I have three weeks to come up with something. And now I've got Elizabeth wandering around smoking and sleeping and having endless baths.'

'Okay,' Jansen accepted the apology, 'let's get some sleep.' She snuggled into her.

'And I can't work in the sitting room, in case she turns up.'

'I'm really tired,' Jansen said. She was annoyed again.

May attempted not to talk.

'I've just driven all the way down to Bexhill-on-Sea, back up to Gatwick, and from there to Waterloo. The traffic was – terrible; you have no idea. Then a passenger asks me if I would drive her over night to Brussels! She'd missed the last Eurostar, and wanted to be back for her son's birthday. The tip would've been good . . .'

May had a thought.

'I'm exhausted,' Jansen said.

'What about if I was sick on Friday?' May suggested. 'Then we'd have a weekend together. We could do something special.'

Jansen reminded her, 'I'm back at work on Sunday.'

'I know. That's what I mean. We'd have Friday and Saturday.'

'I'm giving blood on Friday,' Jansen said.

'I could come with you.'

'If you want, but, May –'

'Or I could take tomorrow off, but I don't suppose it'd be realistic for me to be sick tomorrow and Friday.'

'I'll think about it. May, just to let you know: if you spend the day with me on Friday, I'm seeing Tamsin in the afternoon, so you'd have to decide whether you want to see her (which would be nice – that would be fine), or not; in which case I could drop you somewhere near a tube station.'

'Drop me somewhere? Why would I want you to drop me somewhere? If I'm taking the day off, it would be to spend time with you.'

'I'm just letting you know what I'll be doing.'

'We never have any time together, and now you're using up a free day spending it on Tamsin.'

'We've still got Saturday together.'

'Hmm.'

'Why don't we plan to do something really nice, the following week, once you're on holiday? We could take the train down to Bexhill-on-Sea – if I can get Thursday off.'

'And you couldn't cancel your Tamsin thing?'

'I'm not cancelling it.'

'(I was asking a question; that's all.)'

'She's got an interview,' Jansen said, 'and she's going to call when it's over, so we can arrange somewhere to meet – it depends on the weather – she's quite keen on a wander along the South Bank. We might go as far as the cathedral, and stop at the café.'

'Are we going to spend the whole day with her?'

'You don't have to come at all, if you don't want to. I'm telling you what I'm doing.'

'I may as well go to school, I suppose.'

'That's fine. Let's go to sleep.'

'What time did you get back last night? I didn't even hear you come in. It must've been very late.'

'Yes, it was late.'

'How late?'

'Yes,' Jansen replied. She was already falling asleep.

'No, I said, "How late was it?" When did you get home?'

'Hm?'

'I had a bad dream last night.' It was nearly quarter to seven. Jansen looked as if she might be awake (May had seen some movement) – or if she wasn't, she should be; she had to leave for work in less than an hour. And the alarm was about to go off. 'I dreamed I was in the bedsit, and the pipes were being eaten away by all these rats. I had to sprinkle white stuff on them to make them stronger (the pipes), but that started causing a blockage in someone else's flat –'

'What's the time?'

'It's seven o'clock.' It was ten to seven, so more or less. 'She was going to have to leave because of me, and –'

'May,' Jansen sighed with exhaustion, 'you've woken me up.'

'You have to be awake now anyway. It's seven o'clock . . . I had a scary dream.'

'Hm.'

'What do you think it means?'

'I don't know what it means.'

'You don't have any idea?'

'I don't understand you: sleep is really important to you, and yet you wake me up. Why do you do that?'

'I thought you were awake,' May said. 'And I had a bad dream,' she added.

'Hm.'

'I'm worried about the PhD; I have to come up with a fucking outline. It's giving me nightmares.'

'Mm-hmm.'

'And I'm sending Francine some more stupid fucking comments tomorrow, on that bloody fucking Mardrus book that I can hardly the fuck understand!' May heard the sitting-room door being opened. 'Oh, fuck! Elizabeth's up.'

'May, I think you've used up your "fuck" quota for the morning.'

'She can't be going to have a bath?' May listened. 'She is! She's having a bath! Fucking hell!'

'It's not very enjoyable being woken up, raved at, and then sweared around,' Jansen said.

'"Sworn", you mean. It's no fun being "sworn" around.'

'I'm going to go back to sleep for a bit. Please wake me up in half an hour,' Jansen pulled the duvet up to her chin, 'and not before half an hour.'

19

The Invitation

It was Tuesday evening: in less than a week it was the beginning
of Easter break; which meant that in just over two weeks, it was
the book launch. May got herself a coffee and some peanut butter
on toast, went back to the front door, and picked up the pile of
letters lying on the mat. She had walked over them as she came
in, leaving them there until she was ready to cope with them. An
electricity bill (Jansen would open that), she went back to the sitting
room, a letter from Amnesty International (Jansen), and – it had
arrived – an A4-sized envelope addressed to Mlle. Woodlea: from
Francine. Inside were two bookmark-sized invitations:

PAUSE LECTURE BOOKSHOP INVITES YOU TO MEET

FRANCINE BRION

AND TO CELEBRATE THE PUBLICATION OF HER COLLECTED ESSAYS

TROISIÈME PERSONNE SINGULIÈRE

(ÉDITIONS ÉQUIVOQUES).
READING AND BOOK SIGNING
THURSDAY, 20 APRIL AT 20.00.
RSVP

———•··•———

There were also a photocopy of the interview with Francine;
flyers about her book and the launch; and a note (no unnecessary
verbiage, as usual) on a slip of paper:

Ma chère May,

Two invitations – one for you, and one for your supervisor. (You can photocopy the flyers.)

Je t'embrasse,

Francine Brion.

PS Thank you for returning the book, and for the card. I am still waiting to hear what you think of my article on Delarue-Mardrus.

Why, May wondered, had Francine put her surname? May stared at the note as she sipped her coffee. Was Francine angry with her? Perhaps she was; she probably was. Because May hadn't mentioned the article, she hadn't written anything much in the card, and she'd taken over a month to do all that: none of her notes had been good enough; they were not good enough. But perhaps she should have sent them. Because now it looked as if she hadn't even read the book.

Well anyway, her rate of progress on the PhD was unimportant – in that she wasn't enrolled anywhere and she didn't have a supervisor.

Sometimes – May finished her toast – she wanted to take a brick and knock herself out for a while. She would go to bed early – she really couldn't stand herself – and redraft her notes on the Delarue-Mardrus article while she waited for Jansen to get back. May put Jansen's mail on the stool next to the bed, and went to the bathroom to brush her teeth.

Two redrafts later, she heard the key in the door. May clicked off the light and lay down, pretending to be asleep. She heard the front door open and close – gently. It was Jansen, definitely: she was always careful to pull the door shut quietly; she was considerate. May listened: Jansen was brushing her teeth.

'Jansen?' May called out. 'Jansen?' There was no reply. May could hear her putting their toothbrush back in the cup. 'Jansen?' she called out again, more loudly. May got out of bed and opened the door.

Someone with long ringlets of dark brown hair was standing in front of the basin: a man; he'd turned to dry his face on the hand towel. May let out a yell, and he jumped, pulling the towel off the rail.

Elizabeth came running. 'May, this is Mark; Mark, May. Sorry! Sorry! Oops!' This was so amusing, to her.

'Hello,' Mark said. He looked tired and pasty. 'Shit, you gave me a fright there.'

'I think I got a bit more of a fright than you did.'

'I was making us coffee,' Elizabeth said. 'D'you want one?'

'No, thank you,' May said. 'I've got work tomorrow, so – goodnight.' She shut the door and, still breathing fast, climbed back into bed.

There was a tap at the bedroom door. Elizabeth came in. 'Sorry 'bout that,' she whispered in the dark. 'He's feeling totally gross; he's just been sick round the corner, in front of the twenty-four-hour shop. He was driving me back home from a party at his place and we had to stop all of a sudden, so he could throw up. The van's parked on a yellow line. Anyway, I'm gonna give him my mattress. He's not capable of going anywhere . . . And you won't see him; he'll still be fast asleep when you get up . . . You're having an early night,' she observed.

'Yes: because I need to get up in the morning. That gave me such a fright.'

'Sorry. Sorry again.'

'Whose toothbrush was he using?'

'The blue one, don't worry.' Elizabeth went back to the door. 'I'd better go and see how he is. Hey, I can take that letter to the post office for you tomorrow if you want, if you've still got it. Or anything else. I'm going there after the Jobcentre.'

'No, I haven't got anything.'

20

The Bargain

'When people write "RSVP", do they really mean it, do you think?' It was eight thirty on a Monday morning, and May was still in her pyjamas; it was the first day of her Easter break. Nearly a week had passed since she had received the invitation to the book launch, and now she had less than a week to reply (if she was going to).

'What?' Jansen put on her chauffeur blazer. She picked up her bag, went to the kitchen, got an apple out of the fridge and washed it.

'When they put "RSVP" on an invitation, do you have to reply, or does it not really matter?'

'Is this a specific question, May? Because I'm in a hurry.' Jansen put the apple in her bag, and went to the front door.

'If you get an invitation to something, and it says "RSVP" –'

'Where are they?' Jansen checked her blazer pocket. 'Just a moment.' She went past May and back to the bedroom, where she looked on top of the chest of drawers, then put her bag on the floor and started rummaging around in it. 'You haven't seen the car keys, have you? I hope I didn't leave them in the sitting room.'

'Behind you – on the stool.'

Jansen turned round and picked them up. She put them in her pocket. 'Thanks,' she said. 'Thanks. Right, I've got to go now, or I'll get a parking ticket.'

The phone rang.

'Could you get that? Bye, darling.' Jansen went to leave.

'I don't want to; I'm not answering it,' May said. 'I'm not in the mood.'

'May, I've got to go!'

'I haven't had breakfast yet.'

'For God's sake!' Jansen dropped her bag and picked up the receiver. 'Hello. Oh, hi!' Her face transformed into happy surprise. 'Yeah, I am actually – no, that's all right . . . um, yeah okay well let's . . .' She gestured impatiently over to her diary on the writing desk, and May handed it to her. 'You're in this morning, are you? All right.'

May watched her; she knew she was being clingy.

'No, no, no.' Laughter. 'Yeah, great, fine. No that's fine. Bye!'

Jansen put her diary into her bag, and went to the front door again.

May followed her. 'I'm talking about the book launch. Obviously,' she said, talking fast. 'She knows I'm coming anyway, doesn't she? So, do I need to reply, or not?'

'I think it's polite to reply. Yes.' Jansen opened the door. 'Just give her a call, May. It's quite simple.'

'So you think I have to?' May said. 'But she might ask me about my supervisor; she'll expect me to have written that covering letter to the universities; she might want to hear it.'

'I think it's up to you. Bye –' Jansen gave May a kiss on the cheek, 'bye, darling,' and went out of the door.

May went to the National Gallery; she hadn't been there for a while, she needed distraction, and it was her Easter break: she had the right. Anyway, it was educational – and Francine was busy until one. May got a headset and walked – 'Spain and Venice 1700–1800', 'Canaletto and Guardi', 'British Portraits', 'France 1700–1800' – from room to room in no particular order, tapping in the number next to various paintings, listening to the recordings, and noting . . . *how vivid . . . finely rendered . . . just visible, under . . . an astonishing range of . . . almost translucent . . . holding wreaths . . . and at the centre of the painting* . . . gap after gap in her education.

After an hour or so, she returned the headset, went to the shop and bought a book on French painters of the eighteenth to the twentieth centuries; over coffee, she would take some small steps towards self-improvement.

She left the Gallery with her new book, pushed open the large doors into the bright daylight of Trafalgar Square, the noise of traffic and police sirens, and crossed the road to St Martin-in-the-Fields. She sat on the steps of the church.

In her journal she jotted down: *Fragonard, Courbet, Vigée-Lebrun*. She'd cover them first; then she'd start at the beginning of the art history book and have the pleasure, at that point, of having already read certain scattered sections. Of course, she shut her journal and put it away, to do this properly she should also revise her Greek and Roman myths and legends.

'Sweetheart.'

It wasn't Jansen speaking.

May focused on the blurb at the back of her new book. If she didn't look up, maybe he'd go away.

'Sweetheart.'

She looked up. A man wearing a striped sweater whose colour was lost under various stains leaned in towards her, as if he were about to confide. 'I'm reading,' she said.

'I'm sorry to disturb you,' the man began, 'but I only wanted to ask if you had a couple of pounds to spare, so I could get home . . .' May opened her book at a painting of two women in a small boat on a lake: by Morisot, *a leading figure among Impressionists*, '. . . and as long as you're doing okay – I had it all, I had the fast car, I know what I'm talking about – people like you.' The alcohol on his breath was strong as aftershave. 'But if things go wrong: they don't want to know.' He addressed a few passers-by, who ignored him. 'I don't suppose you want to hear this,' May was engrossed in her book, studying a parasol, 'but everyone's shit stinks, sweetheart, you can't get away from that, darling, and you can't hide in that book of yours either; that's not gonna save you. People don't give a damn about each other,' he continued to himself. 'It's just me-me-me: "good to see you", "keep coming back",' he smirked through his rotting teeth, 'but they won't give you any bloody money; they're not gonna give you what you actually need. What are you reading? You haven't got any change, have you? I only need a pound.'

'No, I haven't.' May looked up again, then returned to her book.

'I'd only need a fiver,' the man told her, raising his voice, as if she were deaf. 'Or a pound; that would get me somewhere anyway. A pound? Thank you for listening to me.' He started walking off, then changed his mind. 'You know why I'm talking to you?'

May put her book in her bag, and the man gave up, leaving her with a parting: 'Bitch.'

She should have stayed at home; this was how people never did anything. She was wasting time, being undisciplined; flicking through art books and acting as if she were on holiday.

She felt ill: either she was getting another cold or it was just that she was exhausted. She went down to the café in the Crypt and bought a cappuccino and a bread-and-butter pudding drowned in custard. As she ate under the dim blue ceiling-lights she watched the lunch queue grow longer. At a nearby table a girl sat flicking through *Hello!* magazine. May envied and despised her for this mindless and purposeless activity. Just to do anything that was a complete waste of time, and not feel guilty about it. The hours, the minutes ticked loudly away in May's head – 'That's one minute gone, that's another' – reminding her to use time well. If only she could return to those unconscious days, she could drift along, and die at some point, happily unaware of any ambitions unfulfilled. It was just so painful to know that in nine years (eight really) she'd be forty, and she wouldn't have done anything with her life.

May now sat growing a headache as she breathed in other people's colds. She put her jacket on the chair opposite hers. She'd finish her cappuccino and go home.

⋆ ⋆ ⋆

Elizabeth was *out shopping with Mark, xx.* May stood in the sitting room. She had the place to herself; it was late in the afternoon. Now was the time to call Francine. May would keep it short: I'll be at the book launch; I'm looking forward to it; and how are you?

And perhaps she would also say she was thinking of deferring the PhD.

There was a knock at the door and the sound of a key in the lock.

'Oh, hi there.' It was Mark, letting himself in. He had a large carrier bag with something square inside. 'Elizabeth's gone to get milk. She'll be here any minute.'

'Oh,' May said.

'Shall I put this in the sitting room?'

'Yeah.' May stepped aside, and then followed him.

There was a tap at the door, and Mark went back to answer it.

'May, you're home already.' Elizabeth came in and leaped onto the sofa. 'Yay!' she said, pulling a carton of cigarettes out of the carrier bag, and setting it on the rug in front of her. 'Forty packets per carton: that's thirty pounds we've saved,' she told her.

'Something like that, yeah,' Mark said.

May said nothing; she tried to show lack of interest. Now that Elizabeth and Mark had taken over the flat, she would have to take the phone and shut herself in the bedroom.

'One-fifty times forty: that's thirty pounds,' Elizabeth went on.

May let the maths slide over the top of her brain. Thirty? That wasn't right? No, she had to work it out: ten times one-fifty is fifteen, times two is thirty, times two is sixty. 'That's not right,' she said aloud.

'Oh sixty! I've saved sixty, I mean . . .' Elizabeth focused on dislodging one packet from the carton. 'Great!' She laughed (she was stoned perhaps; she had to be, to be finding any of this amusing), and emptied out the cigarettes into her palm. 'Twenty in a packet.' She splayed them on the table. 'Each one,' she picked one up, 'every time you smoke one, you're making a saving of 15p.'

That definitely wasn't right. May didn't bother working it out; it was the logic itself that bothered her.

'Would you like a cigarette?' Elizabeth offered. 'You look like you could do with one. Mark, perhaps you'd make us a coffee?'

'You know I don't smoke,' May said. 'And no coffee for me, thanks.'

May went to the bedroom. What she'd do, she decided, was jot down what she wanted to say to Francine, and then she'd feel prepared. May opened up the writing desk and found a scrap of paper. She smelled smoke. They were smoking in the flat. She went back to the sitting room.

'It's all right. Don't panic. We were just lighting up. We're going for a walk.' Elizabeth stopped to point dramatically at the door. 'For God's sake.' She raised her eyebrows at Mark, and they left.

May went back to the bedroom, got a pen and made a few notes; three bullet points:

- Am going to defer
- But am coming to the book launch of course (looking forward to it)
- (only if asked) Supervisor isn't coming

Fine. May went over what she'd written: she would mention the deferral straight away, and then (if Francine wasn't angry with her) May would be able to go to the book launch in a relaxed sort of way, all pressure off. She picked up the phone.

'Tiens, c'est May! How are you? You're well?' Francine was delighted to hear from her. 'Your dissertation's progressing?'

'No. In fact, no.' (Bullet point number one – attempted.)

'You're coming up against some difficulty.' Francine understood straight away.

'I won't be able to bring it to show you it yet. It's not at all ready.'

'Fine. We can arrange another time for you to bring it. After this book launch is over I'll be far more available in any case. So, don't worry. Just keep going.'

'I really don't think I can do the PhD.' May tried again; she told Francine about her latest rat dream.

'There is something gnawing away at you, a desire. Look up the word "rat" in the dictionary,' Francine told her. 'The rat is a survivor. It's a very good sign, this dream. You can be happy with it.'

May listened. She didn't believe what Francine was saying, but she listened anyway.

'You are quite capable of doing this PhD: I know that, but you don't; and you won't know it, you won't know you can do it, until you've done it; so you must persevere. It's the only thing to do when it's like that. Come to the book launch,' she concluded. 'You need to meet people.' (Bullet point two was covered.)

'And what about you? Have you had any dreams?' May enquired.

Yes, Francine had had two *very* interesting dreams: one was about a smashed ceiling and the Cyrillic alphabet flying out. 'It was as if there was no centre of gravity,' she said.

'Did the dream mean something?' May asked.

'Of course it meant something.' Francine did not go on to explain what; either May was supposed to know what the dream meant, or it wasn't her business to know. 'I'll see you at the launch. You can come to dinner at my place the following evening.'

'Wonderful.' May's throat hurt.

'You have read *L'Ange et les pervers* – now I suggest you think about the status, or the "value", of the feminine in this novel. I also recommend you get hold of a copy of *Gabriel*. There are comparisons to be made between the two works.'

'*Gabriel*.'

'By George Sand. Your supervisor, is she coming to the book launch?'

'No.' (Bullet point number three. May folded up the scrap of paper, leaned over and dropped it in the waste-paper basket.)

'No? Well, you'll report back to her, no doubt, you will tell her what she has *missed!*'

'Yes.'

Francine laughed. 'Bon courage!' she said. 'Until very soon.'

21

The Little Holiday

'This is heavy! What have you got in here?' Jansen flipped open the suitcase.

'Some books to read.'

'How many? We're only going away for two nights.' Jansen started rifling through the bag like a Customs Officer.

'I won't know what I feel like reading until I get there, so I've taken a selection.'

'You've taken a library!' Jansen pulled out a large book, and held it in her palm, as if she were trying to guess how much it weighed. '*Histoire du féminisme français?* – no, May, you're not going to read this.'

'I am.' May took the book from her, and put it back into the suitcase.

'*Lélia, or the Life of George Sand!*' Jansen read out. '*Methodology in Qualitative Research*: I feel as if I'm going on a study weekend. This is meant to be a holiday. Take one book, and I bet you won't even read that. You're not going to read all of these.'

'I will. I'll read bits from all of them.'

'What's this?' Jansen had discovered Francine's essays. 'You're taking all of her articles?' She pulled out the folder. 'I'm not helping to pull this bag, unless you get rid of something.'

'I can't get rid of that. That's the most important thing.' May took the folder from Jansen and put it back into the suitcase.

'Put it in another bag, May – I'm not carrying her essays.'

'You've got a real problem with Francine, haven't you? What's your problem?'

'If you want to take all these books, and her essays, you can be in charge of the bag. That's all I'm saying.'

'You've got these heavy shoes here – I'd say that's as heavy as three books at least.' May held up the plastic bag with Jansen's shoes in them. 'And you've got these slippers; why do you need these? Ah! And there's a book in here: *The Gnostic Gospels*.'

'I'm taking one book.'

'Wait a minute' – May hovered her right hand over the book, touching her forehead with the other, in feigned concentration – 'I'm picking something up here . . . I'm sensing this is a gift – from a Christian? I'm picturing someone in a checked shirt –'

'I bought it myself, May. I found it at the bookstall under Waterloo Bridge.'

'That afternoon you were with Tamsin!' May completed Jansen's sentence. 'I knew it: she didn't buy it for you, but she recommended it though, didn't she? And you're reading it because she thought it was interesting, and you want to please her.'

'That's really insulting, May. I'm reading it because I would like to read it, because it interests me.'

'And because of Tamsin.'

'Tamsin is not particularly interested' – Jansen delved into the suitcase again, and took out Francine's essays – 'in Gnosticism, if you want to know.'

'Could I –' May made a failed grab for the essays. 'Could I have that back, please?'

Jansen shook her head.

'Please, would you give it to me!' May tried to wrench the folder out of Jansen's grip. 'It's MINE!' Jansen wasn't going to give it to her. 'Okay then.' May kneeled down abruptly on the floor next to the bag. 'Okay,' she said, as if she were dealing with an unreasonable toddler. 'Perhaps I just won't go.' She took out the history book and thumped it onto the floor. 'I'm too busy for this anyway.' She took out the George Sand, her pyjamas, the boring methodology book . . . 'And you can have a nice empty bag all to yourself.' May wanted to go on the train with Jansen. She loved going on little weekends away with her. They'd had an amazing few days in Wales one time; they visited the house of the Ladies of Llangollen, and read out bits from *Under Milk Wood* together in bed. 'I'll see you in a couple of days,' May said.

'If you don't want to come – here is your precious folder,' Jansen made a grand gesture out of handing it back to her – 'I'll go on my own.' She took her jacket off a hanger in the wardrobe, put it on, and wrapped a scarf around her neck.

Now, if May wanted to go to Bexhill, she'd have to back down immediately; she'd have to apologize about her Neanderthal communication skills. 'I just don't like being bullied,' she began – it was better tactically, she decided, not to come across as entirely in the wrong – 'into deciding, in advance, what I'm going to read.' She put everything back into the bag. 'I would still like to come.'

'Right.' Jansen left the room; she was going to be in a bad mood for a while, possibly the whole train trip – as long as she hadn't just decided that May could go on her own . . .

May followed her to the other room: Jansen was sitting on the sofa, she still had her jacket and scarf on, and she was staring ahead at something.

'What are you doing?'

'What do you think I'm doing? I am waiting for you to get ready. We have to leave in five minutes.' She looked at her watch. 'Choose what you'd like to take with you: either you bring a book, or Francine's papers.'

May went back to the bedroom. She took the history book out of the suitcase again, and the one on research, hesitated, then put the history book back, and took out the biography, and finally, after thinking about it some more, swapped the biography for the history book again. She put Francine's articles back at the bottom of the case. 'Okay.' She appeared, tight-lipped, at the door of the sitting room, with the bag standing next to her. 'I'm ready.'

Jansen got up off the sofa. 'You've chosen one thing?' she verified.

'One book, yes.'

'Thank you.'

They left the flat.

'But I didn't take out Francine's articles,' May added, once they were sitting on the train, and the suitcase was lying on the seat in front of them. 'Because they don't count.' May smiled. 'I took out two books.' She made the peace sign.

'Fine. Then you'll be the one in charge of the suitcase.' Jansen took the cup off the Thermos, unscrewed the lid, and poured tea into the cup.

'No! You've got your shoes in there, if you remember. We're both in charge.'

Jansen smiled at May's reaction. 'Sorry,' she said, 'but I did tell you I wouldn't help with it, unless you took some things out.'

'I took out two books,' May repeated.

'Mm. I'm not interested, May.' Jansen had a sip of tea.

'I wanted to have the option of reading something other than Francine's writing, *and* I couldn't not bring her work: because I'm going to the book launch on Thursday, and she said to bring questions.'

'I'm not interested.'

'And because I might be quizzed on her writing. So I need to be really familiar with it. Before Thursday.'

'No one's going to quiz you on her writing. You're going to a book launch!'

'Well, anyway. That's why I had to bring her articles.'

Jansen said nothing.

'So, we'll take turns with the bag.'

'I don't want to talk about this, May. I'd like to enjoy the journey.'

'So would I. And I'd just like to know you're going to help with the suitcase.'

'Are you going to stop talking about this? Because otherwise I'm moving to another seat,' Jansen said.

'Are you going to be fair about the bag? Because otherwise I'm changing carriages.'

'You always have to go one up, don't you?'

'You've got a pair of heavy shoes and you've got that book Tamsin wants you to read.'

'Do you want this tea?' Jansen asked.

May shook her head.

Jansen started pouring the rest of the tea back into the Thermos.

'What are you doing?'

Jansen screwed the lid back on, and stood up. 'I'm changing seats.'

May raised her eyebrows, she clicked her tongue. 'Don't bother.' She stood up. 'I'm changing carriages.' She heaved the bag off the seat, and started pulling it down the aisle, past a man and a woman and probably their teenage daughter. 'You're being unfair,' May called back to Jansen, who had sat back in her seat. 'I don't see why I'm the one who's taking this.' May went into the next carriage.

They met up again at Bexhill. Jansen was further down the platform; May went past, pretending she hadn't seen her.

'Hello,' said Jansen, walking alongside May. 'Do I know you?'

May kept on walking.

'Can I help you with your bag? It looks heavy.'

May ignored her.

'Windy weather, isn't it? I'm spending a couple of nights here,' Jansen continued. 'I'm staying at a bed and breakfast. What about you? Where are you going?'

'Very funny,' May said. 'You know I have no idea.' She stopped walking, and passed the bag to Jansen.

'What's in here?' Jansen asked.

'Ha-ha,' May said. 'Thank you for taking it.'

'I'll pull it halfway,' Jansen specified.

They left the station.

'It's not very warm down here, is it?' Jansen said. 'I'm glad I brought my slippers; your bones feel the cold when you get to our age.'

'I'm still feeling annoyed with you,' May warned her. 'I'm not in the mood for jokes.'

'And I am still annoyed with you – just to let you know. This morning, I was that close to calling Francine. I am not going to put up with this for much longer.'

'Is that a threat?'

'I am letting you know – how – I – feel.'

'You're threatening me, that's what you're doing.'

'No, I am not threatening you. I wish you would listen.'

'This is a lovely holiday. Relaxing.'

Jansen stopped, unzipped the suitcase, and took out a map.

'Could you not have worked that out earlier?' May said. 'Now we look like tourists.'

'We are tourists, May. That is what we are: tour-ists.'

'Speak for yourself.'

'Would you like to be in charge of directions?' Jansen asked.

'No, I would not like to be in charge of directions,' May said. 'As you know.'

'Right. So please leave me to work this out. Can you see any street names?'

'Do you want me to answer that? Even though it would mean I was helping you?'

'Sea Road,' Jansen had found the name. She looked it up on her map.

'Isn't it just towards the sea?' May said. 'We just head towards the sea.'

Jansen continued studying the map.

'How hard can it be?' May added.

Jansen handed her the map.

'What?' May had the map in her hand now.

'Over to you,' Jansen said.

May didn't look at it. 'You know where you're going,' she said, 'so let's go.'

Jansen said nothing.

'You know where we're going, so there's no point in my looking at the map.'

'The street you are looking for is Albany Road,' Jansen said.

'You know the way,' May said, 'and you know I hate maps.'

Jansen sat down on the suitcase.

'Hello, ladies!' the owner of the bed and breakfast greeted them in a plastic voice.

'Hello,' said Jansen. 'We're booked under "Andersen",' she told the woman.

'Oh yes!' The woman remembered the name; she opened her A4-sized diary at the desk. 'Oh?' She paused. 'I could offer you a twin – if you'd prefer?'

'We have booked, haven't we?' Jansen verified. She leaned forward a bit and looked at the large diary on the desk.

'Yes, oh yes, you have booked, that's fine,' the woman said, 'but we're actually not quite fully booked this weekend, so if you'd prefer a twin, I could offer you a twin.'

'No thanks. We're happy with the double,' Jansen said.

'You haven't got two singles?' May enquired.

The woman had another brief look in her diary. 'No, I'm afraid not,' she said. 'We've only got one single left, but I could offer you a twin and a single, for the price of two singles,' she proposed. 'If that's helpful.'

'What would be the difference in price between that and the double?' May asked.

'Oh, yes, it would be a bit more expensive,' the woman regretted to say. 'But the twin would be exactly the same price as the double. And they're both en suite.'

'How much would two doubles be?' May asked.

'Two doubles?' The woman was trying to work this out.

'We'd like one double,' Jansen said. 'The one we've booked, please.'

'No, yes, of course.' The woman smiled; she looked nervous. 'Room three then.'

May smiled; she was still angry with Jansen.

'Good!' The woman turned round to take key number three off its hook; and May aimed a brief over-accentuated smile at Jansen, who did not smile back.

'Who should I give this to?' the woman asked brightly.

May reached out to take it. 'Thank you very much,' she said, and she smiled again.

Sachets of coffee, tea and sugar, mini plastic containers of UHT milk, and two china teacups cradled together on a couple of saucers on a tray; a black leather folder next to that, containing pamphlets about Bexhill's restaurants and attractions. The bed was puffy-duvet soft; there was a large armchair; a view of the sea; and a desk with a television on it. Jansen lay down on the bed with the remote.

'We're not going to watch television, are we?'

'I'm seeing what's on.'

'There's nothing on!' May said.

Jansen flicked through the channels – four or five of them – and landed on *Trisha*.

'No! Oh God I can't bear that!' May said.

Jansen flicked back to an advertisement for hair-removal. She switched off the television. 'May, I need a bit of space. If you want to go out, I'm going to stay here for a bit and watch TV.'

'It's the middle of the day.'

Jansen switched the television back on, and May sat in the armchair; she took out her *Life of George Sand*.

Later they had lunch at a little café on a road that had an Oxfam, a Cancer Research and a British Red Cross on it; so they browsed in those for a while, and Jansen found a cookbook. Then they walked in the wind all the way along the beach of stones; Jansen zipped up her windbreaker and gave her scarf to May, who snuggled into her, and they sang Bee Gees songs into the wind, and Abba. Jansen sang 'The beach is alive with the sound of seagulls' and 'What are we going to do about Booboo?' And then they found a tearoom – Jansen paid.

In the evening, May bought Chinese takeaways, and they went back to their room and lay in bed, watching the news: a crumbling cottage somewhere near Belfast was being saved, as the result of a local campaign; May and Jansen got all weepy together over that, and May made them their second cup of coffee.

22

Tamsin Again

The morning after they returned from their weekend away, Jansen suggested they stay inside all day: the weather was grotty – grey and rain – and Elizabeth wasn't back from wherever she'd gone the night before last.

At about three in the afternoon, Jansen went out to get them something yummy from Arif's on the Walworth Road, while May stayed at the flat to set the table and put the kettle on, and then wait around for Jansen to get back.

Tap-TAP! May went to the door. She was still in her pyjamas. She had thought it would be Jansen of course.

It was Tamsin, dressed as if she'd just been for a jog, in green tracksuit pants and yellow wet-weather jacket.

'May!' Tamsin shot her head forward, like a goose. She put a note back into her jacket pocket, and started taking off her rucksack. She was expecting to be invited in. 'I didn't think anyone would be at home! Are you here on your own?'

'Jansen's just gone off to get lunch; she'll be back in a minute.'

'Oh, great!' Tamsin was thrilled. She put her rucksack on the ground, knelt on the doorstep, unzipped her bag, and pulled out a bottle of water.

'Come in,' May said.

'Is that all right?' Tamsin put the bottle back into her bag, and stepped inside. 'I hope I'm not disturbing you,' she said.

They went to the sitting room. May turned on the gas heater, and opened the curtains, while Tamsin, taking off her jacket and settling herself on the sofa, explained that she had 'heard back' already: she'd got the job at the YMCA near Tottenham Court Road! 'I'm going to be at the front desk, on reception. I can see it getting really busy. I'm going to have to keep my sense of humour!' she laughed. 'Well, it won't be boring, that's for sure. And I can even have a room there until I get a flat.' She took a swig from her bottle, and passed it to May, wiping her mouth with the back of her palm.

Tamsin was, May conceded as she shook her head and mouthed 'Oh, no thanks', attractive – in a conservative sort of way; and some women do find conservative women attractive: because they seem to need protecting; they need guidance and an interpreter at times.

May smiled politely into the silence. 'Would you like a cup of coffee? Tea?' She heard the front door open.

'Tammy!' Jansen appeared at the sitting-room door, holding some paper bags of food.

'Hey! Jan! Whoo!' Tamsin swung up off the sofa, and cupped her right arm around Jansen in a version of a hug: something she might've learned in the army perhaps, a sort of side-on 'semi-hug'.

'Jan': May tried the name in her head. Definitely not the same effect; there was less substance to it. May attempted, with a pocket-sized smile, to look on happily at this mini ex-soldiers' reunion. 'Tammy' was now perched on the sofa next to 'Jan', telling her about her first day on reception. May sat, redundant, at the table. She was hungry. Jansen was holding on to the paper bags, laughing. May took the bags from her, and opened them: in one, a coconut cake (Jansen's) and a carrot cake (May's); she folded up the bag, and opened the other one: one mushroom and one spinach pastry; they'd been heated up. May went to the kitchen, divided up the pastries, put them on three plates, and brought them back to the sitting room.

'Oh, this looks good. Thanks.' Tamsin took her plate.

'Thanks, darling,' Jansen said.

May sat down at the table with her plate.

'You two have just been on holiday, haven't you?' Tamsin asked, addressing them both.

'Yeah, Bexhill-on-Sea,' Jansen said.

'Yes.' May nodded obediently. The afternoon had been hijacked.

'A bit of quality time together,' Tamsin said. 'That's important, isn't it.'

'It was pretty cold and windy on the beach, but there was a café in the pavilion that was sheltered, and we bought a cake and hot drinks there.' Jansen had put the plate next to her on the sofa, and was pulling off her jumper as she spoke.

'Hey!' Tamsin exclaimed, pleased. 'You're wearing that shirt I gave you years ago!'

Unfortunately, this was true. Jansen happened to be wearing that ugly old army shirt; it was all frayed around the collar, so Jansen only ever wore it in bed now, which was all right, but sometimes at the weekend, when she couldn't find anything else, she'd say this one would do.

Tamsin smiled a goofy little smile. Then, 'So, how's the driving going?' she asked. 'Any more famous people to dazzle us with?'

'Not since Sean Connery.'

Tamsin took a bite of her pastry. '"Congratulations on your Oscar. And may I just say",' she said through a mouthful, '"that you look great in a kilt": brilliant!' She laughed.

'I had a New Zealand rugby player, too, just the other week,' Jansen remembered. 'What was his name? You can't remember, can you, May? Umm . . .'

'Let's think . . .' Tamsin said.

'Sorry to be rude,' May cut in, 'but I've got to go and get some work done.'

'You teachers are such hard workers,' Tamsin said.

'Not really.' May shrugged. 'Anyway, nice to see you.' She went to the bedroom, flipped open the suitcase and pulled out Francine's articles. There were four more days to go before the book launch; perhaps she should get on with the covering letter, so she could take it to show Francine.

Francine Brion has asked me

Francine Brion, whose work I have been researching, has asked me

Francine Brion has asked me

(Yes, better to keep it simple.)

Francine Brion has asked me to send you these flyers, as she thought you might like to obtain copies of her articles. A collection of . . .

Was a covering letter even necessary though? What about just:

With compliments, Francine Brion: (address, telephone number). UK contact: May Woodlea (address etc.)

That would mean they might contact May. She decided to make herself a coffee, and have some of the carrot cake.

Half an hour later, Tamsin 'had to be off'. Walking past the open bedroom door, she waved at May in a vaguely military-but-friendly way. 'Oh!' May feigned surprise and disappointment. 'You're going now?'

Once she was sure Tamsin had left, May returned to the sitting room. 'She's invited you on a silent retreat?'

'Yes, May.' Jansen collected up the plates and cups.

'So you can stare at each other all day? I think that's creepy.' May held her stomach, as if she were in pain. 'There's something really illogical – don't you think? – about inviting someone on a silent retreat.' May followed Jansen to the kitchen. 'I think it's quite rude, actually; she didn't mention me.'

'Would you have wanted to go?' Jansen started washing the dishes, running them under the hot tap, and putting them on the drying rack.

'Possibly.'

'Oh, yeah . . . for sure.'

'How would she know? Perhaps I like going on silent retreats.'

Jansen pulled out the plug.

'And she probably expected you to say yes.'

'She's allowed to ask.' Jansen handed May a tea towel. 'She's lonely.'

23

The Book Launch

May arrived half an hour before their arranged meeting time. The reading was in the basement. She went downstairs. Rows of chairs filled nearly half the room. A few women were still wandering around the bookshop with glasses in their hands, but most people had already secured their seats.

Francine was sitting at a table at the back, wearing a comfortable-looking jacket, rich dark brown, with a strip of velvet around the collar; she had a pile of books in front of her, and she was sitting, one hand cupped, mock-ironic, under her chin, in a listening pose, next to another woman; they were laughing. May went over to them. She would have preferred it, she would have felt more comfortable (perhaps), if Francine had been alone, but at a book launch that couldn't be possible.

'Tiens! Te voilà, toi!' Francine pulled a chair towards herself for May. 'Anne, this is May; May, this is Anne, a very dear friend of mine. The writer I told you about.' Francine got up as she finished her sentence; 'I'm going to circulate.' May was being fobbed off onto the extraordinary Anne Béranger: Parisian-chic, May observed, in that ill-looking gaunt-faced way.

May smiled and came up with a sentence: she said, 'Francine's told me so much about you.' She didn't want to be there. She hated her hair at the moment, too: it was turning into a mushroom, and she should have done something about it.

'How do you know her?' Anne Béranger was younger than Francine – perhaps by about ten years – and had a smoker's voice.

'I rang her.' May kept her answer brief; she didn't like being interrogated, especially not by this 'very dear friend' woman.

'Quite simply!' Anne was both impressed and mocking. 'And she asked you if you'd read her latest *œuvre?*'

'I told her I was thinking of doing a thesis on her.' May tried to maintain her dignity.

Anne laughed. 'She'd have been flattered!'

'I was doing research for a PhD, but I'm not now. I'm dropping the PhD idea . . . for now.' Why was she telling this to a complete stranger? Sometimes she had an honesty problem. 'Well, I've been thinking about deferring for a while, so . . .' May watered down her confession, 'I'm going to have to let her know.'

'That would be a mistake, I think. She adores playing Pygmalion. When I told her I would be continuing my job as a translator, she accused me of ambivalence; she said I was incapable of fully assuming my writer identity, whereas, on the contrary, it's the financial security I need in order to write. Of course, she has a private income, so . . . In here,' Anne tapped the side of a leather satchel sitting on a chair next to her, 'is the manuscript of my first novel. It's taken me over five years to get it all written out, then one more year with the editing and the revising. Francine's offered to read it once more, before I send it off. I want to be sure I've captured the era.'

May said nothing. Anne continued.

'I did a lot of research: Evelyne Le Garrec, Françoise d'Eaubonne, Monique Wittig . . . I went to the Marguerite Durand library, scoured the seventies publications – I spent hours in there; and I read relevant history books, Françoise Picq, et cetera, Marie-Jo Bonnet – have you read her work?'

'Do you mean *Les Relations amoureuses entre les femmes*? Or *Les Deux Amies*, which has just come out?' May asked; she was being competitive; she was showing off. Her heartbeat sped up.

'Francine knows her, of course.' Anne ignored May's question.

'Yes, I know,' May said, not to be outdone, although she had probably just sounded defensive.

'Oh, look: they're going to start.' Anne stood up. 'I'm going to go and get that front seat.' She rushed off.

May found a seat at the end of the second row, next to a string of carefree chatting women. Francine had taken off her jacket now, and she was scanning the room; she looked supremely relaxed, she looked superb; everything about her: how she stood there, and what she was wearing, the cuff of her shirtsleeves slightly folded over; she was relaxed, and yet smart. She looked . . . 'stunning' was the word. Noticing May, she raised her eyebrows, pleased with herself and conspiratorial. That was it; May could no longer deny the obvious: she was in love with Francine; she was in love. And, naturally, naturally, she had just ruined things by talking to Anne; May wished she'd never met the woman. She felt like leaving. She felt like crying. She would have to tell Francine she was deferring now, now that she'd blurted it out – how had that happened? – to this Anne-writer-friend, to someone she had only just met; May would have to tell Francine this evening.

A woman was gaining attention by tapping the side of a glass with a pen. 'S'il vous plaît! S'il vous plaît!' she called out.

All talking stopped.

'Welcome, all, to Pause Lecture,' the woman began. 'We are very happy to see you gathered here in such numbers in order to hear Francine read from her work *Troisième personne singulière*. Francine has published articles in various magazines too numerous to list. *Troisième personne singulière* brings together these articles in one volume. At last, I think you will all agree.' She smiled, turning to Francine. 'But now, I shall let her introduce her work to you more fully.'

Francine rubbed her hands together, and then she yawned into them. 'Excuse me,' she said, and a few people laughed, as if she had just made a joke. Francine smiled, took off her glasses, wiped the lenses on the cuff of her sleeve, and then she spoke: 'I always like to begin . . . gently,' she said, putting her glasses back on again. She had a small cold sore, May noticed, on her bottom lip. 'When

I wake up in the morning, I lie there with my eyes closed for at least half an hour. Half an hour, at least. I feel it sets me up well for the day. It centres me.' She turned to the woman who had introduced her. 'Shall I perhaps choose one of my previously unpublished essays?' Francine asked her. 'No one is going to want to hear me read from the old ones, are they?' The woman offered this question over to the audience, who nodded their enthusiasm, and Francine opened her book somewhere near the middle. She coughed, took a small sip of water, and began.

And then May began: worrying – about having to tell Francine (the evening of her book launch) that she had deferred. May heard nothing of what Francine said: not because May wasn't interested (she was interested; in fact, she wished she had the text in front of her), and not because she couldn't understand the words; she understood each individual word; it was all the words put together, all strung together so fluently that was the problem. It required a certain level of concentration. Francine could clearly have thrown the book onto the floor and continued to the end of the essay, without any difficulty; she knew it all by heart; every now and then, she stopped for a few significant seconds, looked out at her audience, repeated a word, and went on. May prepared her response: she was keen to go back and reread the text now, she would say; she would look forward to reading it once more for herself; she didn't want to comment until she had read it properly, of course; she'd say that the rhythm, the rhythm of the text, it had such a beautiful rhythm; it had distracted her. May looked at the stairs just behind Francine, and imagined herself floating away, up the stairs and out of the door, up, up, up into the sky, above the Parisian rooftops.

Francine had stopped speaking. 'It is this *recognition*,' Francine went on, after the pause. 'This recognition, and this recognition alone,' she was now looking directly at May, and May blushed, 'that will allow it.' Francine smiled. There was a respectful silence, Francine closed her book, and the applause started. What recognition?

May clapped. Francine had looked at May for a reason: it was a gift, and May had missed it.

Eventually, May went to buy the book, then queued up to get her copy signed. She waited until last, so as to have no one behind her, and because she was in no hurry to go back to the hotel. She wanted to make herself available to leave with Francine – should Francine want to go out for coffee – so that she could tell her how much she had enjoyed the reading, how glad she was to have been there. She had to mention the deferral, too, of course. After getting the book signed, May lingered near the English section while women drifted away, up the stairs.

Anne, too, was hovering, much to May's annoyance.

'So, Anne, shall we go for a drink? May will come with us.' Francine was ready to leave.

It was dark outside. They walked down narrow streets, south towards the Seine, past closed patisseries and jewellers: Francine and Anne speaking; May listening.

'You who are an eclectic reader, Anne – have you read *L'Ange et les pervers*?' Francine asked.

'Oh yes yes of course, but many years ago now. If I am remembering it well, there was a good deed leading into a tidy "happily ever after". For me it lacked spice; there was no sensuality. In fact, I do think I found the tone rather moralizing.'

'Moralizing? You must be thinking of another novel. In this one, no one ends up on the narrow path of righteousness; no one is punished. All the characters are entirely free.'

'Apart from the children.'

'That's true – you're right.'

'And the pregnant woman,' Anne added.

'Yes, obviously, the pregnant woman; but what you need to know is that she was based on Renée Vivien: Mardrus's *rival* in love.'

'That's interesting.'

'It's revenge,' Francine told her. 'An attack via literature.'

'Fascinating.' Anne turned to May. 'And what about you? Have you read this book?'

'Of course she's read it,' Francine said. 'She has read a great deal, our May.'

She had read it, but she had no thoughts right now; she had no ideas about anything. She wished they would just ignore her.

'Did you find the tone moralizing?' Anne asked.

'Perhaps slightly . . .' May ventured.

'Really?' Francine was surprised; she was put out. 'And in what way?'

'Careful. You are going to have to defend yourself now!' Anne warned.

'Perhaps,' this wasn't going to be good enough, 'the fact that the main character – the angel – chose to adopt the unwanted son –'

'Exactly!' Anne agreed. 'The angel corrects the sins of the perverts.'

'The adoption was an act of selfishness. No, if there is a moral of the story – and it is rather a moral *within* the story – it is not to be found at the end. That would be an over-simplistic reading.'

'I'm not saying I disagree with you,' May defended herself – not that she knew what she thought, of course.

'Who did you identify with in the novel?' Francine now asked her.

'I don't think I identified with anyone . . .' Or had she? May tried to think.

'Ah! That's revealing. So the story meant nothing to you at all? It didn't touch you?'

'Yes, it did.' May tried to remember which of the characters she had identified with; there was more than one . . .

'In that case, you identified with one of the characters – necessarily. Perhaps you saw yourself in the angel.'

'The poor girl! Leave her alone,' Anne said, and she let out a little laugh.

May said nothing. She probably identified with the pregnant adulterous woman, the pathetic crying one; she couldn't say that. 'I'd have to think about it,' she said in the end. She felt like just walking off; she felt like leaving them.

'She refuses to tell us,' Francine concluded. 'She doesn't want to tell us, for fear of being judged. It's too sad.'

'Perhaps she couldn't identify with anyone,' Anne proposed. It was possible she was being supportive; May couldn't tell.

'There is always a character with whom one can identify – if only one is willing to admit it – at least one, usually more than one. For centuries we have been reading literature about heterosexuals, translating the genders to our own experience (I can do that of course: I identify with both the man and the woman), since for ever. No, I'm sorry' (Francine rarely, or never, apologized, and this was not an apology), 'I'm sorry, but she is merely refusing to tell us,' she continued. 'She is too frightened.'

'I think I can identify with such a fear,' Anne said, and she gave May a sad little smile of commiseration.

'You can laugh, Anne, but maintaining a childish desire always to please, expecting all the while to be spoon-fed, *there* is the true risk; one had better be careful what one takes in, while sitting there, passively swallowing!' Francine looked at May: 'Perhaps you could at least tell us what you thought of the reading this evening?' she asked her.

'I think I would have to read it once more for myself before I could comment intelligently,' May replied. She was an idiot, and a dimwit, and she'd fallen in love.

'Yes,' Francine was impatient, 'but what is your overall opinion? Your impression?'

'I was so pleased to have been able to be there,' May said – stupidly. She was going to start crying, and she really didn't want to. 'The rhythm, as you read, was so . . . beautiful that I –'

'Let's go in here,' Anne said, and they went into the café; its windows were all steamed up.

Anne led the way to a table.

'May is doing a thesis on me. Did she tell you that?' Francine announced, once they were seated.

'Yes, she told me,' Anne said. She looked over at May.

'I'm thinking of deferring, though,' May said. Francine would hate her now.

'You've made a decision, then?' Francine turned to Anne. 'What are you having?' she asked her.

'For the moment,' May continued. 'I'm going to buy the occasional magazine on university courses, maybe work out which university really appeals to me. I'll continue taking notes. I haven't stopped taking notes. I'm just deferring it. That's all. It's going to be a slow process . . . I've realized.'

'You have returned to the preparation phase.' Francine looked up from the Drinks menu. 'Well, don't hang around too long,' she could now advise.

'I'll defend slow people. I'm slow,' Anne put in.

'No, but you are awake, you know what you want, and now you're about to send off a manuscript.' Francine dismissed Anne's comment.

'It's true. At the age of forty-five. But you're . . .' she turned to May, and considered her, '. . . you're not yet thirty?' she guessed.

'Continue to flatter her, Anne, and she'll never achieve a thing. She needs shaking up.'

'I'm just leaving writing the thesis for now,' May drivelled on – she wished she'd shut up. 'Perhaps next year,' she went on anyway, in a convoluted attempt at positive thinking, 'I'll go part-time in order to read and do a course or two. There may be some courses that would be interesting and useful.'

Uncommitted, vague, but Francine did not, in any case, take May's verbal peregrinations seriously. 'You don't seem to know what you're doing. What are you going to drink? Water?' She closed the subject.

24

Tough Duck

Wandering along the Seine in search of books the following morning, May found a book for just five euros: a first edition of *Nouvelles pensées de l'amazone*, a rare find. She held it against her heart, letting the book seep into her; she was being enriched and she hadn't even opened it yet. She realized she stunk, both her tops did. The next hour she spent, unbelievably, instead of opening her treasure, hunting in vain for a simple T-shirt. Most of the shops were shut. The ones she found open were geared towards tourists; glittering Eiffel Towers and gaudy Mona Lisas. She walked past a smiling cardboard figure with a T-shirt stapled to it. Just inside the sparse wooden-floored shop, were piles of T-shirts on a low table. Perhaps she'd find something there. Hopeful, she went in. With nothing, she came out. The women's were too skimpy, the men's too big – they all started at 'M'. She tried and tried on T-shirts (only six in fact). Finally a shop assistant said:

'So, are you taking this one?'

'How much is it?'

'Thirty euros.'

'Okay, thank you.' (She wouldn't take it.)

'Any of them any good?'

'No, thank you.'

'If I had served you, I'd never have let you try *one* on, you know!'

'Il fallait me le dire avant,' May defended herself, pleased to have drawn from her memory files the ideal French phrase for such an occasion.

She was at the wrong end of Paris. She had wanted a five-euro T-shirt from Belleville.

'You didn't find anything among all these T-shirts!'

'No.'

She left under attack from the three shop assistants, who conversed loudly about how she wasn't at Les Galeries Lafayette. Perhaps this had happened because she had let herself get dehydrated in her single-minded search for a T-shirt. She was guilty of unfolding six tops. A thoughtless, annoying tourist. (A tourist, she was not. She would not wear that label.) She had wasted precious time. That was her worst sin. She told herself she was useless, that Francine would never waste her time hunting for a T-shirt. She rang her:

'Was it nineteen hours or twenty hours that I was supposed to arrive?'

'Twenty. Come at nineteen rather. I need to rest.'

Francine had been writing all day.

'You don't like duck, I imagine,' were Francine's first words.

The moment May had entered Francine's apartment, she had sensed anger hovering. She had hardly wanted to proceed into the kitchen where Francine had gone quickly ahead in order to turn on the electric elements.

'Yes, I do. I do like duck.'

'Good . . . good. Look, you can help me by cutting up these beans.' Francine handed May a small knife.

'Should I cut them like this?' May cut on an angle half a finger-length, keen to show she could take the initiative.

Francine was standing on the kitchen bench now, reaching for a saucepan.

'*You* are doing it. *You* decide. Really, May, just do it!'

May cut.

Her throat hurt. She needed to say something. She *should* say something. Silence. Silence. Her vocal cords seemed to have sucked themselves together like plastic straws. May wished she had never told Francine about the deferral.

'So, are you going to talk to me this evening? You have nothing to tell me.'

May searched, like a student in front of an examination paper, with a pain in her stomach. She'd be accused of *mutisme* before long. She tried to think: I'm reading . . . That would do. 'I'm reading *La Folie en tête* at the moment,' she said.

'Mm-hmm.' Francine wasn't interested. After all, what was there to say to that? It was a dead-end statement. 'Yes, and what do you have to say about it?' Francine asked calmly; she was getting cross; she was in a bad mood. That was clear.

May would have to comment meaningfully on the book now. She couldn't. 'I really like Leduc,' she said.

Francine poured the beans into the pot of boiling water, went into the sitting room and put on some music. She announced the opera singer's name. 'This is [. . .].' A complete blank. Immediately. May heard Francine say the name and forgot it straight away: another missed opportunity to learn.

'I haven't brought the letter with me,' May said; she thought she'd better say so.

'Which letter?' Francine was impatient.

'The one to send to the universities; that I would put in with the information about your work.'

Francine pulled a roasting dish out of the oven, and placed potatoes and a chunk of meat on each plate. Then the beans.

They sat down to eat. Silence. May was in trouble. She thought quickly, desperately. Perhaps she could find something to say about Leduc? What did she like about Leduc? She went through the book so far in her head. A jumble of events. What one thread of thought could she remember? What did she like about it? Francine was licking the cold sore on her bottom lip.

May began her struggle through tough duck. 'C'est très bon,' she lied politely, wondering how she was going to cut into the leathery mass, wishing she'd been given a smaller chunk. Had Francine cooked it to a rock deliberately, in order to achieve some sort of symbolic message?

'Who taught you to be so soft? Your mother?'

'No.'

'It is not a quality.'

It occurred to May she was going to be in trouble, whatever she did, however she held herself, however well she achieved a self-contained, non-demanding, outwardly focused presence. Her heart tightened now as she sat in front of her duck.

'Your invisibility. It's exasperating. "I'm not saying I disagree with you" – Don't you have any opinions of your own? You bow to me. Do you think it is the behaviour of a woman of thirty-two?'

'Thirty-one.'

'To play the obedient little girl, to nod and smile. Do you know how old you are?' Francine marked a pause. 'It is the behaviour of an eight-year-old!' She stopped to sum May up in one look. 'You don't invest yourself in this world. That is your problem. Worse than a shadow, you just follow people around, agreeing, agreeing. From there stem the worst atrocities.'

They ate in silence. This could be leading nowhere good. May was definitively in Francine's bad books; she had displeased her by trying to please her. Several past moments where she might have comfortably disagreed with Francine now aligned themselves, as though stored in a single compartment, entitled: 'moments where I lacked integrity'.

May continued to attempt to eat the duck, but it was like chewing gum, and refused to get any smaller. No amount of chewing helped.

Francine looked at her. 'I shall accompany you to the Métro,' she said.

'That would be kind.' Francine was trying to get rid of her. May's stomach hurt. Francine seemed to be waiting for her to say something. But May could think of nothing safe to say.

'Are you waiting to be dismissed?' Francine looked briefly at May, then stood up suddenly. 'You've finished,' she stated, taking May's plate, then her own, and putting them on the bench. May started to help clear the table. 'Leave it. Leave it. I'll do it later.' Francine went purposefully to the front door where she began hauling coats off the hook and onto her left arm, looking for a suitable jacket. May got her coat and stood by, student-like; she kept herself completely still, hoping to become invisible.

'There's nothing like the oppressed to come across arrogantly. There's where being oppressed leads you: to this arrogant observation of those around you. It's very unpleasant, I assure you, *very* unpleasant.' Francine pulled on her long leather jacket as she spoke, doing up the buttons; like a snake putting on its skin, May thought.

'So, what can I do to change it?'

'You speak; that's all. You *speak*.' She picked up some shoes from under the sofa. May followed her back into the kitchen and sat opposite Francine, who was now slipping on the shoes.

'Okay, so I will say thank you for dinner . . . although the meat was a little overcooked.' May risked saying this. She was feeling a bit tearful.

'Oh that's very easy: "the meat was overcooked"; that's far too easy.'

'And you seem angry with me; I don't know why.'

'You don't know why? You're going to have to grow up a little, my dear.'

'Is it something I said yesterday evening?' May knew she was being imprecise.

'A question: that's a start, but it's more than that. You say what you think, because people can tell what you're thinking in any case. One can read it on your face.'

Francine got up, and looked at herself in a mirror hanging behind the kitchen door. The dark green trousers – linen, May noted – were a bit short.

'What do you think? Do the shoes match the trousers?'

'Yes, fine.' May couldn't say otherwise. 'But . . . thank you very much – it's kind – but I can walk to the Métro on my own.'

It was dark outside. Late. May wished she was back in London already. She passed a telephone box. Jansen would still be out driving. No one to call. She ran across the road, *not* getting run over, as it happened; not that she was ready to die – which would be selfish – but an accident would be acceptable. That much further to walk, she looked ahead, until she was at the river: too far. The tourist shops were open, some restaurants. She walked on. Finally, the riverbank, naked now – with no bookstalls out – the stretch of large green boxes all latched up. What would she do once she got to the hotel? Her tongue was dry against her palate. Was Francine in love with her? It was what she was starting to think. Or why was she so furious with her?

Back over the bridge. The water was, of course, beautiful; the white-grey bridge, beautiful. She walked through all this beauty, past the fountains at the Hôtel de Ville, and finally got to the Métro. Once below, the bright lights accentuated the heavy feeling under her eyes. There'd be quite a wait at this time of night. Well, she sat down, being there was as good as being anywhere else. What would she do once she got to the hotel? She looked at her watch. Perhaps Jansen would be home soon? The platform was fairly empty. Silent. A few people sitting alone on her side.

The train for the other side arrived, disturbing the silence momentarily, before slithering away.

'Allô.'

'Hello, it's May . . . I'm sorry, I hope it's not too late to call. I was just about to go into the hotel, but I thought I should give you a quick call first.'

'What do you want to say? You have made this call; it's supposedly in order to tell me something.'

'Yes . . .'

'What do you have to say?'

'There is something –'

'Good. Tell me. Take a risk.'

'I'm sorry,' May said, 'that I didn't tell you before that I was planning on deferring.'

'So you have not deferred yet: is that what you're telling me?'

'Yes, I have; no, I mean, no, I am not now enrolled at university, no. That's right. I am no longer doing the PhD.'

'Is that everything?'

'And just . . . I find it difficult . . . that is to say, I think Jansen can find it difficult, I think she's been finding it difficult when I'm so obsessed with . . .'

'Allô?'

'(Yes, I'm still here) with the PhD . . .'

'And?'

'I'm really always thinking about it and . . .'

'No, May. Either you speak –'

'And sometimes,' May rushed on, 'I can be quite obsessed with the PhD, and perhaps because of that, no doubt, I talk to Jansen quite a lot about you, which she doesn't like very much –'

'Of course she doesn't like it; she must feel afraid.'

'No. Why? Why would she be afraid? No, she isn't afraid.'

'That surprises me.'

'It's not because of you in particular; it's that she doesn't like the subject in general – the PhD, I mean, not the subject. When I say I've been thinking a lot about you, it's all to do with the PhD.'

'Fine. In which case, speak to Jansen. You are explaining yourself to the wrong person. We are not in a relationship, you and I.'

'No, of course not. I'll speak to Jansen. But what do you think? Should I stop teaching? Should I be in Paris, studying, in your opinion? Would that be a good idea?'

'You have to decide that for yourself – what you really desire – and discuss it with Jansen, surely, since it would affect her. This is your problem, in any case,' Francine said. 'Now, I am very tired; so I wish you a good night.'

'Could I just ask –'

'Good night.'

'Whether I could call you later, another –'

Francine had hung up.

25

The Break-In

The hook on the bathroom window was unlatched. May went round the flat, saying, 'That's odd, that's weird.' Until she realized: the spare key was missing; someone had broken into the flat, and they'd gone out the front door, taking the spare key. May gasped, put the snib on the front door, and then called Jansen, who was somewhere in Wales, looking for her passenger's house.

'Maybe they just were just having a very thorough look around – as part one of the burglary process,' May worried aloud. (Nothing had been taken.)

'Well, anyway, now they've seen we've got nothing, they won't be back,' Jansen reassured her.

'What should I do? Should I bother calling the police?'

'Yes, you have to report it.'

'Couldn't you do it when you get back?'

'May, you can do it. Just call 999.'

'I can't do it. I hate ringing people.'

'I'd like you to call them. I can't. I'm in Wales. May, I've got to go. I don't know where I'm supposed to be, and I need to find out. Call me later, and let me know how you got on. And call a locksmith.'

What was the point in calling the police when nothing had been taken? If it was 'probably just children from the estate', as Jansen seemed to think, why bother? May made herself a Tranquillity tea, sat on the bed and finally called the police.

The police said they'd send round a scene-of-crime officer. Half an hour later, there was a knock at the door, and May went to answer it: a trim woman in jeans and what looked like a bullet-proof vest introduced herself. She was carrying a shiny black briefcase. May showed her to the bathroom. The policewoman clicked open her briefcase, and set to work sprinkling powder over the surfaces near the window, then dusting them with a tiny soft brush. The woman went outside after that, and managed to find fingerprints on the outside window ledge; she took a copy on a small square of glass that she then put into her bag. However, the woman turned to May – and to Elizabeth, who had arrived halfway through the print-taking – even if they did manage to match the prints against someone else's, they wouldn't be able to make a conviction, she explained, because it was actually not illegal to touch the outside of another person's property. Elizabeth stood there nodding, fascinated, and asked various questions, as if she were planning on a career in forensics. The policewoman, it turned out, had combined forensic science with drama; in fact, she had an Arts degree (she had changed career). Cool! What college had she been to for that? Elizabeth asked. Saint Martin's, she'd done sculpting and installation. Elizabeth was also into art, she told the woman as she lit herself a cigarette, and she was thinking of Goldsmiths – inhale, inhale – what was the policewoman's opinion on that place? No, the policewoman didn't want a cigarette, thanks. *Well* – the woman was packing up her briefcase now – she didn't know much about that place, just that it was supposed to be a bit more theory-based, or so she thought, but at the end of the day, it depended on what you were really looking for, didn't it? Yeah, it was a matter of taste, that was what Elizabeth thought, too; it was what you were looking for, wasn't it?

Et cetera. May went back inside and rang a locksmith.

Two hours later, May sat in bed with *Troisième personne singulière* opened at the 'Recognition' essay Francine had read out at the book launch. Although May had not yet responded to the reading, that was quite acceptable, as long as she did respond – within a week would be acceptable. What she would do – she made her humiliated resolution – was write a letter completely dedicated to the essay, with all her thoughts and questions et cetera; and at the end of the letter she would write a tidy little line (or two or three at the most) concerning the deferral of her PhD, as well as an apology for having telephoned so late at night and keeping Francine on the phone; and she would also apologize for not yet having written the covering letter to the universities. (She could include a photocopy of that covering letter, if she had managed to write it by then.) And then maybe Francine would like her again. May read the first paragraph of 'Recognition', flicked to the end, and read the last paragraph (this was a reading technique proposed in *Methodology in Qualitative Research*). After this, she began skim-reading the whole essay. She was incapable of concentrating; however, when she read it tomorrow, it would nevertheless be more familiar to her than if she hadn't even glanced at it, and that would –

There was a quiet tap at the front door. May climbed out of bed.

'He didn't get here until quarter to eleven,' May told Jansen as she held the door open for her.

'I'm sorry I couldn't have been around.' Jansen came into the bedroom, clattered her keys onto the writing desk, and took off her jacket. 'How long did he take?'

'Not that long. Elizabeth made pizza and invited him to dinner.' May shut the bedroom door.

'Oh, that's kind of her.' Jansen sat on the end of the bed, and took off her shoes.

'Fortunately he couldn't though,' May said as she got back into bed. 'He had to go straight to another job, so she gave him a slice to take away and she was all smiley and grateful. It stresses me when she does that sort of thing.'

Jansen made one of her non-committal 'mm' sounds. She undid her shirt buttons, and pulled off her trousers. 'I'll say hello to you properly in a minute.' She put on her pyjamas and went off to brush her teeth.

It made May anxious when Elizabeth invited strangers in off the street, like that. (It would have been all right if they'd been cats.) She was always befriending people. When Elizabeth was five or six she once brought home her best friend's older brother, and fed him cornflakes in order to keep him there until May got back from secondary school. She thought he could be a boyfriend for May (he was only twelve or something); May got rid of him politely. It was so tiring going anywhere with Elizabeth, because she had to talk to people – at the shops, at the park – and then May would have to join in. If Elizabeth had gone to Francine's book launch, May pictured it, she'd have been mingling happily away. Francine would think she was fantastic.

'I'm exhausted!' Jansen came back into the room and got into bed. 'Hello, darling.' She kissed her on the cheek and climbed into bed. 'Thank you for waiting up for me.' She straightened up the blankets and pulled them up. 'Oh, did you find something when you went to bed?'

'No . . .'

'Lift up then!' From under May's pillow, Jansen retrieved a crumpled card:

A Birch Tree has been planted for you – Happy Easter, darling. Love, Jansen.

'Oh, that's lovely!' May's eyes watered up. Jansen was so kind to her, and loving. 'But I've crushed it!' She set the card on the stool next to the bed, and gave Jansen a hug. 'Thank you. That's so lovely!' She wished she could delete her messy late-night phone call to Francine.

Jansen smiled. 'I'm glad you like it. So! Let's get some sleep now.' She went to turn out the light.

'Can I just quickly tell you how the book launch went?' May asked.

Jansen turned out the light behind her and lay down.

'Or are you not really up to it?' May added.

'You could tell me briefly,' Jansen offered.

May said nothing.

'How did it go?' Jansen prompted. 'Was it okay?'

'I told her I've deferred.'

'Ah.'

'What do you mean by "ah"? Was that a judgmental "ah"?'

Jansen sighed. 'Do you want to tell me how it went or not?'

'You're too tired to really listen, though, aren't you?' May felt awful about the call; it was so embarrassing, she couldn't bear thinking about it.

'May, I'd love to be able to listen, but I'm so tired, I'm falling asleep while we talk. Can you tell me about it tomorrow morning? And then I'll really be able to listen.'

May said nothing. She wouldn't be able to talk to Jansen about the phone call anyway, so what was the point?

'Can we talk tomorrow?' Jansen suggested. 'Before I go to work.'

'You're not working tomorrow, are you?' May needed her.

'Yes, I am.'

'But that's illegal, isn't it? That's dangerous! How many hours did you do today?'

'I didn't start until twelve. I agreed to do a swap with someone.'

'And you still have to work tomorrow?' May said. 'So we won't be able to have a day together.'

'I don't start until twelve.'

'But you're going to have to sleep all morning.'

'I'm going to need to sleep in, yes, and then we can have breakfast together before I go.'

'It'll be just like a weekday,' May concluded.

'The longer you keep me awake; the longer I'm going to have to sleep in. Let's just get some sleep now, and see what happens,' Jansen said.

'Someone else could have offered to do the swap, but they asked *you* because they knew you'd say yes. What does that mean for *you* the rest of *your* week? You've got Tuesday to Friday off, now. And then you'll be working over the weekend, and we won't get to see each other. That's what it means.'

'Yes.'

'Oh God I've just remembered: the mock exams are coming up; how boring! How boring!' May was a stupid primary-school teacher, and a boring nobody.

Jansen said nothing.

'And then come the real exams and then I'll have the reports to do: "blah-blah is a hard-working, conscientious pupil. She listens carefully in class and –"'

'May, you're raving on.'

'"She always hands in her work on time, and obtains –"'

'I'm *very* tired.'

'You don't want to know what she obtains then – just quickly? Before you go to sleep?'

'No, I don't.'

'"Full marks",' May told her anyway.

Jansen said nothing again, only more loudly.

'"In all her spelling tests",' May completed her sentence. She laughed a little hysterically, and then she cried.

'I've had enough of this,' Jansen said, and she got out of bed.

'Where are you going? I thought you were tired. I'm not happy,' May said.

'Neither am I.' Jansen put on her slippers. 'I'll be back in five minutes – leave me alone.' She left the room.

26

Victim Support

'Hi-there!' Elizabeth, still glowing from a recent bath, was sitting in front of the gas heater, cutting her toenails onto that day's *Guardian* – onto the G2 section, the most interesting part. Jansen was at the table, reading the rest of the paper.

'Hi.' May took off her coat, and put down her bag. No one had made dinner.

Jansen looked up from the sports page. 'Hello,' she said, and handed May a letter.

It was from Victim Support. '"Dear Ms Woodlea",' May read out.

'I opened it.' Jansen returned to the football. She was still annoyed from the other evening.

'We were curious,' Elizabeth added. She picked up a piece of nail that had flown off onto the carpet.

May skimmed through the letter: '"I was sorry to hear from the local police . . . free and confidential support." Gosh, that's nice. That's nice, isn't it? It's nice to know they send these out.' May sat at the table next to Jansen.

'Mm-hmm.' Jansen wasn't listening. 'Do you want to make me a hot drink?'

'I'm the one who's just got in,' May said.

'I'll do it. I'll do it. No squabbling, now!' Elizabeth folded up her newspaper of nails, and took it out to the bin in the kitchen. 'Whadd'ya want?' she asked as she left the room.

'Green tea!' Jansen called out.

May looked at the Victim Support letter again. 'There are good people out there, aren't there?' she said. 'We should keep this. It's a memory.'

Jansen ignored her.

A few minutes later, Elizabeth returned with four cups on the breadboard. 'I've made you a coffee,' she told May. 'And an ordinary tea for Tamsin, right? Well, this is cosy. Tea to your liking, Jansen?' Elizabeth faked an American accent.

'Tamsin's here?'

'She'll be here any minute. She's gone to the Fish Bar to get us some fish 'n' chips.' Jansen spoke to the page she was reading.

'And now, it's presents time!' Elizabeth kneeled on the rug, got a plastic carrier bag from next to the sofa, and pulled out some books: 'Yours –' she handed Jansen *Friendly Food*, a cookbook; 'mine –' she placed a large book, *Sculpture: My Way*, next to her on the floor; 'and May's –' she handed May a book. 'All for less than ten pounds.'

Women of Iron and Velvet: And the Books They Wrote in France. Colette was on the front cover.

'Great title, isn't it?' Elizabeth said. 'What d'you think? It's old, but the pictures are still good.'

Copyright, 1976. May flicked through the book, looking at the portraits and photos: Monique Wittig with a bob, Minou Drouet the child poet, Françoise Mallet-Joris. 'Thank you,' she said. 'It looks interesting.' She hated it when Jansen was angry with her.

'Could be useful for this PhD,' Elizabeth specified. She got off the floor and went and sat on the sofa. 'That you're apparently doing,' she added.

There was a knock at the door. Jansen left her book and went to answer it. Pleased sounds, laughter, Tamsin appeared. She'd got a free Coke. Polite greetings. She and Jansen went off to the kitchen to get plates.

'I'm not "apparently" doing it, by the way; I am doing it,' May told Elizabeth while they were alone. 'Thank you for the book.' She wished Jansen hadn't mentioned the PhD to Elizabeth.

'There's something else; it turned up a few days ago.' Elizabeth handed May *The Angel and the Perverts*. 'I got it through Abe.books; actually, Mark ordered it for me, but you can have it. Your need is greater than mine.'

'I've already read it.'

'*Oui*, but not *en anglais*.'

'I don't need to read it in English. I've already read it in French. Why would I want a translation?'

'Dunno. Maybe you missed something. There's a rather interesting introduction in here, as well.'

May took the book. 'Do you want it back?'

'No, it's a present. I've read it now anyway. Waste not, hoard not.'

Jansen and Tamsin came back with glasses and plates, salt and vinegar and tomato sauce. 'I'm still amazed we bumped into you!' Jansen said. 'London's so small actually, when you think about it.' She opened up the large fish 'n' chips package and, with one hand, craned out the chips onto the plates.

'Thank you,' May said to Elizabeth, and she placed the books on top of the bookshelf.

'Mon plaisir. Enjoy.'

Tamsin poured the Coke.

'None for me, thanks,' May said. 'I've still got my coffee.'

A tap at the door: 'That'll be Mark.' Elizabeth bounced off the sofa. 'He's having a hard time at the moment, with Kate. Everyone, be nice to him.' She went to answer the door.

Jansen got him a plate and a glass. He came in. Re-round of greetings.

'Mi-um, mi-um,' Elizabeth said, and burst out laughing, choking on her chip; Tamsin thumped her on the back. 'Ta.' Elizabeth coughed and took a glug of Coke. 'Mark, I was just um,' she said, 'Tamsin's been filling us in with her and Jansen's brief stint in the army: I've learnt how to dig trenches –'

'Power tools are better than pickaxes, it shouldn't be more than half a metre wide . . .' Tamsin supplied the details good-naturedly.

'How to starch-iron clothes: really useful stuff (not)!' Elizabeth laughed.

'The collar's all I bother with,' Mark said. He had tomato sauce on his chin.

'Women like a well-ironed shirt,' Elizabeth told him. 'A bit of insider information for you.' She stretched and yawned. 'We had such a great day! Pity you couldn't make it,' she said. 'Jansen and I spent a few profitable hours in the second-hand bookshops on the Charing Cross Road, and then we wandered down to the Portrait Gallery, where my personal guide introduced me to a few of her favourites – Marie Stopes, the Brontës, Beatrix Potter – before taking me to afternoon tea at the caff at the top. What a view! I felt like Mary Poppins.'

May looked at Jansen. 'Great,' she said.

'How was your day?' Elizabeth asked.

'I had a boring English teachers' meeting to go to.'

'Boring teachers only?' Elizabeth said, unscrewing the Coke.

'Some idiot thinks we should be changing the exam paper more often.' May ignored her. 'That's going to slow down my marking.'

'It might be an improvement,' Jansen said. 'Yes, please.' She passed her glass to Elizabeth.

'No, it's not going to be an improvement. They're not changing it for any reason. What they're doing is putting in a different boring reading comprehension, a different boring story topic, and different boring grammar questions. It's just so that if one of the children has managed to take home a paper, their younger sister won't get a hundred per cent when they sit the exam.'

'May, if this is all so boring, do we have to hear about it?' Jansen laughed.

'Oh yay that I'm not at school any more!' Elizabeth said. 'Mark?' she asked, and he gave her his glass. 'And none for you, May?'

'I've got my coffee.'

'Ooh. You look a bit grumpy. Have I said something wrong?'

'I'm tired,' May said. 'I'm not grumpy; I'm tired.'

Tamsin focused on her chips. Mark glanced over at Elizabeth.

'Actually, I'm sorry but I really am exhausted,' May told everyone. 'Sorry, Tamsin; thanks for the dinner,' May spoke to her 'adult-to-adult', ignoring Elizabeth, 'but I'm going to have to be rude and go to bed. Good night, everybody.' She got her books from the bookshelf. 'I had such a late night last night. And my feet are tired.'

'Sleep tight!' Elizabeth waved at May's feet. 'No talking, you two.'

'Good night, May.' Jansen looked up briefly.

May went to bed, and Jansen didn't follow her to come and say hello or good night. May waited for about ten minutes; she opened *The Angel and the Perverts* at the introduction, 'Lucie Delarue-Mardrus and the Phrenetic Harlequinade', but she wasn't reading, she couldn't read: she was too hungry to read. And she was waiting for Jansen.

May got up, and went to the kitchen to get herself some toast. On her way back to bed she looked in at Jansen, Elizabeth, Mark and Tamsin; they were all reading books or parts of newspapers; the 'hiss' of the gas heater was providing them with gentle background music.

'You're still awake.'

'I wish you hadn't told Elizabeth about the PhD.' May slid *The Angel and the Perverts* off the bed and onto the floor.

'I didn't know it was a secret, May. I thought she already knew about it. If you'd told me it was a secret, I wouldn't have said anything.' Jansen put her *Friendly Food* book on the bed, and pulled off her jumper.

'It wasn't a secret; I just wish you hadn't told her about it. Because, now, what if I don't ever do the PhD?'

Jansen nodded, and started unbuttoning her shirt.

'I just didn't want Elizabeth commenting on it,' May went on.

Jansen paused to say 'hmm', and then continued undressing.

'Which she will now, now that she knows about it.' May wanted to talk to Jansen about the phone call to Francine. But she couldn't.

'May, she's bought you a book. Two books. What does that say to you?'

'I wish you hadn't told her.' May shook her head.

'Yes.' Jansen had her pyjamas on now. She went to the bathroom.

May hadn't said everything she needed to say; there was one more thing. She waited for Jansen to get back and shut the bedroom door.

'And did you tell her it was our special café?'

'No, I didn't.'

'But you took her there, anyway?'

'So I'm not acquitted?'

'You could've taken her to the basement café.'

'Yes, but I didn't.'

'Why didn't you?'

Jansen sat on the bed, and pulled off her socks.

'You think I'm being unreasonable,' May said.

'Do you think you're being unreasonable?'

'Oh, "yes I'm being unreasonable": that's what I'm supposed to say, isn't it?' She hated herself at the moment.

'We had a lovely day, and it was a pity you weren't there,' Jansen summarized, closing the subject.

'I was at work.' So how could she have been there?

Jansen nodded again. She put her cookbook on the writing desk. 'Can we turn out the light now?'

'You can turn it out if you want.'

'You're not pre-menstrual, are you?'

'I thought it was our special café.'

'It is our special café.'

'It's not that special to you, obviously.'

'May, you're not jealous of Elizabeth?'

'I'm jealous of her? She's doing nothing with her life, she's using us for free accommodation, and I'm jealous of her? No, I am not jealous; I just think we could keep some things special to us.'

'May,' Jansen smiled, 'it is very special to me too, and I didn't say anything about the time we went there.'

'She'd only laugh. She'd think it was soppy.'

'Well, I don't know that she would, but it's our business and I haven't told her about it.' Jansen turned out the light, and came to bed.

'You can cuddle me, if you want,' May said.

27

The Missing Bear

A paving stone of clay wrapped in plastic. May watched Elizabeth take it to the kitchen, and dump it down on top of the carrots, in the vegetable rack in the cupboard next to the sink: 'the coolest spot,' Elizabeth explained. 'Gotta keep it cool. Cool clay, cool clay,' she said, clearly enjoying the sound. 'It's hard to say . . .' She tilted her head to the left, briefly holding a quizzical pose, then to the right. 'Cooool clay.'

May left the kitchen, without making any comment.

'By the way,' Elizabeth called out. 'I identified with the angel. Who did you identify with?'

'What?' May returned to the kitchen.

'"L'Aannge" –' Elizabeth broke off into hysterical laughter. 'Minus the asexual bit; that bit really didn't appeal very much. Merci. But the young for ever, adorable, attractive to both men and women? Objectively, I'd have to say "oui".' She grinned.

'Of course.'

'And the child – oddly enough,' Elizabeth added. She went to the hall and got a fresh towel out of the airing cupboard opposite the bathroom.

'Or not oddly enough,' May said.

'Who were you?' Elizabeth hunted around for a flannel, messing up the folded towels.

'Who was I? No one. I don't read books, looking for myself in every character. I don't have to place myself in every book I read. I enjoy the language.'

'You were one of the perverts, weren't you?' Elizabeth found a purple flannel. She shut the cupboard door.

May opened it again. The towels were all mixed up with the sheets. She put the hand-towels back on top of the towels, and took out a sheet to refold it.

'That's not an insult: the angel liked the perverts, remember – for they had "surprisingly spotless minds",' Elizabeth misquoted from the translation. 'Now,' she pointed to the middle of her forehead, 'which pervert were you? Let's see . . .' She closed her eyes for a second, and flipped them wide open again – 'Ping! You'd be the pregnant one.'

'Oh, is that right?' May put the sheet back in the cupboard in the right place.

'I'm sorry to have to tell you this,' Elizabeth said, 'but that is right. I'm right, aren't I?'

'No, you are not – right.'

Elizabeth smiled. 'What's wrong with being Aimée? Yes, she was a little unhappy, yes, she needed help –'

'So you're the adorable hero, whereas I'm the pathetic –'

'Adulterous one?' Elizabeth shrugged French-style, and opened the bathroom door.

May followed Elizabeth, who was now dunking her elbow into a newly run bath, testing the water temperature. 'Excuse me?' May said.

Elizabeth hummed 'Home, Home on the Range' as she turned on the hot tap – although the water looked hot enough; the whole room was steamed up.

'Excuse me?' May repeated. Elizabeth was humming that tune for a reason; she was insinuating something.

'I'm just winding you up. Don't worry.'

'What about?'

'Relax. It's a joke. I'm making a joke.' Elizabeth held her hand under the tap.

'Well it's not funny.'

Elizabeth turned off the tap. 'Shall I leave the bath in for you? I've just used up the hot water.'

Three hours later, Jansen finally got back from driving.

'She's really settling in well now, isn't she?' May sat up in bed. 'She's just had another bath. She spends at least an hour in there every evening. Never thinks to open the window (the obvious thing to do). No, she turns the place into a steam-sauna. I go in there afterwards, and the walls are literally dripping! There is water liter-ally *running* down the walls! Every evening.'

'May, I've just got in the door.'

'She could open the window just a little bit, and it would help, but does she? She doesn't. She doesn't worry about condensation or mould. It doesn't enter her head to worry about it!'

'I have just done twelve hours' driving –'

'That's because you agreed on the last pickup. That was up to you.'

'Yes, it was up to me.' Jansen put her blazer over a hanger, and slipped off her navy-blue trousers.

'There's no more hot water, by the way.'

Jansen folded her trousers and hung them under her blazer.

'If you wanted a bath,' May continued.

'I don't want a bath, May; I want to go to bed.'

'There's never any hot water now, after ten o'clock.'

'You never have a bath in the evening.'

'But I might have wanted a bath, though, and if I had wanted one, I wouldn't have been able to, would I?'

'You're going to grow a wart on the end of your nose quite soon.' Jansen leaned towards May to give her a kiss on this nose, and May leaned away from her.

'What a mean thing to say.'

Jansen got her pyjama bottoms from under the pillow, and pulled them on. From the bed, May watched, waiting for an apology. Jansen flung her shirt and bra in a pile on the floor, pulled a large

T-shirt over her head, and went to the bathroom. May got out of bed and followed her.

'What a horrible and mean thing to say,' she whispered.

Jansen put paste on her toothbrush, and held it under the tap.

May sat down on the edge of the bath. 'So, you're quite happy with her moving in? Indefinitely.'

Jansen began brushing her teeth – up down, up down, round and round. She took her time. She put the toothbrush back in the cup, and picked up the floss. That should really have been done the other way round, May observed: floss *then* brush was logical.

'How often is she actually here?' Jansen asked as she drew out a long string, and snapped it off.

That wasn't the point at all. 'We have to have that bin-liner of hers in the corner of the sitting room all the time, and now there's a huge great lump of clay in the vegetable rack, bruising the carrots.'

Jansen looked interested. 'She's bought some clay?'

'Yes, anyway I'm sick of not knowing when or if she's going to be around – and Mark. I never know whether I'm going to get the place to myself, or not.'

'Ask her if she can start looking for another place.' Jansen continued flossing her teeth.

'Very funny! Very funny!' May raised her eyebrows as far as they'd go, tipped her head back for emphasis, and, losing her balance, nearly slid into the bath. Jansen offered her hand to May, who steadied herself, and went on: 'You *know* I can't do that. I have to look *after* her until the Eliza-bath finds somewhere . . .' she trailed off into a mutter.

'"Eliza-bath".' Jansen tried the expression. 'I like it; it's apt.' She turned out the light, and they went back to the bedroom.

There May noticed something: 'Ted's missing. Ted's gone! I knew the burglars would've taken something. They couldn't have just gone off without taking anything, could they? They didn't find anything of value to *them*, so they just grabbed something of value to *us*. They've gone off with Ted.'

'I've lent him to Elizabeth.' Jansen climbed into bed.

'He's sleeping with Elizabeth?'

'Yes, that's correct.' Jansen nodded, and reached for her book.

May stared at her. 'You've lent out your teddy bear.'

'I have.' Jansen shut the book and put it back on the stool next to the bed. 'May, I'm not up to talking. I'm turning out the light now.'

'And how do you think Ted feels about that?'

Jansen switched out the light behind her, and lay down.

'How d'you think he feels?' May sat on the bed.

'May, I'm tired.'

'I can't believe you've lent her your childhood teddy bear.'

'Mm-hmm.' Jansen registered the disbelief, and curled up with her back to May.

What did this mean? May climbed into bed, but there was no point in lying down. There was no way she'd get to sleep now; she had to work this out. She sat there, thinking. Eventually she said, 'In a way . . . in a *way*, it's as if you're sleeping with her.'

'May, I was asleep.'

'Are you aware of that, though? She'll take it like that, y'know.' When Jansen said nothing, May persevered: 'It means you're sleeping with her. You do realize that?'

'If you like,' Jansen said at last.

'That's the message you're sending out.'

'Yeah, probably.'

'So you agree then?'

'I think you're really disrespectful.' Jansen was suddenly sitting up. 'When you need sleep I wouldn't dream of keeping you awake.'

'You wouldn't dream of it.' May laughed. 'Get it? You "wouldn't . . . *dream* . . . of it."' She laughed again, but she knew she was in trouble.

'I am really angry.' Jansen clicked the light back on. 'You know I'm tired, and you know I have to get up at seven tomorrow –'

'And I'll get woken up, too.' May tried to get in a grievance of her own.

'You can go back to sleep. The point is: I've got eight to ten hours of driving to do. I was so tired this evening – do you know? – that I nipped a cyclist coming over Waterloo Bridge. She didn't press charges. But she would have been perfectly in her right to. I was lucky not to be prosecuted.'

'Sorry.' May was contrite. 'Get some sleep. Go to sleep. Go to sleep now,' she said. If Jansen had an accident the next day, it would be May's fault.

'And I am fed up with this jealousy thing. She's your sister! I am not going to go out with your sister, May.'

'Would you be quiet?' May whispered.

'She can't hear us.'

'Would you be quiet, please?'

The next morning Elizabeth was up early, rummaging in the pockets of her army jacket. 'Yes! I have found a "super plus". I think . . . yes! I have found my last remaining tampon.' She went off to the loo.

On the breadboard sat a freshly made sculpture: a bird lying on its back, with outstretched wings. May noted its stomach looked split in half. She'd keep her comments to herself, she decided.

'Have you got it?' Elizabeth had returned.

'It's a vulva,' Jansen said.

'Aha.' Elizabeth sat on the stool in front of the sculpture. 'I'm gonna melt some red and blue glass in there. That'll be the second firing. For now, I've just got to leave it to dry under a cloth, ready for the first firing.'

'How did you come up with the idea?'

'There's the mystery.' Elizabeth stared at her creation. 'Woke up just before five, got out the clay, and dot-dot-dot.'

Jansen clearly liked the result. She kneeled in front of the table, looked intently at the clay bird, smiled at it, warmly, like a visitor at a maternity ward.

'You like her,' Elizabeth stated.

'I do.'

'Thanks.' Elizabeth leaned across and kissed Jansen on the cheek. 'I do, too.'

Elizabeth in her casual sculpting attire, Jansen in her chauffeur's uniform: it was like watching some sort of pagan marriage. A three- or four-minute silence was observed; then Elizabeth covered up the sculpture and went outside for her morning nicotine intake.

'It doesn't matter, May. We can get another breadboard.'

'*She* can get us another breadboard.'

'Okay, yes, but a breadboard costs nothing. I'll pick one up tomorrow anyway. I'm starting a four-days-off.'

That was a problem too quickly solved. 'She doesn't *ask*; she just *takes* the board, and now, if we want to cut anything' – Jansen was leaving the sitting room – 'we'll have to use a plate.' May followed her to the bedroom. '"How did you come up with the idea?"' May exaggerated a look of friendly interest. 'You're feeding her ego.'

'May, I need to make a quick call, before I go to work,' Jansen said.

'I was in the middle of speaking and you wander off.'

'Yes. I need to make a call, and would like to have the room to myself for that.' Jansen had the phone in her hand.

'You're going to ring someone and tell them how petty I am about the breadboard.'

'No, I'm not. It's true I don't feel like listening to a non-problem about a breadboard, but no, I am *not* ringing anyone to talk about you.' She was now pushing May gently out of the door into the hall.

'This is my bedroom, too. What if I feel like being in here?'

'Which room do you want to be in?'

May thought. She didn't care. She wanted to be in the room in which Jansen was making her call. 'Which room are you calling in?'

'I'd prefer the bedroom, but I don't mind.'

'The bedroom,' May said.

'Right.' Jansen stormed past May to the sitting room.

'Who are you calling?'

'None of your business.' Jansen shut the door.

28

The Death Threat

'Urggh! That's so creepy.' May let her tongue hang out in an appalled vomit. 'That's scary.'

Elizabeth, who had finally emerged from her post-creation nap, and who was making her way to the bathroom – again – with a towel and a pile of clothes, made a point of 'ignoring the performance'.

'Yuk! That's disgusting,' May went on. '"This was your life!"' she read out.

Elizabeth grabbed the booklet, and flipped through it. 'Oh, one of those angry, evangelical publications.' She slapped the mini comic book back into May's palm. 'They put these kinda things through the door all the time.'

'It was in an envelope addressed to me, hand-written. Look, it's even got the first letter of my middle name.'

Elizabeth glanced at the envelope. 'They've got it off some electoral list. I wouldn't worry about it.' She dropped her towel and clothes on the bathroom floor.

'But I do; I am worried about it. It's not about possibilities – this *could* be your life.' She flicked to the back of the booklet, where a man in a starched, fifties suit sat with a child on each knee, reading them bedtime stories. His boss, whose voice bubble was filled with praises for the reformed worker, had a Hitler-style moustache. 'It's a death threat.' She stated the obvious. Elizabeth stood in front of her, indicating she'd like to get past. 'What worries me' – May stepped aside – 'is that the burglars might've got some sort of information, and now, for some reason' – she lifted her shoulders up – 'they hate me.'

'No. It wasn't the burglars. You can rest in peace on that one.' Elizabeth laughed at her joke.

'Oh, thanks. And you know that for sure?' A rhetorical question.

'Yeah.' Elizabeth was certain. 'Hey, listen, I'm gonna have a bath. Need the bathroom?'

'*How* do you know?'

'Okay . . . if you can promise not to overreact.'

'What?' May was promising nothing.

Elizabeth stared at her. 'May –'

'What? What-what-what? What?'

Elizabeth held her forehead in her palm. She waited. She kept May waiting. She sighed. 'Are you going to interrupt me? Because forget it, I'm not saying anything if you keep interrupting me like that.'

May opened her eyes wide. 'Go on – I'm not speaking – go on.'

'I came back to the flat one night, without my key. No one was home . . .' She made three dots in the air with her index finger.

'You broke in?'

Elizabeth mouthed a slow, definite 'yep', and walked off to the loo, leaving May in the hallway, holding on to her death threat.

A minute or two passed. The loo flushed, and Elizabeth reappeared, on her way back to the bathroom.

'We had to pay for the locksmith to come round, and for a new set of keys,' May told her as she went by.

'Didn't the landlord do all that?'

'Yeah. Yes, someone had to pay for it. That's right,' she told Elizabeth, who was putting the plug in the bath, ignoring her. May couldn't believe the attitude. She pictured her levering open the bathroom window, climbing in. She hadn't even left a note to explain what she'd done. 'Do you know,' May had to raise her voice now, in competition with the water that was gushing into the bath, 'that your fingerprints are on record?'

'Well, I'll be sure to wear gloves next time I break 'n' enter.'

Elizabeth squirted some of May's special Liquorice Extract shower gel into the bath.

'I can't believe it!' May would call Jansen and tell her about it. She shouldn't have to keep this a secret.

'Yes, you can tell Jansen if you want. That's fine.' Elizabeth seemed to have read May's mind, and was giving her permission.

Why was it that May was standing there feeling as if she was bad for looking tight-lipped, a spoilt sulky child who hadn't got an ice-cream, and that Elizabeth had the role of the adult, totally unaffected, but tolerant.

Elizabeth laughed in May's face. 'Oh, come on. It's funny! *"Dear Ms Woodlea,"*' she faked a concerned voice, *'"I was sorry to hear you were recently a victim of burglary –"'*

'YOU!' May screamed, 'are wasting people's time!' She pointed her finger at her. 'Is that funny? It's funny that Victim Support's wasting its time because YOU behave out*ra*geously.'

'Mea culpa, mea culpa.' Elizabeth stood up, putting her hands in the air as she edged past May and out of the bathroom. 'Don't shoot,' she said, backing into the sitting room.

'No. You're the one judging *me*.' May followed her. 'Making comments all the time about how I am with Jansen; deciding *I've* got something in common with the most pathetic character in *L'Ange et les pervers*. Well, I know what that's about: projection.'

'I'm sorry?' Elizabeth fished a tea-light candle out of the pocket of her army jacket. She performed a cross-eyed smile-frown of comic confusion.

'You find this so so funny, don't you? Well I don't. I don't *like* you projecting your problems onto me. I don't *like* you suggesting horrible things about me, attacking me via a book. I could say horrible things about *you* if I wanted to: like – do you contribute? Do you pay rent? Do you put money in for food?' May looked over at the newly made sculpture taking up space on the table, and scowled at it. 'I hate that vulva-thing sitting over there. I didn't tell you that before, but I will tell you now. I think it's *risible* (which is not a compliment, by the way). That's not art.' May walked over to it. 'This isn't – art. Don't tell me this is "art". (I hope not.)'

Elizabeth was sending love across the room to her sculpture, as if silently defending and comforting it.

'And where are you going to put it?' May continued. 'Not in the flat. I don't want it in the flat. You will have to take it somewhere else to dry. Because I don't want it around. I don't want to have to look at it. And I really don't want it on the table, staring at me while I *eat*!'

Elizabeth put her hand to her mouth, trying to keep her laughter inside. 'Thank you,' she said, 'for your . . . feedback? So you don't like it then?'

'This is what I think of your sculpture –' May picked up the vulva and, deciding that yes she would, she said, 'It's junk,' and dropped it – th-thud! – onto the floor.

The wings collapsed skew-whiff and the body spread out. Elizabeth jolted back, as if whiplashed.

Outside, a few cars went by.

May was standing in front of the disaster area. She stepped away from it.

Elizabeth walked over to the small clay mess on the carpet, and crouched down beside it. She touched the tips of the flattened wings, before gently and gradually lifting them off the floor, carefully disengaging the damaged bird from the carpet. 'I'm going to tidy this up,' she said quietly.

May left the room. She turned off the taps in the bathroom and went to ring Jansen. Whose phone was switched off. She waited five minutes. She tried again. Eventually she got through.

'Darling.' Jansen was concerned. 'What's happened?' she asked. 'Hello? Hello?'

Eventually, May could try to speak.

'Oh.' Jansen clicked her tongue. 'May,' she sighed, 'you didn't!' Jansen left some silence after that, in order to emphasize the gravity of the situation.

'Yes, I did.' May twisted the telephone cord round her index finger. 'I just wanted her to stop laughing all the time. She makes me so furious!' May wiped away her tears angrily. 'She thinks she's so "quietly" funny, but what she is, is rude.'

Jansen said nothing.

May freed her finger from the telephone cord. 'If she moves out – all the better.'

Nothing.

'I'm sorry I did it.'

'Hm.'

May felt like a child at the headmistress's office. 'She is the one who broke into our flat,' she enunciated each consonant, 'and did not let us know about it.'

'She was probably too scared.' Jansen was on Elizabeth's side.

'Oh, yeah. Right. Ri-ght!' May laughed out her disbelief. There was no point in talking to Jansen about this. 'Thanks for your support.' She heard the front door slam. 'Just a second.' She dropped the receiver onto the bed, and ran out to the external landing. 'What are you doing?' she shouted to Elizabeth.

'I'm going to buy some cigarettes – I'm out. Is that permitted? Or do I sign a form first?' Elizabeth disappeared down the stairwell.

May went back inside. She picked up the phone again. Jansen had hung up.

29

The Disappearance

Then the week began. May went to work and Jansen slept in and went shopping; and May came home to find no Elizabeth; and Jansen – when May rang her from school in her breaks – said, 'No, she's not back yet' and 'No messages.' May called Elizabeth's mobile: no answer. Monday. Tuesday.

Wednesday.

'I don't think Elizabeth will have disappeared for ever,' Jansen said. 'After all, she's left all her stuff here; she'll have to come back and get it, won't she?'

Thursday.

Friday. May was alone in the flat: Jansen wasn't there; she was out driving, and Elizabeth wasn't there – she was either at Mark's (according to Jansen) or she was somewhere else (Jansen's other idea). May was alone. She was alone with her head, and because of that she picked up the phone. It was without thought. She just picked up the receiver.

'Allô, c'est May.' She was sending herself out on stage unprepared. She'd improvise. 'I'm calling you . . .' She didn't know why; she didn't have a reason. She wanted to hear Francine's voice.

'Ah, c'est toi.' It was impossible to know whether Francine was in a good or a bad mood.

'I wanted to explain why I decided to defer.' Yes, that was the reason – that's right – and this call was probably a mistake.

'I don't see the interest in that, quite frankly. You have already made the decision. All alone, like a big girl.' She was in a bad mood. 'You might have talked to me about it before you took your decision, and there perhaps, speaking about it would have served a purpose.' She was in a very bad mood. 'Now you want me to understand something perhaps. You want me to understand you.'

May tried to think of something to say.

'What does your supervisor say about this?'

May said nothing. She didn't like to lie, not actively.

'You've discussed it with her, at least?'

'No.' No, because there was no supervisor.

'She doesn't know about it?' Francine processed this. 'In her place, I wouldn't be exactly delighted to learn that I'd been kept in the dark.'

More silence.

'I have an idea,' Francine said. 'Come and see me when you can be more open.'

May tried again to think up something to say.

'Right. You have nothing else to add?'

May was still thinking. Her lips were dry.

'Very well. Goodbye.'

'Okay. Goodbye.'

May looked in the cupboards: tinned tuna, rice, tinned pineapple, honey, salt, flageolet beans, couscous, pepper. She looked in the fridge: milk, cheese, leeks and a jar of black olives. She took the jar to the sitting room, sat on the sofa, had a couple of olives, and then rang Jansen.

'Is she back?' Jansen asked.

'No,' May said. She put a third olive stone next to her on the arm of the sofa.

'Hmm,' said Jansen.

'There's nothing to eat.' May put another olive into her mouth. 'I'm really hungry and there's nothing to eat.'

'What are you eating then?' Jansen asked.

'Olives,' May said. She added another stone to the pile. 'I wish there was something to eat. I feel like something real. We've only got tins of things.'

'We've got leeks in the fridge, haven't we? And I'm pretty sure we've got some potatoes left. Why don't you have a look?'

'I don't feel like cooking,' May said. She put the lid back on the jar.

'Well, I'd really appreciate it if you would. I'm going to be home by half past eight tonight, and we could have dinner together. Why don't you do wedges?'

'Boring.' May stared at the jar. 'I feel like something spicy and light,' she said.

'We've got spices,' Jansen told her. 'Cumin, paprika, I think we've got some Cajun spice – have a look in the bottom drawer.'

'Mm.'

'You could do some couscous, if you feel like something light.'

'When is it you're getting home?' May asked. 'Eight thirty?'

'I should be there by about eight thirty, maybe a bit later.'

'Eight thirty, or a bit later? I'll be starving by then.'

'Well, eat something. Have some muesli. Are you going to cook?'

'Probably. I suppose. Maybe. I'm not promising that I will,' May said.

'Are you going to cook something, or not?' Jansen asked.

'I have to promise that I'm going to cook? I really don't feel like cooking.'

'Fine, don't cook.' Jansen said. 'If you don't want to, please don't. Don't bother.'

'Are you annoyed now? You want me to, don't you?'

Jansen sighed. 'I'll pick something up on the way home.'

'Singapore Fried Rice?' May suggested.

'Okay.'

'Yay!'

'Actually, May, this really annoys me. We've got food at home. It's a waste of money getting a takeaway.'

'I don't feel like cooking,' May said. 'I'm feeling flat.'

'You never feel like cooking.'

'I'm worried about Elizabeth.' May didn't have the energy to mention her call to Francine.

'I know you are. Why don't you try her mobile again?' Jansen suggested.

'Why?'

'You don't have to. It's a suggestion ... May, I've got to go. I'll see you in a few hours. Eat something, and I'll see you around eight thirty.'

30

Some Space

Saturday morning. Elizabeth had left her bags – the rubbish bag and her cardboard box of art history and modern art theory books; she'd left the mattress folded in half with all its bedding still on it, and her towel hanging over a chair; she had also left a couple of bras and knickers in the airing cupboard in the hall, and the remaining clay in the cupboard next to the sink: she would have to come back, as Jansen said, 'to get all her stuff'. Nearly a week had passed.

'How can I relax my jaw when I'm asleep! If I'm awake, I can try to remember, but not while I'm asleep.'

'Welcome to the day,' Jansen said.

May dropped her jaw open, practising a relaxed, slouched mouth.

'You look like someone pretending to be dead,' Jansen said.

'It hurts to relax my jaw. It doesn't come naturally to me. And it doesn't help that Elizabeth's disappeared. She had to go off straight away, didn't she? So as not to give me the chance to apologize. She wants me to feel terrible. When I get my dentist's bill, I'll send it to her.' Already there was Francine, who was angry with her; it was too much. May put her tongue on her top right molar at the very back of her mouth. She was being punished. 'A root canal doesn't hurt, does it?'

'Yes,' Jansen said.

'Yes, it does hurt?'

'Yes, it does.'

'No, it doesn't.' That was a question really. How did Jansen know, anyway?

May pictured someone in a white coat pulling out nerves with something like tweezers. It was logical that they couldn't anaesthetize you, because perhaps they'd need to know they'd got a nerve, and not something else. 'Who do you know,' she said, 'who's had a root canal?'

'You don't need one, May. You don't need a root canal.'

'What d'you mean, I don't need one? How do you know? Are you a dentist?'

'She didn't say you needed a root canal. Did she?'

'When I asked her, she said she didn't *think* I'd need one "yet" – she used the word "yet". She said if my teeth were hurting all the time, that might indicate I needed one.'

'So you don't need one,' Jansen concluded.

'They're really sensitive. I can't drink cold water any more. I'm going to need one.' She was going to need all her molars done, eventually. She imagined strings of nerves shrieking out of her gums. 'It's just a matter of time. The dentist said there was some sort of plastic thing she could give me to fit over my teeth at night. I'll probably choke on it.'

'It's amazing how much more talking you do than me. You've only just woken up.'

'Why aren't you worried about Elizabeth? You don't seem that worried. You don't seem the slightest bit worried.'

'She'll be at Mark's.'

'Yes probably, but she isn't answering my calls. It's so clever: she manages to disappear, leaving me guilty of something. I could be enjoying her absence, but I can't, because I'm a criminal. It's amazing how I end up being the criminal.'

'She obviously needs space. That's all. You'll work it out.'

May couldn't begin to explain how wrong Jansen was; there were too many points to cover at once, her system jammed up thinking about it. She pulled the duvet over her head, and curled up. It was good Jansen had the day off. May needed her to witness how bad things were.

'You could always apologize over the phone,' Jansen said. 'You could leave her a message. That's what I would do – in your position.'

'I'm not the only one in the wrong.' And Francine could be more understanding, as well; she could be less harsh. Francine was in love with May, that's what it was: and she was disappointed in her because of the deferral, she was embarrassed to be seen to have expended so much energy on someone so stupid.

'May, you dropped her sculpture on the floor: you owe her an apology.'

'Elizabeth' – May stuck her head out of the duvet again – 'is the one who's been breaking into people's homes, and not telling them about it.' She couldn't feel bad about two things at once. 'It was really stressful: thinking we'd been burgled and having to worry about whether or not they were perhaps going to come back, and take something.'

Jansen laughed.

'Could I have some "space"?'

Jansen ruffled May's hair. 'You just look so funny with your little head poking out!'

'Could I have some *space*, please?' May jerked her head away from Jansen.

'Booboo, it's not that serious. You've got to learn to laugh at yourself.'

'Could you go away, please?'

Jansen got out of bed, pulled on some socks, and left the bedroom. She was making a statement. May would have to get up now, if she wanted to talk to Jansen. She would not get up. She'd lie there, wasting her life.

May picked up the phone and dialled:

'Allô, oui.' She was French, but she wasn't Francine.

'Oh *bonjour* . . . is Francine there, *s'il vous plaît?*'

'No, she's just gone out. Can I help you perhaps?' It was Anne. May recognized the voice.

'No. Thank you. Could you –'

'Ah! I know who you are: it's May. You don't recognize me. It's Anne Béranger. How are you?'

'Oh yes. How are you?' May replied.

Anne laughed. 'That's so English: "How are you? How are you?"' She repeated the question in deliberate French-student English. 'And nobody answers the question. I adore it!'

May waited for Anne to move on, to say something else, and then she'd get off the telephone.

'Oh, it's difficult, isn't it?' There was sympathy in the tone. 'Excuse me. I am not polite: I am not English; I cannot talk about the weather. When I meet someone I want to know: are you happy? Are you in love with your husband? Or do you just pretend?'

'Mm,' May said, to indicate she'd been listening.

'So, how are you, in any case?' Anne continued. 'And I would like to know the answer. Because I am French.'

'Fine, thank you. Very well.'

'And I am also extremely well,' Anne said. 'That's excellent. Shall I ask her to call you?'

'No, I'll try again later. Thank you.' It was only ten thirty in the morning in France; had Anne stayed the night at Francine's?

'You know Francine finds you enormously frustrating, are you aware of that? You really made her come off her hinges.'

'I haven't yet made a decision about the PhD,' May said. 'Anyway, thank you very much, I'll call her back.'

'Shall I tell you a secret? Before you escape? Ha-ha! Yes! You are curious. All right, I'll tell you: I am of the opinion, I intuit rather – which is far better – that you have not had "no effect" on Francine. Don't forget that you are English. You speak French very well: just a hint of English. It's quite charming. So, there you are ... I'll tell her you called.'

It was true then. May took out her diary. What was Anne saying? Was she being ironic? Was she being subtle? She was French, after all; she'd have read *Le Cid*: *'Vas, je ne te hais point.'* ('Go, I hate you not' – that is to say, 'I love you.') And why would Anne have used a double negative unless she had wanted to express something stronger than what she was literally saying? No one goes to all that effort to express nothing, do they? May sat up in bed, and wrote:

Chère Francine,
I am going to write you a short letter.

Chère Francine, (she started again)
I am writing to you . . .

Chère Francine,
A postcard from London, for perhaps . . .

May stopped once more. She crossed out that sentence. She decided she'd write a letter she wouldn't send. Or maybe she would send it.

Chère Francine,
I don't know what you meant by 'more open'. . .

May stared at her beginning. Perhaps she wouldn't write to her at all. Silence would be stronger. It would show she had nothing to be defensive about. And how could she defend herself against Francine, anyway? 'That's right. Invent excuses for yourself': Francine didn't believe her, but it *was* more difficult in French; May couldn't express herself as clearly in French as she could do in English. She decided she'd write the letter in English first, and do a translation later:

Dear Francine

A note appeared under the door. May tiptoed over, and picked it up:

Dear May,
I can see you're not feeling great. When you want to come out we can
talk.
Love you,
Jansen
PS What about going out to a café for brunch?

May was touched. She was also hungry. She opened the door, and went out to the sitting room. Jansen was on the sofa, with her knees tucked up to her chin, waiting for her. She looked over to May, who stood in the doorway, staring back. Jansen placed her feet on the floor, creating a lap for May, who went over. A few minutes later, she slid off Jansen's lap, onto the sofa.

'I'm hungry,' she said.

'Let's go out for a walk together, and get some food.'

May scrunched up her face. 'I'm exhausted!' She collapsed herself over Jansen in a Sarah Bernhardt swoon.

'Come on.' Jansen heaved her slowly back into the sitting position, and got off the sofa.

May lay down again, keeping her eyes closed, even though her audience seemed to have just left. She was tired: breathless. She opened her eyes: Jansen had left the room. May got up, and found her in the kitchen, getting money out of the kitty tin in the cupboard. 'I was asleep just then,' May announced. She slid herself down the wall onto the floor, and slumped there, drooping her arms and head.

'Do you want to come with me? Come on. It'll do you good.' Jansen pulled her up.

31

Some More Space

The waitress had just brought them tea, a cappuccino and scones.
May, like a restaurant columnist preparing a report, made her initial
appraisal of the place:

'It would be a lot more pleasant if they turned off the loud radio.
Do they really think they're adding to the atmosphere, bombarding
us with this popular junk?' she began. 'The music's blasting my
ear-drums,' she went on. 'Could anyone like this? It really lowers
the tone of the place. A bit of gentle classical music,' she offered
her suggestions, 'and the kitchen closed off from the rest of the
café, would improve the atmosphere. It's really not relaxing.' She
looked around at the other tables. People were struggling to be
heard above the music and advertisements; they were more or less
shouting at each other; some of them were smiling or laughing,
stupidly oblivious to the noise. 'We could ask them to turn it down?'
May turned to Jansen.

'We could? You can, if you'd like to, yes.'

'Why me? Why should I do it?'

'Because it's a problem for you.'

'So, you don't mind the noise? You don't mind,' May lowered
her voice, speaking just too softly for Jansen to be able to hear,
'the fact that, if I talk normally, you're going to miss everything
I say.'

Jansen pulled a book out of her bag: *Fever Pitch* – another
Hornby.

'I thought we were coming here to talk.' May took out her
books. She took out her mobile: no messages.

Jansen poured herself some tea. May had a sip of her cappuccino; at least it was as she'd asked for it: 'Very, very hot and weak,
please.' May looked up. Jansen had gestured to the waitress, who
was now coming over to their table.

'Excuse me. We're finding it hard to hear each other. Would you
mind turning down the music?'

'Oh, I am so sorry,' said the waitress. 'I'll turn it down.'

'Thanks.' Jansen smiled at the woman, and then she went back
to her book. She was going to continue ignoring May.

Fine. In that case, May would continue ignoring Jansen.

When they first used to go to cafés, they never used to ignore
each other. The first time they went to a café together, they
went to the National Portrait Café; it was expensive, and it was
Jansen's suggestion and she had paid. They talked and talked,
and they both smiled a lot, they couldn't stop smiling. May said
to Jansen (because she was living in an army camp), 'I think
you need a teddy bear'; which was quite forward of her – they
hadn't even slept together at that point. 'Are you offering to buy
me one?' Jansen asked her. 'I could do, if you like,' May had
replied; she'd meant it, too. And then Jansen said, 'May, that's
a lovely idea. Thank you. But I've already got one.' And May
felt embarrassed; she thought maybe Jansen was kindly rejecting
her. It was awful.

And then it wasn't: because Jansen said, 'Perhaps you'd like to
come and meet him some time, at the army camp?' And a couple
of weeks later, May had received a proper invitation by mail, and
a tiny pewter bear – who was now lost somewhere in a small back
garden in Pimlico.

The music had been turned down; May called Elizabeth and left
her a message: 'I just wanted to say that I am sorry about your sculpture – but that I am not worried about you, so please don't think that
I am worried about you. Because I am not worried. Thank you.'

Jansen looked up from her book.

'What?' May asked.

Jansen raised her eyebrows and gave a hint of a smile, then returned to her book.

'What?' May asked again, and then she received a text message from Elizabeth:

Am at Mark's, so u can stop not worrying. Ex

'She's at Mark's,' May said.

'Hm,' Jansen said. 'Good. I'm glad she sent you a message.'

'Did you know she was at Mark's?'

Jansen sighed. 'I didn't know she was at Mark's. Although I did say that's where I thought she would be.'

Dear Francine

Jansen and May were back at the flat again. Jansen was in the sitting room and May was in the bedroom. She looked at her letter so far:

Dear Francine

May didn't know what to write next. She sat there, staring at her beginning for a while. She added:

How are you? I hope you are well.

She crossed out the greetings, and started again:

Dear Francine,
I am writing to explain why I have deferred, and why

No, she couldn't write that, because then she would have lied in writing. In which case, she couldn't write anything. She threw the piece of paper into the waste-paper basket.

There was a tap at the door. Jansen pushed it open, passed the phone to May, and left.

'Hello?'

'So, you haven't been worrying about me.' It was Elizabeth.

'Of course, I've been worrying about you.'

'Well, thank you. That's very sisterly of you,' Elizabeth said.

May nodded. 'Mm.'

'I haven't told Mark about the flying vulva, by the way – just to reassure you.'

Was that another dig? May pulled herself up in bed. 'I am very sorry,' she said, 'that I dropped your sculpture. And about criticizing you. I don't think you're a user.'

Elizabeth inhaled heavily on her cigarette.

'We invited you,' May went on.

Elizabeth exhaled.

'Sorry,' May repeated.

'No problemo.'

'What did you do with the vulva?'

'Yeah I took it with me. I've turned the wings into an oyster shell. I'll show it to you some time – once I've had it safely fired perhaps.'

'I want you to know that you're very welcome to come back and stay,' May said. 'If you want.'

'Sure. Okay. I'll be back Saturday week then.'

'Good. Well, I'll look forward to seeing you.'

May went to the sitting room. Jansen looked up, and shut the book she was reading.

'Elizabeth will be back next Saturday,' May announced. 'I have just invited her back. Why did I do that?'

'Yes, why did you?'

'Because! Because I'm a criminal. Because she's my hopeless sister. Because she's doing nothing with her life and she makes me feel guilty. I am responsible.'

'Did you set a time limit?'

'No, I didn't set a time limit!'

'Why not?'

'Because I didn't. I didn't think to. Okay?' May sat down on the sofa. 'I would just like to get on with my PhD, if I was allowed! We've got a week without her, and then she's back again. Do we have a life together? Or are we just the owners of a free –'

Jansen made a dramatic stop sign with her hand, as if she were helping someone manoeuvre out of a tight parking space. 'I would like to say something.' She marked a pause. 'I would like you to know – that I have been finding this situation impossible, and I have been very seriously considering moving out for a bit.'

'Oh, great. I'm having a difficult time, so you think you'll move out just when it's all at its worst. I think you should move out right now. I think you should go and stay at the YMCA with Tamsin. I guess you've already spoken to her about it, how awful I am to live with.'

'No, I haven't.'

'You haven't spoken to her?'

'No, but I did think of moving in with her for a while, though. She's got a new flat with a spare bedroom –'

'Oh, well that's perfect then. I wouldn't hesitate.'

Jansen let May finish, then left a little space of silence, before she continued, 'And she was even looking for a lodger, so then I thought –'

'Perfect! Perfect!'

'I *thought* Elizabeth might be interested, so I asked Tamsin about it, and she said she had decided against getting in a lodger for the time being.'

May didn't speak.

Neither did Jansen.

'May, I understand you want to help your sister – she is your sister – but I would like you to tell her that she can't keep on staying with us indefinitely. It's already been over a month; that's far too long. I could tell her myself, but I would prefer it if you would tell her; she is your sister.'

'You find her annoying, too?' May asked; she was pleased – as well as still being upset. Her stomach hurt, and she felt a bit weepy.

'I *like* Elizabeth,' Jansen said. 'I enjoy her company. She's very likeable. And yes, I am beginning to find it slightly annoying not being able to use the sitting room, it can be frustrating that she's in the bathroom when I want to get in there, but most of all, May, I am sick of you going on and on about her.'

'Well, you can ask her to move, then,' May said.

'I have just asked you to do it. I would like you to do it. And now, I would like some time on my own, so please decide which room you want to be in.'

'Are you planning on leaving me?' May said.

'I am not planning on leaving you.'

'You're not?' May verified.

'I need some space,' Jansen said. 'Right now I need some space.'

'You mean as in "a few minutes, or an hour"?' May asked.

'Please give me some space,' Jansen said.

'How long for?' May asked.

Jansen didn't answer.

32
Scones and Jam

May baked scones the next morning – she had had the idea at about three o'clock in the morning when she wasn't sleeping. She sneaked out of bed early, at six thirty, and quietly made cinnamon scones, with half a sachet of sugar in them and a coating of egg white to make them go golden. And then she went back to wake up Jansen.

'What's the time?'

'It's seven o'clock,' May whispered in the bedroom darkness.

'I'm not going to work today.'

'You're not working? Why? What are you doing?' Jansen was going to spend the day packing her things; May scared her stomach, picturing it.

Jansen reached for the clock.

'I've made you scones.'

'. . . Thank you.' Jansen put the clock back on the stool.

'Do you want to go back to sleep then?' May wanted her to stay awake with her, and eat the peace offerings and reassure her that she wasn't moving out. 'I could bring you tea and scones in bed if you like . . . I thought you were working today: that's why I woke you up.'

'It's okay – thank you; I've decided to take the day off.' Jansen pulled herself up in bed, and clicked on the light. 'And I need to call someone now anyway, to let them know. Could you pass me the phone?'

May got the phone from the chest of drawers and handed it to her. 'So we can spend the day together?' She was starting to feel a bit happier. Nothing drastic was happening after all.

'We could spend the day together if you want.' Jansen was dialling her work.

'Yay!' Everything was fine again between them. May smiled as
she listened to Jansen making her call, and then she took the phone
back and put it on the chest of drawers. 'Perhaps we could go
somewhere interesting in the car? We could go to a teashop in the
countryside somewhere, or we could go for a walk in a forest. We
could take a picnic.'

'I'm not up to driving, May. That's why I've taken the day off.'

'We could go on the train somewhere then. We could go to
Windsor Castle.' May felt like doing something exciting. 'Or
Brighton.' Jansen loved the sea.

'Maybe another day.'

'I'll make tea.' May went to switch on the kettle. They would
have a boring day, but it didn't matter. Everything was back to
normal again; and that was good enough. No one was leaving
anyone; Jansen wasn't moving out, and Elizabeth was moving back.
And May was going to try to be more relaxed and pleasant to be
around.

'It looks sort of rococo, doesn't it?' Elizabeth lifted up a corner of
the cloth to give May a last look at the reconstructed vulva in its
pre-fired state. It was Saturday morning, she had just moved back,
and Jansen was driving her to the pottery shop in Vauxhall. 'We'll
see you in a bit.'

Which could mean anything. May decided to clean the flat; that
would make Jansen happy. She would tidy up the place instead of
writing to Francine; she didn't know what to write in any case, and
she was so tired of Francine always being angry with her.

One day – she took the vacuum cleaner out of the cupboard
in the kitchen – she would be interviewed about Francine by
someone writing a biography; May would be among a group of
people who had known Francine in some way. She wouldn't be

able to say she had known her well; she'd nevertheless give a few factual details about her personality, her behaviour and what her working space looked like. What might be May's exact words? (She was vacuuming the bathroom now. Elizabeth had left a wet towel on the floor; May picked it up.) 'Francine Brion . . . made of ambition a moral issue; to fall short of self-fulfilment, for her, was' – May went to the sitting room and flung a few of Elizabeth's belongings, a plastic bag of her paintings or something, onto the sofa – 'criminal.' Or it might be what she ate that would be of interest: 'radishes with salt'. Would May have to be 'someone' in order to be asked about Francine though? 'I was a disappointment to her in the end.' She plugged in the vacuum cleaner next to the sofa. Even if she'd only known Francine for a year and then had a falling out, what she had to say would be of interest. Because Francine would perhaps only be a blip in May's life. It was not a friendship that could last; it wasn't a friendship, in fact. What was it?

May unplugged the vacuum cleaner and took it to the bedroom. She wouldn't be interviewed of course, because she wasn't someone; she wasn't doing anything. If she did the PhD or something more than teaching nine-year-olds that 'is' is a verb, she could be interviewed; but otherwise (unless they found her letters to Francine with her embarrassing notes on a non-existent PhD) they, or 'she' rather (the biographer), wouldn't – May put Jansen's leather bag onto the bed – know where to find her.

Elizabeth and Jansen returned about three hours later.

'Borough Market,' Elizabeth explained, coming through the front door past May. 'Expensive, but delicious.' She set various bags on the table, a flat square box and a couple of bottles in brown paper bags. 'Chocolate pie,' she announced. 'Organic apple juice' – she pulled a bottle out of one bag – 'and *vino!*' She took the other bottle out of its bag. 'We sampled everything: olives, wines, dips,' she continued unpacking jars and little plastic tubs, 'fudge, chutney, jams . . . I'm not hungry any more. Who's getting the plates?' She looked at May.

'Where's Jansen?' May asked.

'She's parking the car.' There was a knock at the door. 'Oh there she is! I'll get it.'

'Bread!' Jansen came into the sitting room with Elizabeth.

'And lots of cheese.' Elizabeth took a plastic bag from Jansen, and placed it on the table; she drew out various cheeses: Camembert, a wedge of Brie, some blue vein . . . 'We're gonna have enough left over for a picnic! Hey, that's a great idea: we should go on a picnic! Are you working tomorrow?' she asked Jansen. 'What about driving us down to Brighton?'

'A picnic . . .' Jansen considered the proposition.

'We could get up really early and go down for the day,' Elizabeth elaborated on her plan. 'And make our way back up to London some time around four or five. Whadd'ya think? Fun?'

'The traffic will be bad on a Sunday evening,' May said. 'There's probably no worse time to think about coming into London.'

'The traffic would be okay if we left a bit later, around about seven,' Jansen said. 'We should probably allow three hours, but if we're lucky the traffic won't be that bad.'

'Hey, let's do it!' Elizabeth said.

'Sounds good,' Jansen agreed. 'Sounds fun.'

'That would mean a late night, though, wouldn't it?'

'Oh, don't be boring, May!' Elizabeth turned to Jansen. 'She's being boring again, isn't she? All work and no play make Jill a dull girl.'

'I've got school the next morning; I really don't want a late night.'

'We could be back by nine thirty, or ten at the latest – definitely,' Jansen reassured her.

'And then we have to get ready for bed.'

'You could go straight to bed, May, if you wanted to,' Jansen said.

'We never go straight to bed. It always takes us ages.'

'We'll send you straight to bed,' Elizabeth promised, 'as soon as we get in.'

'I am now looking forward to a whole week of exhaustion,' May told Jansen. 'You want her to leave and then you say "Hey yeah, let's all go to Brighton": isn't that a double message?'

'No, I think it would be enjoyable to go to Brighton. And it might be a good distraction for you, too. I thought.'

'What from?'

Jansen ignored the question as she pulled off her jumper. 'Didn't you say you wanted to go to Brighton last weekend?'

'With you! Obviously.'

'Okay, well I guess you'll have a horrible time then.'

'I feel as if I've just been bullied into a fun day at the beach. I knew I had to say yes; I had no choice, did I? I have to pay now for having dropped her sculpture; that's what this is.' May climbed into bed. 'It's fine for Elizabeth; she doesn't have to get up in the morning, does she? I can't just decide to have a nap in the middle of the day. "Sorry, spelling is cancelled, while I go to sleep."'

Jansen nodded. 'I'm going to the loo.' She picked up the newspaper on the chest of drawers.

May waited for her to get back and shut the bedroom door, and then she said, 'Did you ask her about moving out?' She had to whisper this, because now Elizabeth was in the kitchen, making herself another hot drink.

'What?' Jansen unbuttoned her jeans and pulled them off.

May repeated herself.

'May, I can't hear you.'

'Did – you – ask – her – about – moving – out?' May silently mouthed out the question.

Jansen looked puzzled. 'I can't lip-read, May. You'll have to speak up.'

May ripped a piece of paper out of her diary, scrawled on it and passed it to Jansen, who took the pen from her and wrote: 'no'; 'why not?' May scribbled out. Jansen shrugged, and opened the bottom drawer to get out a fresh pair of pyjamas.

'Well, you could have.' May decided to risk talking – softly. 'You could have talked to her about it in the car, on your way to the pottery place. Or at the Market.'

'And I didn't.'

'Because you want me to do it?'

'Yes. I want you to do it. Correct.'

'Why? So that I can be the nasty one? I'm already the nasty one. Why can't you do it?'

'If you want her to move out, you're going to have to say something. She's your sister.'

'You could say something. You want her to move out, too.'

'May, it's perfectly reasonable. This is a very small flat. She'll understand.'

'Why hasn't she moved out already then – if she's so understanding? Why didn't she only stay a couple of weeks or something? I don't get it! Can't she see this place is too small for three people?'

'Obviously not.'

'It's so obvious!'

'If you want her to know how you're feeling, you're going to have to let her know.'

'You could do it. Why don't you do it?'

'And I would like you to tell her this week, because it's been too long.'

'Have I got an ultimatum? Is that another threat? My "second warning" or something?'

Jansen was in her pyjamas now. She climbed into bed.

'I've got other things to think about right now. And to worry about,' May said. 'I can't deal with several things at once.'

'What "several things" are we talking about?'

Jansen drove down the Parade, and eventually found a car park in Regency Square. They walked back along the beach – the sky was brighter on the coast, sandstone-blue – towards the pier; it put them all in a cheerful holiday mood: May and Jansen hand-in-hand, crunching over the pebbles, Jansen carrying their lunch, and Elizabeth dancing around them, back and forth.

They went back up onto the promenade, found an empty bench and stared out at the murky-green sea, dark blue on the horizon. Then they ate their Brie and lettuce sandwiches, taking swigs from the half-empty bottle of organic apple juice, and ending with fudge. May felt sick now – and guilty: lazy. Elizabeth, though, who still had energy, wanted to visit 'the Lanes'.

So they went towards the shops to walk off all the food, and to T.K.Maxx: summer was on its way, according to Elizabeth, and if you didn't mind looking you could find some great stuff in there. Elizabeth tried on gaudy dresses à la Dorothy in *The Wizard of Oz*, because you never knew if you didn't try things on and she was looking for a bit of colour: did Jansen like this? (An army-type shirt from the men's section.) Or this? (A glittering evening jacket.) May? (A short tailored jacket.) And what about this? (Pencil-lined trousers.) With this? (A light cotton blouse.) Elizabeth bought a flattering green woollen shrug in the end (for cool summer evenings), at half-price, and May and Jansen bought nothing.

A teashop break at Tallulah's: they had scones and jam and clotted cream; May had a nutty-flavoured Colombian coffee, and Jansen and Elizabeth shared a pot of Earl Grey.

Then they wandered down the North Laines – handmade jewellery, posters and toys – May started to feel frantic with the purposelessness of the day – one-pound books and seventies-style tops and dresses – it was terrible how she was wasting her time. They wandered and wandered and wandered. Jansen went in and out of shops, patiently browsing – cards and knick-knacks and bright green kitchenware – and Elizabeth stocked up on felt-pens and glitter, and chatted at stalls with the creators of studded belts, sequinned purses and elaborate earrings.

Finally, they made their way to the Regency Restaurant, because Jansen knew May loved seafood and Elizabeth had never been there, and it was near to where the car was parked. They got a window table that looked out towards the sea, into the evening sky. Jansen ordered a large bottle of sparkling mineral water and a seafood platter for the three of them.

May smiled at Jansen: this was so lovely; in fact, it was magical. 'It's good to relax now and then,' May said. 'I think it's good for you. For your system.'

'And fish is good for the brain,' Elizabeth added; she was wearing her elegant new shrug.

'What's going on?' Jansen wondered aloud. They were in a traffic jam on the M23.

'There must've been an accident,' Elizabeth said. 'Shit.'

May sighed. 'What time do you think we'll get back now?' She looked at her watch. 'It's already nine-fucking-twenty. Fantastic. Wonderful. I'm so glad I came.' She couldn't be pleasant all day.

Jansen turned off the engine for a while. 'It's pretty bad,' she said.

'God! I knew it!' May slumped back into her seat. 'I've got school tomorrow, and I'd like not to be tired for the whole week, if that's possible. I wish I hadn't come. Damn it!'

Elizabeth yawned out a cheerful arpeggio. 'I might stretch my legs,' she told Jansen, who nodded and went, 'Yeah, okay.' Elizabeth unbuckled her seatbelt, and got out of the car.

'"Yeah, okay"?' May turned to Jansen. 'It's dark outside, and she's walking down the motorway – in the dark. That's not "okay"; it's dangerous. And stupid. What if the traffic suddenly clears?' Elizabeth was walking on the verge, alongside the car. May wound down the window. 'Will you get back in, please?'

'Yeah, when it starts to clear I'll get straight back in. Of course. I'm not too keen on walking all the way home.'

May wound up the window again. She shook her head.

'Time for a mint, I think.' Jansen opened the glove compartment, got a mint out of the tin and popped it into her mouth. 'I really liked that tearoom,' she said. 'What did you think of it?'

May got herself a mint. 'Are you trying to change the subject?'

Silence.

'It was okay. It was good. I liked the scones.' May sucked on her mint.

The car in front of them went forward a bit; then its brake lights went on, and it stopped.

Again Jansen moved the car forward slightly.

The car in front went forward another half-metre or so, its brake lights went on . . .

May glanced over at Elizabeth, who waved and smiled as she continued strolling – she looked as if she were on a treadmill – alongside the car.

'I wish she'd get back in the car,' May said. 'It makes my stomach clench up.' She wound down the window again. 'Would you please get back in the car?'

Elizabeth opened the car door, and jumped in. 'That was fun,' she said.

'It was dangerous,' May corrected her.

'There's a jam on the other side, too, isn't there?' Elizabeth said to Jansen.

The car in front edged forward, stopped.

They edged forward, stopped.

The car in front edged forward, stopped.

They edged forward, stopped.

The car in front edged forward, stopped.

They edged forward, stopped.

Then Jansen suggested they play 'twenty questions'.

Five musicians, two actors, three writers, four feminists, two cartoon characters and the Pope later, the road narrowed from two lanes to one, and they passed a tow-truck loading on a crumpled Ford Fiesta, and, behind it, a police car with flashing blue lights.

33

The Explosion

'Third, second or first choice. Yeah, well, they . . . I'm an idiot because I put Goldsmiths as my first choice because it's supposed to be excellent, but really I prefer Saint Martin's . . . yeah, but you don't get your second choice unless your first choice rejects you . . . True . . . yeah, true . . . (Hiya!)' Elizabeth mouthed at May, who had just got back from work, and discovered the shattered oyster sculpture on the sitting-room table. 'No, yeah probably not . . . What about you? Yeah . . . Yeah . . . Yeah . . .' Laughter. 'No way!'

May went to the bedroom. On the pillow, next to a bar of Divine chocolate, was a note:

Hi, darling. Hope you got through your day okay. Give me a call. Jansen xx

May sat on the bed, eating the chocolate – without a hot drink, which was a stupid thing to do – and waited for Elizabeth to get off the phone. In the end, though, she had to go back to the sitting room, and say something. She said, 'Could I use the phone? I'd like to use the phone.' She wanted to call Jansen and thank her for the chocolate and the note.

Elizabeth held up her left hand, her fingers spread out like a starfish. 'Five minutes,' she mouthed. 'She's back, yeah. Hmm, yeah.' Elizabeth laughed. 'Yeah . . . yep . . . ah-hah.'

May went back to the bedroom.

'Yeah . . .' Elizabeth continued. 'You are not! You're not, Mark. No . . . No, you're not. Yeah . . . yeah, well *yeah*! You are that – definitely, yeah. Hmm . . . Thanks, Mark, yeah, thanks. You're a babe!

Hmm . . . hmm, yeah. Cool.' There was a silence, and then, 'I'm off the phone!'

May returned to the sitting room.

Elizabeth was standing at the table, fingering the pieces of her shattered sculpture. 'I brought her back by taxi this afternoon. Tragic, isn't it?' she said. 'D'you want to attend the funeral?' She carried the breadboard to the kitchen, and May followed her – not in order to attend the funeral; she wanted to make herself a drink. 'DA. DA. Da-DA!' Elizabeth hummed the first few notes of Beethoven's *Funeral March*. 'Clay to clay,' she said as she tipped the debris into the bin. 'Et cetera!' The service was over. Elizabeth ran hot water over the breadboard, scrubbing it briefly – and inadequately – with a cloth. 'That was nice and quick, wasn't it?' She put the board onto the draining rack. 'News flash!' she then announced. 'I have just put in a late application to do a Fine Arts degree. And if I don't get in, I'm gonna do an intensive foundation course somewhere, and then try again the following year. It's all happening.'

'Good. It's good you're getting on with it.' May filled up the kettle, and clicked it on. She still felt guilty for dropping the vulva.

'What about you?' Elizabeth went cross-eyed.

'Tea?' May ignored her.

'No, I'll try this stuff.' Elizabeth got the organic, Fair Trade decaffeinated out of the cupboard, and sat it on the bench. 'And what about you? How's the PhD going? Jansen told me you weren't really doing it . . .'

'Well, actually, I am – "really". I'm just not enrolled, is what she meant.' May got out two cups.

'Yeah, she said you weren't enrolled.'

'I'm doing the background reading at the moment,' May chose a camomile teabag, and put it into her cup, 'which means that once I do enrol, it'll take me less time to complete it.'

'Are you ever going to enrol?' Elizabeth tipped an estimation of a spoonful of coffee into her cup.

'Next year, yes,' May lied. This was what she hated about Elizabeth, and why she didn't want her around: she was so perceptive sometimes, she was almost psychic.

'And what does the French woman you're besotted with think about that?'

'A French woman I'm "besotted with"?' May put on a puzzled look.

'Yeah, well, whoever it was you were blushing at on the phone that time – the one you keep visiting in Paris . . .'

'Oh, that's just someone who's been helping me a bit with my research – I hardly know her!' It was like living with a spy. 'Why would she think anything about when I enrol? Anyway, I make my own decisions.'

Elizabeth shrugged knowingly.

'What does' – May shrugged – 'mean?'

'As long as you're doing it because you want to do it; not 'cos you wanna please some woman who you've decided is better than you, that's all.'

'I'm not a child,' May said.

The water came to the boil, and May poured it into the cups. 'I'm going to take my tea, and go and make my call now,' she said. She got the telephone from the sitting room, took it to the bedroom and shut the door.

'Hi, May!' Jansen was in a cheerful mood.

'Why did you tell Elizabeth about Francine?'

'I didn't.'

'You didn't? Well, how come she seems to know all about her?'

'I haven't mentioned anything to her about Francine,' Jansen said.

'You have told her about "a French woman" though, that I've been visiting in Paris and who I'm apparently "besotted" with?'

'May, Elizabeth has been living with us. She'll have worked that out by herself.'

'How?'

'She's not stupid.'

'So you didn't tell her?'

'No.'

May nodded.

'Is that all you rang me about?' Jansen said.

'But you did tell her,' May continued, 'that I wasn't really doing the PhD. Why did you have to say that? I am doing the PhD, as you know; I just haven't enrolled yet.'

'Yes, that's what I told her: I said you hadn't actually enrolled. Why do you have to be so secretive?'

'I haven't been secretive; it just didn't come up.'

'Oh. Well it came up when we were talking,' Jansen said. 'And, as the subject came up, I told her the truth. I'm not going to lie.'

'Thank you so much for telling her that I am not doing a PhD – not that I ever wanted her to know that I *was* doing a PhD, even though I *am* doing one.' She was supposed to be thanking Jansen for the chocolate; instead she was on the phone being horrible again.

'Until you have enrolled on a PhD, May, you are not doing a PhD,' Jansen said. 'And I don't think you should be pretending – to yourself, or to anyone else – that you are doing one.'

'I am not pretending to be doing a PhD,' May corrected her. 'In fact, I've told Francine that I've deferred, as you know, even though I have been working on the PhD and I am still working on it.'

'Have you been doing a PhD, or not?' Jansen asked.

'I have been constantly working on it, as you *know* – worrying about it – and I've been doing background research.'

'Are you enrolled on a PhD, or not?' Jansen asked again.

'Am I in court?'

'I think you're in denial, May.'

'I'm "in denial"? I think you're in denial.'

Jansen laughed. 'Would you like to know why I told Elizabeth about the PhD?'

'No, I wouldn't.'

'No, of course you wouldn't. I told Elizabeth you weren't doing the PhD –'

'I am doing the PhD.'

'Okay, fine – I told her about your PhD "quandary" because I felt she needed to know that your behaviour, destroying her art-work, for example, wasn't all about her.'

'Oh? Because it's about me – I'm the failure?'

'I wasn't saying you were a failure, May. That's not what I –'

'What were you saying then?'

'I thought she needed to know it wasn't all about her, and –'

'You *thought* she needed to know –'

'And, *and* – before you interrupt,' Jansen said.

'You interrupted me!'

'Just listen, May! Listen!'

May hung up.

'For your information,' May spoke angrily at the telephone. 'Last week – if you want to know – I saw a post advertised in the *Times Higher Education Supplement*: research fellow, six hours teaching, eighteenth- or nineteenth-century literature.'

May had been flicking through various magazines and newspapers – *Floodlight, Hot Courses, TES*, et cetera – at WHSmith, browsing her life away. Would the post be for a PhD student (or for someone who wanted to do a PhD)? Or was it for someone who already had a PhD and wanted to do more research? Perhaps she should ring and find out. It was a thought.

But really that was all it was.

She picked up the phone. And put it down again.

If she was going to call Francine, she should think about this carefully first. She sat down on the bed and took a sip of her camomile tea, and stared at the writing desk: a thick layer of dust lay on its surface. May went to the bathroom, pulled off a piece of loo paper, and came back and wiped the dust off the desk. The chest of drawers was dusty too; she picked up books and papers, pens, and dusted around them, the various other objects, keys and a bookmark. Then she dusted the stool where her tea was, and had another sip. She had to be honest about the deferral: that was one thing. And what could happen? Nothing. It would just be a bit unpleasant.

She picked up the phone.

'Allô, c'est May.'

Francine said nothing.

'I'm calling because I'm thinking of coming to Paris this weekend – just for the day.'

Still Francine said nothing; she clearly felt May hadn't finished.

'And I wanted to know whether I could come and visit you – on Saturday or Sunday – in the afternoon, some time that would suit you.'

'Sunday,' Francine said. 'If you arrive at two o'clock, I could give you an hour, but only an hour; after that I shall have to get back to work. I've got a talk to prepare and –'

'Oh?' May had interrupted her; she hadn't meant to; she'd meant to show interest.

'Yes. Good.' Francine was about to finish the conversation.

'And apart from that?' May asked. She hoped Francine might fill in the rest of the sentence.

'That's a good start: "and apart from that". What is it you want to ask me "apart from that"?'

'How are you?' It was the first question May could think up.

'What do you think? Well, very well.'

'That's what I thought, since your book's been published.'

'There is more to life than that!'

'That's true,' May said. 'Of course there is, yes,' she agreed. She felt like crying.

Silence.

'See you on Sunday then,' May said.

'Yes, see you on Sunday. Au revoir.' Very formal.

'Au revoir!' May said it cheerfully, as if all was well.

She was very tired. She felt as if she had a rock in her head. She didn't always like Francine that much. May lay down on the bed. Then she sat up, and she called Jansen again.

'Hello. Are you calling to apologize?'

May sighed loudly. 'I'm *tired*, I'm so tired.' She lay back down on the bed.

'So am I,' Jansen told her.

'Are you annoyed because I said I was tired?' May asked. 'Or not?' she added. 'Are you just tired, too?'

Jansen said nothing. Then she said, 'I am just saying that I am also tired.'

'I am sorry about hanging up on you,' May said. 'And thank you for the yummy chocolate.'

'Apology accepted.'

'When do you finish?' May asked.

'I should be back by ten.'

'Ten! Oh God! I wanted to talk to you! I wanted to see you!'

'Why don't you talk to Elizabeth?' Jansen said. 'Perhaps you could have a talk with her, and ask her about moving out.'

'I haven't got the energy to do that; I don't want to talk to Elizabeth. I wanted to talk to you. I've got all sorts of things I wanted to tell you.'

'Yeah.'

No one said anything.

'Sorry, darling, but I've got to go.'

'Drive carefully,' May said. 'I'm sorry about hanging up on you.'

'Yes. See you tonight.'

May got into her pyjamas. It wasn't even eight o'clock, but she was going to get ready for bed anyway. She shut the curtains, she went to brush her teeth, took the phone from the bedroom and then knocked on the sitting-room door. Elizabeth was in bed already. She had set up the mattress on the floor, and she was reading her *Sculpture: My Way* book.

'I'm going to bed now; I'm going to bed early,' May told her. 'If anyone calls, I'm asleep. Here's the phone, if you want to use it.' She passed it to her. 'Please don't wake me up. Good night.'

'Good night.' Elizabeth put the phone on the floor next to her. 'Hey,' she said, just as May was about to shut the door, 'if you want to do that PhD, I think you should just get on with it. It feels good, you know, to make a decision and to take an action.' Elizabeth shared her experience and wisdom.

'Thanks. Thank you.'

'I'm sure you're capable of all the boring research,' Elizabeth added.

'Thank you,' May said.

'I would find it dull sitting in the British Library all day. But if you're into that sort of thing –'

'Good night.' May shut the door.

If you close your eyes and try to relax your face, you are still resting; if you've got your eyes closed. In the dark. That is rest.

Even if you aren't asleep.

You're not sleeping, but it's still 'rest': Jansen had told her that.

One trick, May decided, might be to slow down your breathing: you're sending a message to the body that it is feeling calm and is now about to fall asleep. May forced her breathing to slow down. It was like a plane braking, after it had just landed; it required quite a lot of energy. But that would be to begin with, because if she kept the brakes jammed on, and kept them on, eventually her breathing would slow down and start coasting along until eventually it would dip into a pulsing standstill, and she would be breathing in and out – slowly. And then, in theory, she would go to sleep.

34

The Declaration

May would have to start speaking soon. She sat at Francine's kitchen table trying to begin. Francine sat opposite her, waiting. It was just after two o'clock. May's train was in four hours. She could walk to the station after this, she thought, if she wanted to; she'd have the time.

'You come here with nothing to tell me. You sit there like a bird with its beak open, waiting to be fed.'

There were two glasses on the table, a jug of water, and nothing else.

'I came here to tell you something,' May said.

'Very good. So, tell me. What do you have to tell me?' Francine poured herself some water.

'It's not very easy,' May began.

'Fine. It's not very easy. That's good: so now you are going to do something that's not very easy.'

'I'm interested in what you write,' May said.

Francine wasn't going to interrupt.

'I'm very interested in it, and I don't always understand it,' May went on. 'I admire you. A lot.'

Francine said nothing. She drank some water.

'I've read all your articles,' May told her.

'I know you've deferred,' Francine said. 'You've told me that already.'

'Yes, but in fact: I haven't deferred,' May said. 'Because I never enrolled on a PhD. I never even wrote a proposal. I don't know why.'

Francine refilled her glass with water. 'I see. And now you've told me that, what are you going to do?'

May didn't understand.

'Yes, what are you going to do? What are you expecting from me? That I give you absolution?'

May smiled a tight apologetic smile. Her throat was dry. She didn't drink.

'It's not very amusing all this. Do I seem to you like a thought-dictator? This is your view of me, it appears.'

'No, it's me. I didn't want you to be angry with me.'

'It shows to what extent you lack confidence in me.' Francine looked at her.

'No, I lack confidence in myself.' May knew this was the ultimate in pathetic, but she had to defend herself. She cried.

'Oh, the little baby's crying!'

May kept crying; with or without Francine's approval, she cried.

'Yes. You can always cry, but what are you going to do?' Francine asked her again.

May answered the question; she thought she'd be told to leave, otherwise. 'I could do the PhD,' she grabbed her first thought. 'I've looked into various universities. I've been making notes.'

Francine shook her head. 'Your university course is of absolutely no interest to me whatsoever; it's you who interest me, your path.'

It was like a declaration of love; perhaps it *was* a declaration of love. May wiped away her tears with her fists.

'You lied to me.' Francine drank the rest of her water. What was she about to say? 'And what's more, you put a lot of work into this lie. I've got a folder full of letters from you about my writing. Now you tell me you never started this thesis. It's not very flattering. So, what do you want from me now?'

May looked at Francine. She really didn't know.

'What did you want so much that you put all this effort into maintaining a lie?' Francine asked her.

May tried to think.

'You have no idea? Let us work it out by elimination: are you interested in doing the PhD? That is the first question.'

May couldn't answer that one.

'No – is the answer.'

'It does interest me,' May protested – feebly.

'No, you are not interested. So, what are you doing here? That is the next question.'

May couldn't answer that one either.

'You've had a good many opportunities to ask me to help you, and all this time you have preferred to work it out on your own. You have remained silent: because that is safe.'

'I have asked questions.' What was she supposed to have asked?

'You've asked polished "intelligent" questions about my work.'

'Intelligent ones?'

'You needn't look so pleased. You have never taken a risk, not one; I have no idea what your opinions are: that is where you have failed. Ask me something you really want to know. Let's see if you can do it. There isn't anything you would like to ask?'

'Do I annoy you?' May asked.

Francine looked furious.

'What do you think of me?' May tried again.

'You are uptight,' Francine answered.

'Thank you.'

'Ah, she doesn't like being called that!'

'No, I don't.'

Francine laughed. 'You are a product of England: very Protestant.' She observed May a while, then she asked, 'What else would you like to know? Here is your opportunity.'

'If you despise me, why do you spend time with me?' May asked: a brave question, this one.

'Well done, but you totally misunderstand. I don't "despise" you, not at all. Take a look in the dictionary.'

(May would look later.) 'Why have you agreed to spend time with me?' She simplified the question.

'I haven't signed a contract, as far as I am aware.'

'Will you still want to see me, if I am not doing this PhD?' How many different ways did she have to phrase it?

'I am talking to you now. I could have told you to leave much earlier, but I have not. Why do you think that is?'

May wasn't sure.

'You are in love.'

May said nothing.

'I have shocked you,' Francine said.

May blushed. She was blushing on cue; it was ridiculous.

'You hide it badly. But, tell me – if you dare – that you are not in love with me.'

May stared at her empty glass. 'I am a little "taken" – perhaps?' she said.

'"Perhaps"? You're not sure. Well, if you don't know, no one else can answer that for you. I can't tell you what you are feeling.'

'I don't want you to.' May was supposed to be in love; that was what Francine expected. Of course.

'Listen, May. I am going to have to be very hard on you, otherwise I am doing you no favours. I am not interested in a sentimental relationship with you. I am only interested in an exchange between equals. I am interested only in adult women, in women who speak.'

'I am speaking, I'm speaking now.'

'You are part of the generation who has gone to sleep. You have to wake up now.'

May attempted to look alert.

'At your age I had already done incredible things,' Francine continued.

'I'm not good enough for you, I'm not good enough to be your friend. It's what I always thought.' She was only ever supposed to be the hopelessly enamoured student. Reality, she thought, was such an exhausting disappointment.

'That depends on you. You will have to show me what you are capable of. You have shown me nothing for the moment.'

That wasn't true. Francine had 'a folder full' of notes and letters from her. 'I've shown you things,' May objected.

'Very little. You have to continue.' Francine stood up, took the glasses and put them on the bench. 'I want to place you before your own destiny,' she said. 'You will have to live a long time to accomplish what you have to do.'

May got up, and pushed in her chair. She was so tired of Francine; and she was tired of performing; she was tired! She was going . . . to start crying again. She tried not to. She tried not to. She cried. She was crying again. Francine was not in love with her; and she wasn't in love with Francine; no one was in love with anyone. Her crying slipped into laughter: she was losing control of her face now. Actually, the situation wasn't that funny, but she was laughing anyway; or perhaps it was funny.

'Drink.' Francine poured water into one of the glasses. 'You should drink. You're getting hysterical.' She handed May a glass.

May drank. She stopped laughing, and drank. She put the glass back on the bench. She wanted to leave now; she wanted to go and breathe some polluted outside air, and be on her own.

'When is your train? This evening?' Francine asked.

'Yes.' May took her jacket off the back of the chair.

'You will have your Jansen waiting for you at the station.'

'No,' May said. 'She's working.' She put on her jacket.

'You'll see her later then.' Francine led May to the door. 'You are going to do something extraordinary with your life,' she clasped May's forearms firmly as she spoke, 'you are going to become a fulfilled woman, and then you are going to come back to see me. And then we shall see.'

'Yes, perhaps.' May tried to be honest.

'You say "yes", quite simply.' Francine kissed her on both cheeks. 'Au revoir alors?'

'Yes, au revoir,' May said, although she wasn't sure she meant it. Francine opened the door.

35

The Convalescence

There she was. In her uniform.

'Hello, darling.' Jansen opened her arms wide, and May stepped into a hug. Weepy and limp, she let herself be held. She felt like a five-year-old being collected after a hard first day at school.

'Are you hungry?' Jansen asked.

'No . . . *Yes*,' May corrected herself. 'Yes.' She was so glad to see her.

They walked out of the automatic glass doors, and past the taxi stand.

'The car's parked round the corner; I couldn't park here.'

'Have you finished for the evening?' May said.

'It wasn't that busy. I got the rest of the evening off. I thought it important that I come and meet you.'

They walked on.

'And I don't start until ten tomorrow,' Jansen continued. 'So I could give you a lift to school.'

'Is Elizabeth at home?'

'No. I asked her if she wouldn't mind staying at Mark's for the night, and she said she might not come back until Tuesday or Wednesday.' Jansen smiled at May. 'Anyway, we've definitely got the whole place to ourselves this evening.'

They got to the car; Jansen unlocked the doors from a distance, using her remote – it was a Volvo, 'top of the range', with a central locking system. Then she went over, and opened the door of the passenger side for May, who got in, and leaned over to open up the other side for Jansen.

'Is there anything to eat?' May asked as Jansen got into the car.

'I'm going to make you a quick stir-fry once we get home.'

'Okay, great. Thank you.' May put on her seatbelt. Jansen was so loving and thoughtful, she was such a patient and wonderful woman; May was grateful for her in her life. 'Do you know, it's stupid of me, but sometimes I can wish, I have wished,' she corrected herself, 'that you could be a little bit more like Francine.'

'You want me to be like Francine? Well, I'm not.' Jansen frowned – annoyed.

'I said "I have wished". It's you I want to be with.'

Jansen nodded, and clicked in her seatbelt.

'What I mean is I've sometimes wished that you were a bit of an intellectual,' May said. 'But you're kind and you're very generous, which I appreciate. That's what I meant. I was giving you a compliment.'

Jansen turned on the ignition.

'I appreciate your coming to get me,' May said. 'Thank you.' She sighed. She shook her head, and let out another loud sigh. 'I didn't mean I don't love you.'

'I'm just feeling a bit hurt,' Jansen said. 'I'll be all right.'

Now May had a stomach ache. 'I do love you,' she said. 'I'm sorry. I'm just tired, I'm exhausted, so I can't always express myself that well.'

'It's all right.' Jansen started manoeuvring the car out of the parking space.

There was a message flashing on the answering machine when they got in.

'Don't play it! Don't play it!' May went off to the loo. 'Just give me a chance to go to the loo,' she yelled through the door. Jansen was listening to the message without her. May flushed the loo, and quickly washed her hands. 'Oh, you've listened to it. You've wiped it!'

'It wasn't for you anyway.' Jansen put the remote for the car on the table, and went to the kitchen to make the stir-fry. She was still in a bad mood.

May followed her. 'Are you still in a bad mood with me?' she said.

'I'm not in a bad mood.' Jansen put a very slight emphasis on 'bad'. She took a tin of braised tofu out of the cupboard and put it on the bench.

'Well, you look like you're in a bad mood,' May insisted. It didn't feel fair; she wanted Jansen to be all loving again.

'Excuse me,' Jansen said, and May stepped away from the fridge. Jansen took some courgettes and red peppers out of the salad compartment. 'You could do some onions, if you like, if you want,' she told May. 'And some garlic.'

'Do we have to have onions?' May opened the cupboard next to the sink. The clay was still in there; she heaved it off the carrots and onions. 'Shall I do some carrots, as well?' she asked.

'Yes, that would be good.' Jansen spoke in a stiff, hurt way. She slid the diced courgettes off the new breadboard into a bowl, and started washing the peppers. 'Actually, would you mind finishing this?' She dried her hands on a tea towel. 'I might just make a quick call.'

'Why do you have to make a call?'

'I feel like talking to someone.'

'Why can't you talk to me?'

'I have been talking to you. I feel like talking to someone else.'

'I'm going to have a bath then,' May said. 'You said you'd cook me a stir-fry.'

Jansen went to the sitting room, and shut the door.

May ran a bath. She put some bread into the toaster, and clicked the kettle down. Having made a hot cocoa, she poured a small pile of raisins and sunflower seeds onto the side of a plate, and whistled a medieval French tune as she quietly Marmited her toast. She was relieved to be back at the flat, and glad that Jansen was around, glad, also, that Elizabeth wasn't around, but she wasn't happy; she couldn't be fully happy, because Jansen was annoyed with her. She took the toast with her to the bathroom; she shut the door, turned off the taps and climbed in.

May fed one or two sunflower seeds into her mouth, and nibbled at the lightly buttered, Marmite-dabbed toast: she felt as if she were in early recovery from something; as if she'd been violently ill, and had to take things gently for now. After her exhausting efforts to please Francine, and her final failure, it was all – at last – over. May was in convalescence. She slowly made her way through the raisins and the sunflower seeds, finished her toast, and let the water out of the bath.

As she got into Jansen's pyjamas she gazed apologetically at Jansen's teddy bear, who was sitting on a pillow staring at nothing; he'd lost his pewter bear companion because of her. She went over and kissed him on his little head. 'Hi, Teddy,' she said.

The first time she'd met Ted was at the army barracks, where she had spent the night with Jansen for the first time; the place was like a school after school: deserted, echoing. She and Jansen had made their way in the dark past the NAAFI – Jansen had tour-guided her – to Block A, where Jansen slept; the room was sparsely furnished, May remembered: four free-standing wardrobes and four neatly made single beds in each corner. And on one bed was a teddy bear. 'Everyone's away,' Jansen said. 'So, you have a few choices: you can sleep in this one, this one, this one, or you can sleep with me.'

May went back to the kitchen. 'Who were you on the phone to?'

Jansen looked up from her stirring. 'You're wearing my pyjamas,' she remarked.

'Yes, I felt like it . . . You can wear your other ones, can't you?'

Jansen smiled then – one of her comforting, kind, forgiving smiles. 'It's hard, isn't it?' she said.

May walked into another hug.

Jansen held her with one arm as she stirred the vegetables and tofu around in the pan. 'Did you know: that if you make sure the onions are well cooked,' she said, 'everything tastes better?' She tipped in a dollop of mango chutney.

For a few moments they stood there in silence.

Then, 'Who were you on the phone to?' May asked again.

'Tamsin. I was returning her call: she wasn't there; I tried her at her sister's; they were having dinner, so we didn't talk that long.' Jansen stirred in the chutney, and added a teaspoon of chilli paste. 'Is that everything you need to know?'

'Mm-hmm.' May got some bowls out of the cupboard. 'And what did you talk about?'

'"Did we talk about you" – you mean?' Jansen said. 'No.'

'What did you talk about? Was she ringing about something?'

'Why do you need to know this?' Jansen was in a bad mood again.

'I'm curious, if I'm allowed to be! Why can't you just tell me?'

'May, what are you worried about?'

'I'm not worried.' May was starting to feel worried.

'There is nothing to worry about.'

'Oh, now I really am worried. What am I "not supposed to be worrying" about?'

'She's met someone,' Jansen said. 'She met her on the retreat. That was what the call was about. So now you know.'

May made a face. 'You still had a bit of a thing for her, didn't you?'

'Not really, no.' Jansen turned up the element.

'A "sort of thing", then?'

'Yeah,' Jansen conceded. 'Okay, yes.'

'For a Christian soldier.'

'She was a bit mixed up for a while,' Jansen said.

'Oh.'

'She had a lot going on; I felt she needed looking after.' Jansen turned off the element, and served up the stir-fry.

'You felt she needed looking after?'

'May, this is none of your business, anyway.' Jansen took the bowls to the sitting room. 'Bring water, if you want. And we need some forks.'

They sat down to eat.

'But how could you have fallen for her? How could you have actually followed her into the army? You're an intelligent woman! I'm just trying to understand you.'

'You are not. You're being judgmental, and I don't like it.'

'Sorry.' May hated apologizing.

'You don't have to worry about her now, anyway. She's got someone, and she's very happy.'

That wasn't entirely reassuring. 'So she was after you?'

'Yes.' Jansen started eating.

'What ... so did she ask you directly, or was it just "in her behaviour"?' May made inverted commas with her two middle and index fingers.

'It was "in her behaviour".' Jansen copied May's gesture. 'And she was also very direct.'

'My God!' Tamsin was a real threat.

'She felt she needed to express it. She said she wanted to be frank.'

'God!'

'Could you stop swearing, May?'

'Well, I'm obviously not paranoid, am I?' This didn't feel good.

'No.'

'That's frightening. I had no idea! There I was casually going about my business,' May held her hand to her chest, 'and I should have been worrying.'

Jansen kept eating.

'I should've been really worried! Or did I not need to be?'

'That's right,' Jansen said.

'What's right?'

'You didn't need to be. No.'

May's stomach was hurting again. 'Because you told her you loved me, and that you were unavailable,' May proposed.

'Yes, I did.'

They ate their stir-fry.

36
The Duel

'Just to be clear . . .'

May and Jansen were in bed now. Jansen was coming to the end of her *Gnostic Gospels* book, and May was browsing through the bibliography in *Troisième personne singulière*. She waited for Jansen to finish her paragraph and look up from her book, and then she continued, '. . . So you said, "I love May, and I'm unavailable" – you said those words to Tamsin?'

'Not exactly, no, of course I didn't.' Jansen returned to *The Gnostic Gospels*.

'Oh, so you didn't, in fact. So what did you say?'

Jansen shook her head, still looking at her book.

'You just agreed with me that you'd said that to her, to make things easier for yourself?' May went on. 'That would be easier perhaps than telling me exactly what you really did say.'

Jansen stopped reading. 'Well, I could ask you exactly what you said to Francine on your various visits, if you want. Would you like me to do that?'

'Don't be ridiculous.'

'What's the difference?' Jansen asked.

'You know there's a huge difference. There's no comparison.'

'No comparison? Why?' That was a challenge, rather than a question.

'You know you can't compare them. You're joking. Francine and Tamsin?' May laughed at the absurdity. 'You're telling me they're the same?'

'No, they're different. What I'm saying is: we were both focusing on someone else –'

'In not at all the same way.' May winced theatrically. 'Your thing with Tamsin was on a totally different level, your motivations were on a totally different level,' she said. 'Absolutely.'

'On a "different level"? You can be so arrogant sometimes.'

'You're telling me your thing for Tamsin –'

'It was far less obsessive, anyway.' Jansen picked up the clock, looked at it and replaced it on the stool.

'Your thing with Tamsin was of a different quality,' May specified.

'"Different", or "lesser"?' Jansen raised her eyebrows.

'More dangerous. More likely.'

'Oh, you think so?'

'What I'm unsure about, and what I'd like to know, is whether I should have been worrying,' May continued.

'You want to know whether you should have been worrying?' Jansen dog-eared the page she had been reading, and put the book on the stool beside her.

'What's so bizarre about that?'

'So . . .' Jansen frowned, pretending to try and then fail to under-stand, 'so if you discover you should have been worrying, how useful will that be for you?'

'It'll be information.' May shut Francine's book, and placed it on the floor.

'Ah huh.' Jansen got out of bed. She went to the bathroom to brush her teeth. Finally, she returned with a string of floss.

'You're on the defensive,' May stated, 'which I find a bit disturbing.'

'I'm astounded.' Jansen flossed her teeth while she thought about this. Then she said, 'Francine is worth more than Tamsin: that's more or less what you're saying, isn't it?' She returned to her flossing.

'I *said* – and you can twist things if you like, but that'll be your problem – your feelings for Tamsin were not the same as mine for Francine; I'm sorry but they weren't.' May shrugged. 'Why is that such a problem for you?'

'Okay,' Jansen took up May's point, 'Francine is older than Tamsin, and she's more self-assured' – May refrained from adding to the list of differences while Jansen interrupted herself to do a bit more flossing – 'which, as I see things, would lead to an imbalance in power relations, depending on the persons involved –'

'I don't want you dissecting things, "as you see them",' May said.

'It doesn't feel very good, does it?'

'I haven't dissected your thing for Tamsin.'

Jansen put the string of floss on the stool. 'You call it a "thing", which is fairly dismissive, very disrespectful in fact.'

May laughed, she couldn't help herself, and Jansen left the room. May was in trouble. She got out of bed – Jansen had gone to the sitting room. 'Sorry!' she called through the sitting-room door. 'It was nervous laughter. You can be quite scary when you're angry.'

Jansen didn't reply.

'Sorry,' May said again. She opened the door a crack.

Jansen was sitting on the floor, leaning against the sofa, with her head in her hands, quietly crying.

'Can I come in?' May asked quietly. 'Or would you like me to go away?' She stood at the door for a while, and then she went and got some loo paper and a glass of water, and returned with them to the sitting room. 'I just don't like Tamsin very much,' she said as she sat down next to Jansen. 'That's understandable, isn't it?' She was trying to lighten things up a bit.

'I don't care what you think of Tamsin,' Jansen took the loo paper from May and blew her nose, 'but I do find it really painful that you describe my feelings for her as "having a thing"; it's so demeaning. Aren't you interested in knowing what attracted me to her? You're not even interested in finding out. I feel like –' Jansen's face contorted, and she started crying again – 'I feel like you're n-n-not,' she cried as she spoke, 'not even interested in me.' She shook her head as she continued to cry.

'But I am,' May moved a little closer to Jansen, 'I am interested in you. I love you,' she said. 'I love you! I love you! I love you!' she added. Jansen was still crying; she was unhappy; she was distraught. 'I'm sorry, darling,' May said. 'Sorry.' She felt terrible.

'I'd come home, and want to tell you about how my day's been. But I knew you weren't interested, so I stopped telling you anything,' Jansen spoke and cried at the same time.

'I've been obsessed,' May said. 'I've been selfish and horrible.'

'You haven't been at all concerned that I might go off with Tamsin; you've been so unaware of me. I feel invisible; I'm just your cook and your driver.' Jansen took the glass from May, and drank all of the water. 'And you know what else I find so upsetting?' She put the glass on the floor. 'Is your devotion to Francine. What am I worth? No, I mean it. Where do I come into it?'

'I'm not interested in her,' May said. 'I was just dazzled by her –'

'What were you getting out of it? What were you hoping for?'

'I don't know.' May got up; she was going to get more water.

'You want to know exactly what I told Tamsin?' Jansen asked.

May sat down on the floor again. 'All right,' she said. 'If you want.'

'I told her my relationship with you was a bit wobbly at the moment, so I didn't want to see too much of her for a while. And she agreed that we should only meet for coffee now and then; she understood.'

'Of course she did.' May stood up again.

'You're so threatened, aren't you?' Jansen said. That was an attack.

'No, I am not "threatened".' May sat back down on the floor again. 'I'm just saying,' and she laughed as if someone had told a joke, 'of course she *understood*; you made it so clear to her. You couldn't have been clearer.'

'I could have been a lot clearer – actually.'

'Oooh!'

'I didn't do it perfectly, May; I am not perfect –'

'Oh, no. I think you did pretty well though.' May feigned encouragement.

'I don't know why I'm bothering to try and tell you this,' Jansen said. 'Do you want me to tell you what happened, or not?'

'What do you mean, "what happened"? Did something happen?'

'I am trying to tell you.'

'Yes?' May was listening now.

'Tamsin and I *sort of* almost slept with each other – only sort of – and nothing really happened – at all; we just cuddled and rolled around a bit, and I didn't stay the night. That's more or less it.'

'Oh good! Thank you for the details.' May pressed her lips together, nodding. Tamsin was a creepy Tartuffe; she was a dangerous revolting woman. And Jansen liked her. They'd slept together. May put her hand to her head; she felt dizzy.

'It was quite a few weeks ago, May, and nothing happened.'

'When? And why are you telling me about it?' She felt spaced out, as if she were speaking to an empty auditorium. 'If nothing happened. Although something did happen; you've just told me.'

'It was weeks ago. And nothing happened.'

'Oh, weeks ago. How many?' May could have lost her; she could have lost Jansen; she nearly had: she *had* lost her, in fact; she simply hadn't known about it. She was too stupidly busy being self-obsessive with her reading schedules, and trying to please Francine all the time, and –

'Does it matter? The night before she came back to the bedsit; how many weeks is that?'

May sucked in her cheeks. She was in shock.

'This is not all about you, May. Not everything is about you.'

'I'm not saying –'

'What I *really* like about Tamsin – you won't be happy to know this, but there are lots and lots of things actually – what I really appreciate about her is that she *thinks* about other people, she isn't always focusing on herself. Whenever we meet up, do you know what the first thing she does is? She *asks* me how I am: she wants to know how I am; she asks me questions; and she *listens*. She's kind, she's interested, and she's *very* clever actually. Do you know why she's working at the YMCA?'

May had no idea.

'It's for the flexible hours – so she can be free to get more involved in Greenpeace; it's one of the main reasons she's moved to London, actually: she wants to do things like chain herself to posts; she wants to go to the Antarctic; she'll probably get herself arrested one day. She really cares about the world, May – and people! *I* respect her for it; and I admire it. She's an incredible woman. Incredible. She's got an amazing sense of humour, she always looks for the positive in any situation, but most of all she is *emotionally intelligent*.'

'Everything I'm not, in fact.'

'You see: there you go again. This isn't about you! Can you hear what I'm saying?' Jansen was raising her voice. 'It's about Tamsin!'

'It is about me though. I'm the one who's in the hot seat right now. I'm the one who's being told off.' May was feeling shaky.

'Oh God, would you grow up! "I'm in the hot seat" – where did you get that expression from? I am trying to talk to you!'

'All right. I'm not deaf – she sounds amazing,' May conceded.

'Anyway,' Jansen calmed down slightly, 'Tamsin and I came to the conclusion – years ago – that it would never work between us; we're like two North Poles. It just wouldn't work, and we knew it.'

'Until just recently, until a few weeks ago when you thought you'd try again.'

'It went nowhere, May; that's what I am trying to tell you. She was just slightly upset about how the interview had gone, so I took her back to her hotel, and then I went in with her briefly, because she was still upset –'

'Oh, poor Tamsin! Still upset.'

'And that was when she told me she liked me – please don't interrupt – and she told me she knew I still liked her, and eventually I told her I loved you –'

'"Eventually",' May said.

'(Yes), and I told her I couldn't stay –'

'You couldn't stay with me?'

'With *her*!'

'Thank you: I'm dumb. Thanks.' May was crying now. 'I'm stupid.'

'You're not dumb,' Jansen told her. 'And you're not stupid. And I would even love you, even if you weren't an intellectual.'

'Very funny. You think you're clever.'

'I know I'm clever,' Jansen said.

37

Something

It hurt to swallow.

'I am not going to school today,' May told Jansen the next morning. 'I'm getting another cold. Of course. I've got a cold.'

'How are you feeling?' Jansen asked her.

'Like I've got a cold.' May sat up in bed. 'Unless it's going to be the flu this time,' she said. 'My throat hurts.' She held her hand to her throat. 'It feels all inflamed; it feels like sandpaper.' She swallowed painfully. 'It hurts to swallow,' she said, and she swallowed again.

'Poor you. Well, don't swallow then.'

'Don't swallow? How – can – I – not – swallow?' All this she said thickly, in almost a whisper because of her throat. 'Anyway, I am not going to school. I refuse,' she said. 'Because I am not well.' She got out of bed, found the school's number in the telephone book, left a hoarse message on the school's answering machine, and climbed back into bed.

'I'm sorry you're not feeling well,' Jansen said. 'Do you want a hot drink? I can make you one before I go. I can get you some Lemsip after work on the way home.'

'Maxi strength – thank you,' May said. 'And some cough mixture? Could you not go out and get some before you go to work?'

'All right.' Jansen got up. 'I'll probably have it myself in a few days,' she said, and she went off to have a shower.

On Tuesday, May rang the school again, to say she had the flu (which was what it was – or what it would become, if she went to work), and the morning after that, Jansen had it as well. 'I think I've got it, too,' she announced – 'Whatever you've got.' And she rang in sick.

They spent the rest of the week in bed together, sucking echinacea lozenges and zinc tablets, swallowing time-release 1000 milligram vitamin C pills, sharing Benylin cough mixture, blowing their noses, filling up plastic bag after plastic bag (one on each side of the bed) with tissues and – once they'd run out of that – with loo paper.

Elizabeth, discovering they had bad colds, decided to stay away a bit longer; she was okay at Mark and Kate's, she said, for the time being; she could sleep on the sofa in their sitting room.

On Friday, Elizabeth returned with gifts: lemons and grapes, and a box of aloe vera tissues each; she made them lemon and honey and garlic drinks, and shared her handy tips for breathing. 'What I've discovered,' she said, standing in the doorway of their room, 'is that if you lie on one side, the nostril closest to the bed will block, and if you turn to the other side, the other one will block; one of them's gonna block, whatever side you're on. The best thing,' she concluded, 'is to lie on your back. But you may just have to sit up. Failing that, you could try breathing through your mouth.'

Jansen laughed, and then she coughed and coughed and blew her nose; Elizabeth laughed, too, and then she smiled, like a nurse on duty, before shutting them in with their germs.

Cigarette smoke; it was seeping under the door. May picked up the clock: it was half past two in the morning. Elizabeth was up smoking a cigarette – at half past two: unbelievable. May would have to get up and ask her to put it out, but she was too tired to move.

'Can you smell that?' she whispered.

No reply.

'Are you asleep?'

Jansen said nothing.

May would have to get up. She would have to get up now anyway. Because now that she was awake, of course, she couldn't breathe. She would have to get up and make herself a Lemsip; she wanted to be able to breathe, she wanted to be able to go back to sleep, and her nose was completely blocked – the skin just under it was all crusty and peeling – and her throat was dry. She got out of bed.

The light was on in the sitting room: Elizabeth was up – half-finished cigarette in mouth – sculpting something on the new breadboard. When she saw May she stubbed out the cigarette on the bread-and-butter plate she was using as an ashtray. 'Sorry – could you smell that?' she whispered. 'Mark's broken up with Kate,' she added, pointing over to a lump lying on the mattress.

'Your smoking woke me up.'

'Hey, your sense of smell's not too bad then, is it?' Elizabeth observed. 'Don't worry too much,' she said. 'He's pretty good at sleeping through anything; he can sleep with the light on – amazing!'

'You're sculpting something on the new breadboard.'

'Yep. I don't know what it's gonna be yet. "Something" – that's right.'

May's stomach tightened. 'You could ask,' she said.

Elizabeth looked blank.

'As in: "May I borrow your new breadboard?" – perhaps.' All this whispering was hard on her throat.

'Oh, I thought you meant as in: ask the muses, or whatever,' Elizabeth said. 'I wondered what you meant.'

May half closed her eyes; she couldn't keep them open anyway; the light was too bright, and she was still asleep.

'So you're not doing the PhD now?' Elizabeth stopped working on her sculpture.

'Not for now, no.'

'You're still thinking it over.'

'Not right this second, no; it's the middle of the night.'

'That can be the best time, you know.'

'I'm going to make myself a Lemsip,' May said.

'A coffee for me would be great – thanks.' Elizabeth returned to her chunk of clay. 'Hey, have you thought about asking the muses? Perhaps they could help you out.'

'Have you thought about looking for somewhere else to live?' May replied.

'I think you're both past the contagious stage by now.' Elizabeth crossed her fingers. 'But, thanks for your concern,' she said.

May was still feeling heady; her nose was tickling and dripping; her eyes were watering, and her left ear was blocked. 'I really, really, really need space,' she told Elizabeth. 'I really need to have the house to myself sometimes.'

'Oh, yeah, I understand that,' Elizabeth said. 'I need my space, too, but generally I get tons of space, when you and Jansen are at work, so I s'pose it's less of an issue for me.'

'No-o . . .' Was Elizabeth being deliberately thick? 'What I meant was: would you please start looking for another place?' May said. 'Jansen and I would like you to start looking for another place; we would like to have the use of the sitting room back: is what I am saying. And four is too many people.'

'Oh, right. Sure. This is a tiny flat,' Elizabeth said. 'Got it.' She went back to her sculpting.

'So could you start looking for somewhere else?' May asked.

'Message received.' Elizabeth did a thumbs up. 'Roger! Over and out,' she added, making a static 'khirrr' noise as May went off to make the drinks.

May climbed back into bed. She sat there in the dark, drinking her Lemsip.

Jansen coughed, and coughed; she sat up, leaned forward and hack-coughed some more. Then she clicked on the little light behind her.

'Do you want me to get you a Lemsip?' May asked.

'No, it's all right. I'll just have some of this.' Jansen poured herself a tablespoon of Benylin, drank it, switched out the light again, and lay down.

'Mark's here,' May announced.

Jansen coughed. 'Hmm.'

'I've asked her to move out,' May said. 'And I said four was too many people.'

'What did she say?' Jansen asked.

'Do you want to know? Or do you just feel obliged to ask?'

'May, I'm not feeling very well,' Jansen said. 'What did she say?'

'Nothing – she made a few stupid jokes. She'll probably hate me now. Just like you've probably never forgiven me for losing the pewter bear.'

Jansen sat up again and had a sip of water. 'She's not going to hate you.'

'She said she'd start asking round.'

'And as for the pewter bear, I forgave you long ago – you know that,' Jansen said.

'I don't like the idea of him being lost and alone in that garden.'

'He's probably having an adventure.'

May drank the dregs of her Lemsip.

38

The Surprise

'Was that a real surprise?' May followed Jansen around the flat. They were both completely recovered from their colds now, and had been back at work since Monday. It was Wednesday early evening, and May was back from school. She'd just had a look at the new summer exam paper, in the afternoon, which wasn't that different from the last one; and so she was feeling more organized – as far as 'non-life' was concerned, in any case. Also – as far as real life was concerned – there were only six weeks to go until the end of the school year, mid-term break was two days away, and May had arranged something special, a surprise. 'Was that a surprise?' she repeated, following Jansen around the flat. 'When the post arrived, and there they were just lying on the floor?' May laughed. 'You were surprised, weren't you?'

'Yes, May, I was. I was surprised.' Jansen nodded, tolerating the question once more.

May laughed again. 'Fantastic, isn't it? How I managed not to tell you about it. I'm really pleased.' May beamed. 'I'm so looking forward to it. We're going to do something exciting! Why don't people do that more often?' she wondered. 'Just – you know – make something happen?'

Jansen nodded again, distractedly. She was rifling through some bits of paper on the sitting-room table.

'And I promise not to bring any books or anything,' May said, 'to work on.'

'You don't have to promise me that.'

'No, I do: I promise. We'll shake on it.'

'Okay.' Jansen shook hands with May, and returned to her searching.

'Are you looking for something?' May would help her find it.

'Elizabeth's left you a note.' Jansen looked under the newspaper on the sofa. 'Where is it?' she said, and went to the bedroom. 'That's weird.' She flipped through papers and letters on the stool next to her side of the bed. 'Oh here it is.' She passed her the note:

Bye-bye, May. See you round. E xx

'She's gone?'

'Yeah, she's gone to stay at Mark's.'

'What do you mean? Is she coming back?'

'Yes, May. What are you looking like that for?'

'Well, she didn't say goodbye.' May looked at the note again. '"See you round": is she trying to make me feel guilty?'

'You asked her to move out, and so she has.'

May dropped the note onto the bed. 'But it somehow doesn't feel very good. Maybe she hasn't forgiven me for dropping her sculpture, and now she's really annoyed with me because I asked her to leave.' May sighed. 'I wish *you'd* asked her.'

'She's only gone to Mark's – his number's on the other side. Kate's gone to stay at her sister's, apparently.'

'Hm.' May picked up the note again.

'Elizabeth said she'd pop by at the weekend – Saturday morning, she said.'

'Okay.'

'Thank you for asking her to leave,' Jansen added. 'Are you all right?' She gave May a hug. 'Booboo!'

'I *try* to be a good sister!' May said. She was also trying hard to be a better person around Jansen.

'You are a good sister.'

May nodded through her tears. Sometimes she could be.

'She wants to know if she can stay while we're on holiday,' Jansen said. 'By the way.'

May looked up.

'Does that make you feel better?' Jansen asked.

May shrugged.

'And thank you so much for the tickets. It's a lovely idea. Are you feeling better?'

'You're looking forward to it, aren't you?' May said.

'Let's find out whether I can get the time off.' Jansen took her diary with her to the sitting room.

May followed her. 'You'll be able to get the time off, won't you?'

'I hope so.' Jansen picked up the receiver, and started dialling.

'You hope so?' May sat down on the sofa. 'Tell them you were given some tickets.'

Jansen waited for someone to answer the phone.

'Tell them you've got leave owing –'

'Oh, hi, Louie. It's Jansen. Is Ben in? Thanks. Hi, Ben. How are you? Yeah, well, I know this is pretty last minute, but I was wondering whether I could get the fifth to the tenth off . . . yeah, and start back on the eleventh . . .'

'The eleventh? That's the day we get back!'

'I'm up on time, yeah, and I've got leave owing . . .'

'Say the twelfth, make it the twelfth,' May hissed urgently.

'What was that?' Jansen focused on her call.

May got up and wrote: 'make it the *12th*.'

'Okay, great.' Jansen ignored the message. 'Thanks, Ben. Monday, yeah. Bye.' She put down the receiver.

'Did you make it the twelfth?' May was annoyed.

'He said I could come back on the fifteenth, if I wanted to. I've got lots of time owing, and I'm supposed to use it up.'

'Yay!'

'Please don't interrupt me when I'm on the phone. It's really annoying.'

'I was trying to get a message to you!'

'It's very annoying, May.'

'So, are you taking until the fifteenth off?'

'Yes.'

'Yay!'

Saturday. The smell of cut grass wafted up to the fifth-floor balcony where May stood just outside the front door in the early morning sun, sipping a large cup of hot milky coffee, while she waited for Elizabeth.

Someone was mowing the housing-estate lawns; May could see him, the mower, in his blue overalls and cap, holding an electric cord in one hand, floating the mower over the grass with the other. Someone was sweeping the concrete in front of the block of flats. May smiled. She was feeling tranquil; in fact, she was feeling almost poetic, because it was the first day of her mid-term break, and she and Jansen were going on holiday in a couple of days.

She looked at her watch: ten fifteen; Elizabeth would be here soon.

Or she wouldn't. May went back inside.

Elizabeth turned up in the afternoon. Mark was with her. His hair needed combing; he stood outside the door, in loud unassuming silence.

'Hi,' Elizabeth said.

'Hi,' he said. 'How are you?' He smiled.

'Hello. Fine,' May replied in her telephone voice.

'Shall we come in for a bit then?' Elizabeth turned to Mark.

'Sure. Is that okay with you?' Mark asked May.

'Of course.'

They stepped inside.

'I've got this for you.' Elizabeth handed May something in a plastic bag as she passed her in the hall. 'It's your breadboard – and a couple of other things. You're not allowed to look at them yet.'

They all went through to the sitting room.

'Would you like something to drink?' May offered as she put the plastic bag down next to the sofa. She wished Jansen were there.

'I'll make it.' Elizabeth went off to the kitchen. 'You want coffee, right?' she tilted her head back at Mark, and then at May.

Now May had to socialize. She sat at the table.

Mark sat down on the sofa. 'Sorry we were so late,' he said.

'Oh, no that's fine. I wasn't going anywhere.'

May would rather have been making the coffee. 'How long have you and Elizabeth known each other?' May filled the silence.

'She came to one of my gigs about a year ago; I was playing up in Cambridge. And the first thing she told me when we got talking in a break was that she was an artist; she was all relaxed about it, and I thought, "That's cool," 'cos most people are either really secretive or defensive, aren't they?'

Elizabeth came in with two cups of coffee. 'I'm using up the rest of your fruit,' she told May. 'I'm making us all a yummy fruit salad.'

Mark took his coffee – 'Thanks!' – and put it down on the floor. 'But now that I know her better' – he waited until Elizabeth had gone back to the kitchen – 'I know she's not the slightest bit relaxed,' he whispered to May. 'She's extremely serious, and I think bloody good. What do you think?'

'What have you seen of hers?' May flipped back at him; she ought to know her sister a little better perhaps, take a bit more interest.

'Almost everything, I'd say; the print on glass is gorgeous, isn't it?' He pictured it for a while. 'I wish she'd give it to me . . . Ah well, I've got it for now.' He combed his fingers through his hair. 'Maybe I'll just forget to give it back to her.' He drank some of his coffee.

They listened to Elizabeth chopping up fruit.

'She's helped me out a lot,' he told May. 'I was a bit of a major mess for a while there. As you may have noticed.'

They listened to more chopping.

'You do realize you've been housing a creative genius?' he said.

May nodded, since a reply seemed required. Her stomach contracted.

'Have you got any dreams of becoming anything? Or doing anything at all?' He took another sip of his coffee. 'Or are you happy to be a nobody, like the rest of us?' He laughed.

'No,' May said. 'Nothing. No dreams.'

Elizabeth returned with three small bowls. 'Health!' she said, handing them out. 'So, how's life?' she asked May. 'You're going on holiday soon, aren't you?'

'In two days, yeah.'

'Great! I bet Jansen's looking forward to it. They're going on a ship to Denmark. How romantic is that? My sister is doing something romantic.' Elizabeth sat back into the sofa, clutching her bowl.

'How long are you going for?' Mark asked.

'Two weeks.'

'Two weeks.' He was impressed in a downbeat sort of way. 'Well, I guess you can afford it if you're a teacher – unlike our artist friend here! Who was it who said that artists don't take holidays? They're not capable of doing nothing.' He scooped up a spoonful of chopped grapes and kiwi fruit.

'I don't know – I'm always on holiday,' Elizabeth said.

'You won't be soon though!' Mark attempted a bad imitation of Elizabeth's cross-eyed grin. 'She's got an interview at Saint Martin's, did she tell you?' He turned to May again.

'The letter came this morning,' Elizabeth said.

'Wow!' May said. She was pleased. 'That's wonderful! Wonderful,' she repeated. 'Brilliant!'

'She'll get in, too,' Mark said.

'I hope so. Even a part-time place would be great.' Elizabeth put her bowl onto the floor and picked up the plastic bag. 'May, I've made something for you' – she pulled out the breadboard and leaned it against the side of the sofa – 'Mark, you're gonna have to go away now. You can't be here for this; it's a sisterly moment.'

'Fine,' Mark said, and he got up off the sofa. 'Nice to see you again, May. Thanks for the coffee and the kiwi fruit, and the grapes. I'll wait for you in the van,' he said to Elizabeth.

May heard the front door close. 'It must be amazing,' she said, 'having someone who so completely believes in you. He has absolute faith, doesn't he?'

'Yeah.' Elizabeth pulled out a large envelope and handed it to May. 'Voilà!' she said. 'This one's more for you than for Jansen, but she might appreciate it, too.'

It was a framed certificate, blue on the borders, with pink and red glitter sprinkled around the calligraphy:

May Woodlea
has been awarded 'un PhD'
maxima cum laude

'"Ceci n'est pas un PhD",' said Elizabeth, reading out the caption below. 'Congratulations!' She shook May's hand energetically and gave her a quick hug.

May looked at the certificate, and put it on the table. 'Is it a joke?'

'No, it's a present: a gift from *moi* to *toi*.'

'And what's it for?' May didn't like it. 'If it's not a joke.'

'I thought it might help you to visualize things. Then you can chuck it away if you want. Or keep it. Up to you.' Elizabeth got something else out of the plastic bag. 'Now this one – moving right along – is for both of you.'

It was a glass mosaic on a slate tile: of two tiny blood-red birds, swirling around each other in a grey-blue sky.

'Do you like it?'

May didn't know what to say. 'It's quite beautiful,' she said. 'It's very beautiful, in fact.' She gave Elizabeth a kiss on the cheek. 'Thank you.'

'Cool. Right' – Elizabeth collected up the bowls, and got up – 'I better get moving.' She took the bowls to the kitchen.

'You've got your key?' May followed her. 'Because it's all right for you to stay, just to let you know.'

'Great, cool, thanks – say hi to Jansen.' Elizabeth was at the door now. 'She has enormous belief in you, in case you didn't know: ginormous.'

'She's very open-minded,' May said.

'So am I.' Elizabeth pecked her on the cheek. 'Bon voyage!'

39

The Big Holiday

'What are you doing, May?' Jansen was back from the gift shop.

'What do you mean? I've been sitting here with my shoes on, waiting for you to get back, so we can go and have a look around.' She was sitting at the tiny square table that was attached to the wall of their cabin.

'I thought you said you wanted to stay here for a bit, and rest.' Jansen dropped the *Guardian* onto the lower berth.

'But we're going to go and have dinner now, aren't we?'

'The restaurants aren't open yet. I've just had a look. Why don't we both have a rest, and then go out?'

'I feel like getting going,' May said. 'I feel like getting moving. Shall we go for a walk before dinner?'

'I'm going to lie down for a bit, and read my newspaper.'

'Oh, boring!' May said. 'Could we not go for a walk on deck together?'

'I've just been for a walk, May. Why don't you go for a walk on your own, and I'll come with you later. After dinner.'

'You don't want to come now?'

'No. I'm going to have a rest.' Jansen sat on the lower berth, bending forward slightly, because of the top bunk, and she undid her shoelaces.

May pouted.

'Go for a walk, May. Go and have a look around.' Jansen took off her trainers. 'You'll enjoy it.'

'On my own,' May said.

Jansen pulled off her tracksuit pants, houdinied her bra off, from under her T-shirt, and climbed into the lower bunk. 'Can you tuck me in before you go?'

'I'm not going anywhere.' May took off her shoes, pulled the covers up round Jansen's shoulders, gave her a tiny kiss on the head, and climbed up onto the top berth. 'I'm staying here. I'm going to do nothing.'

'Good. Well, can you please not talk to me, if you're going to stay? Because I'd like to have some quiet time.'

May said nothing.

'Okay?' Jansen asked.

'I'm not talking to you,' May said. 'I am saying nothing – as requested.'

'Give me one hour, and then we can have dinner and go for a walk after that,' Jansen said.

May lay there, staring at her feet. It was scary how capable she was of doing nothing and thinking nothing; she was capable of never doing anything – ever – in her life; it was as if she were holding her breath under water.

Jansen clicked off the little light next to her bunk.

'Are you going to sleep now?' May asked.

'If you'll let me, yes.'

'Can I just tell you something?'

Jansen didn't reply.

'I've had an interesting thought,' May said.

'Tell me about it later.'

'It's really quick . . . It wouldn't take long.'

'No, May. I want to go to sleep. Let me sleep for a bit, and then we can spend the whole evening together. We can talk all evening.'

After a huge buffet dinner – *smørre brød* (open sandwiches) with a variety of Danish cheeses; herring and oysters and mussels; *pommes frites* and *agurksalat* (sliced cucumber); followed by *æblekage* (trifle with apples), *jordbær med fløde* (strawberries with cream), and then *kaffe* – they went for a walk.

They wandered through the disco area and a pub, past cinemas, slot machines and teenagers; up the stairwell to the Saloon Deck, past the children's playroom, a bank and more slot machines; and then browsed around in the gift shop: dolls and mugs, and mini Little Mermaids; Bounty bars and Polo mints and Haribo candies; the English papers, but also *Weekendavisen* and *Jyllandsposten*, children's magazines in Danish, and postcards of the *Dana Anglia*, 'departing Harwich'.

In the Bellevue Lounge, people were seated near the windows, reading or chatting – in Danish or Swedish, or in English – or they were looking out at the blue-grey sea and at the early evening sky.

'Don't you wish,' May said, 'that you were going on a long cruise somewhere?'

'We're going on a short tasteful cruise,' Jansen said.

A short expensive tasteful cruise, May thought. But she didn't say anything, because she'd bought the tickets and she was trying to be nice. 'Shall I go back and buy a Danish newspaper, and we can pretend to read it over breakfast tomorrow morning?'

'No, thank you.'

'You don't want one? Are you sure? It could be fun.'

'May, I don't feel the need to pretend to be Danish.'

They stepped outside onto the deck, through a heavy iron door that didn't go all the way to the ground; they had to step over the bottom part of the door frame. 'This is probably to stop the water from getting in, if there's a storm,' May observed. 'It makes you feel like you're really at sea, too,' she went on. 'With these kinds of doors. Doesn't it? I'm glad this isn't a boring new boat. Isn't this wonderful? The fresh sea air. The "fresh, sea, air".' She breathed in deeply. 'It smells of that, doesn't it? It's "fresh" – apart from the diesel – "sea" and "air",' she said. 'The rumble of the engine, the smell of diesel – it's all part of it; it's all part of the "ship experience".'

'Yes, May.'

'Is there something wrong?'

'No, there's nothing wrong.'

'Hmm.' May thought for a bit. 'So you're just being quiet then?'

'Yes, I am.'

'You'd have enjoyed going on that silent retreat with Tamsin, wouldn't you?'

'Where did that come from?'

'No, I'm just saying: I suppose you'd have enjoyed the silence.'

'Ah-huh.'

'Are you pre-menstrual?' May asked.

'*What?*'

'You just seem in a bad mood, or something.'

'No, I'm not in a bad mood and I am not pre-menstrual. Are *you* pre-menstrual?'

'No.' May said nothing for a few steps. 'Was that an attack?'

'No, it was not an attack. May, let's just enjoy walking together. We don't always have to talk, do we? Let's see what it's like, being quiet together.'

'Do I talk too much? Is that what you're saying? I wish I was one of those calm quiet people. I'd love to be like that.'

'Yes,' Jansen said, 'but you're not; you're a talker.'

'But I'm quiet sometimes; I can be very quiet,' May defended herself. 'Anyway, I thought we were going to talk all evening.'

People were wandering around the ship: mothers and fathers, and children of varying ages, couples, and lone adults; all doing the rounds of the ship. A reconnaissance tour, in leisure time.

'I wish I didn't have to work,' May said.

'You're not working right now. We're on holiday.'

'Am I horrible to be around?' May asked. 'I'm pretty horrible, but not all the time.'

'You have been hard to live with recently,' Jansen told her.

'I wish I was a nicer person,' May said. 'Imagine if I was a nice person, a calm, quiet person.'

'You could be calm if you wanted to be. I think you'd miss all the worrying though.'

'Would you miss it, if I stopped worrying?' May asked.

'No.'

That was the wrong answer. 'You wouldn't?' May said.

They walked past an old wooden lifeboat.

'It can seat sixty-two people,' May noted. 'I wonder how many passengers there are on board right now. What do you think?'

'About one thousand,' said Jansen.

'One thousand? How do you know that? You're just guessing.'

'I read it in a pamphlet: this ship can take about one thousand three hundred passengers.'

May hadn't brought anything to read; she was trying to have a holiday. That was probably a mistake. 'Here we are on holiday: more time is ticking by, and I am accomplishing nothing.'

'May, you're allowed to have a holiday.'

'No, I'm just saying: I'm aware of it.' When would she ever see Francine again? She wasn't about to do anything 'extraordinary': she wasn't good at anything, except lying and putting on an act.

'What about giving yourself some time off?'

'I can't do that: I'm always giving myself "time off". I'm never going to do anything.' May stared down at the waves. 'This is a huge boat,' she said.

'It's a ship, May, not a boat.' Jansen laughed.

'I did have a thought before,' May said. 'I was thinking that perhaps I *need* to do nothing for a bit; perhaps that's what I really need to do: nothing.'

Jansen nodded. 'Yeah.'

'Just not for too long, though,' May added. 'That was my revelation.'

'Hm.'

She thought about actually enrolling on a PhD, but really she couldn't bear the idea. She just wished she could think of something completely different: something *fun*, if that were allowed. If only she could stop worrying a hundred per cent of the time – it would make Jansen happy. 'Maybe I am allowed a bit of time off,' she said. 'Maybe you're right.'

'Good. In that case, let's have a holiday.'

'I just wish I'd never dropped out when I was twenty-two,' May said. 'I could already *have* a PhD.' She sighed. 'And then I'd be a totally different person.'

'Do you know that you've wished about four or five things this evening?'

'Is that not allowed? Am I not allowed to wish anything?' May said. 'All those selfish wishes.'

They were now walking around the stern. It was getting cold; and the sun was about to set. It was late. Most people had gone inside; they were in the seating areas, or they were in the pub, or the cafeterias, or they were back in their cabins. It was quiet. And cold.

'I think if you're happier though, and more fulfilled, you're more likely to be more pleasant to be around; that's what I'm trying to say,' May went on. 'It's cold.'

'Come here.'

Jansen took her hand and led the way up some steps to a higher deck, where there were rows of green plastic chairs all attached together, and they sat down; they were facing in the wrong direction, like the backward seats in trains.

If time could stop now, May thought, perhaps I could stop worrying about doing something or not doing something; I wish time would stop for a while, and I could just sit here next to Jansen, and rest.

A ship was about to pass on the left – 'Yang Ming,' May read out; it was all black with various coloured containers sitting piled up on the deck. 'Here comes another one,' she said; this one was blue, with a white deck, and yellow and green containers. 'It's from ... just a minute ... London,' she said. Then, 'What are your wishes?' she asked Jansen. 'Do you wish I'd stop talking?'

'Yes.' Jansen nodded. 'Let's have a bit of silence. Can we have no talking for five minutes? Let's just enjoy being up here. Look at the sky.'

May looked at her watch: eight fifty-one; she wouldn't talk until eight fifty-six.